BETWEEN FLOORS

The City Between: Book Three

W.R. GINGELL

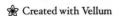

For everyone struggling with JinYeong's Korean, and the romanised expression of the same—

You *tell him to talk in English. See if he'll listen to you.*

CHAPTER ONE

YOU THINK I'D KNOW BETTER BY NOW. YOU'D THINK I'D KNOW not to poke my nose into stuff that isn't my business. Not to go following strange blokes, if it comes to that.

I mean, he wasn't really a strange bloke; his name was Detective Tuatu. I'd worked on a case with him before, and he knew I was following him. I was a bit bored, and I knew he was up to something, so of course I stuck to him and wouldn't let him go alone.

It doesn't sound so bad. It's just curiosity, right? It's not like it's got me nearly killed or anything.

Hang on.

Actually, it kinda has.

Nearly killed, nearly turned into a werewolf—sorry, *lycanthrope*; they're really fussy about that—and nearly vanished away in a way that I still don't fully understand.

Not to mention that *right now* I was trapped Between with a panicking cop attached to my hand and no way of knowing if I was going in the right direction or not.

Hang on. You don't know what Between is, do you?

There are layers to reality. Like trifle, and—

Nah. I'll explain later.

Right now, we were somewhere not quite in the fae world but not quite in the human world, either; a kind of betweenish area that still had a bit of floral to it from the wall paper of the room we'd been in a couple of minutes ago, and a whole lot of menace in it that definitely came from the fae side of things.

"Follow me," I said to the detective. The world was all greenery and dangerous silence around us, and I didn't like the way my words were swallowed up in the stuffiness of that greenery. "Don't let go of my hand. Watch out for goblins and don't touch stuff."

"Goblins?" Detective Tuatu still looked a bit dazed, the whites of his eyes a bit bigger than usual. I wouldn't have been able to notice it so much if it wasn't so gloomy in here and his skin wasn't so dark.

"They're the little mongrels with needles: One of 'em got you that night you came after us into the house across the road."

"That reminds me," said the detective, sounding a bit strained. "The house disappeared that night."

"Yeah."

"*How?*"

"Don't you reckon you've got enough problems right here and now without trying to bring up ones from the past as well?" I asked him. I mean, if that was his way of coping with the panic, fair enough. It didn't make much sense to me, though.

"What's this stuff?" he asked, reaching up to touch a floating bit of moss that drifted by too close for comfort.

"Don't touch stuff," I reminded him. "And don't let go of my hand. What did I just tell you?"

"Why? Isn't it moss?"

"Maybe, maybe not." I threw a look around. "Just don't let go, all right?"

"All right," he said.

He didn't sound very grateful, but I s'pose there's a difference between a hulking great wall of muscled safety like Zero telling you not to let go, and someone as skinny as me doing it.

You don't know Zero. I'll explain that later, too.

I set my shoulders. "First things first," I said impressively, and peeked down at my phone again. There hadn't been a signal before, but there was now.

Well, *that* wasn't suspicious at all.

Detective Tuatu didn't look impressed. "What?"

"Reckon I'm gunna try to call Zero."

"Thank goodness!"

"Oi!"

"Pet," he said. "We're trapped in some sort of hell dimension, and—"

"It's creepy, but it's not like anything's trying to kill you," I protested. "Not yet, anyway. Calling it a hell dimension's a bit much, isn't it?"

"That makes me feel much better," said Tuatu, but he managed not to roll his eyes, which was pretty impressive. "But that was a dead body, back there; and if I'm right about just a very small thing today, it came from in here. I'd rather let the professionals deal with it—and I'm pretty sure that whatever else your three friends are, they're professionals. I don't want to be in here either."

"It's not exactly *in* here," I told him. "And it's not exactly from *this* bit of here that the body came."

I tapped worriedly at the slick surface of my phone, which had blacked out again. It stayed black for just a bit too long, then lit.

"Got reception, anyway," I said. "That's nice."

"That's weird," Tuatu said, but he looked relieved.

"That too," I agreed. He had no idea *how* weird it was. I slowly unlocked my phone, the touchscreen cool beneath my fingertips, reluctant to try and call Zero. I was half afraid that instead of his voice, I would hear something else. Something weird and scary.

"What did you mean, we're not exactly *in* here?"

"There are layers to reality," I said to him, my finger hovering over Zero's number. "The human world—that's the *real* world, so don't let those three tell you different—the fae world, and the bit between where it can be anything it wants to be."

"Where are we, then?" asked the detective. He didn't sound less scared, but at least he was listening. "This bit; is it the Between bit, or a fae bit? And I don't say that I believe in fae, but there's definitely something weird about those three, and we're not in my friend's house anymore."

"We kinda are," I said. "This bit is Between, but it's also your friend's house. Once we start moving we won't be inside the house any more, but we'll still be Between."

"That doesn't make sense."

"Yeah. Sorry." I hesitated for an instant longer, then let the pad of my thumb touch the phone. It lit up, just a bit too late again. "Reckon there's a lag in here?"

"You're the expert," Tuatu pointed out. "Is it ringing?"

"Yeah." The ringing was just a bit too slow, too. "But if I'm honest, I reckon there's about a fifty percent chance that whoever answers won't be Zero."

There was a click on the other end of the phone, then silence.

"Zero?" I said. "Is that you?"

"Yes," said Zero's voice. It was too slow, just like everything else to do with the phone Between, but I was starting to wonder if that wasn't just because we *were* Between. "What's wrong with your phone?"

"I *might* have got caught Between with the detective," I said. "But it's not really my fault because someone threw a body at us and there were cops coming out of the woodwork everywhere, too. Anyway, we need some help because I don't know which way to go."

There was a big silence, and I thought I heard a very carefully let out sigh. If it really was Zero, he was probably pinching his brow about now.

"Listen very carefully," he said. "Can you see anywhere nearby that glimmers?"

"Can we see any glimmers?" I asked the detective.

Detective Tuatu looked sideways at me. "Any what?"

"Glimmers—you know, something that has a bit of a wet glitter to it—hang on, never mind." There was a patch of dark green shadow through the trees across from us; a place that might have been rock but wasn't quite rock, with a definite glimmer of moonlight to it. "Yeah, there's something like that here."

"There will be a door there."

"A door?"

"Not exactly a door, but a way through."

"It'll take us out?"

"No. It will take you to another area of Between. But that will get you out of the house."

"What do we do once we're out of the house? We can't come out too early or the cops will catch Detective Tuatu."

"Once you're out of the house, I can find you," said Zero's voice. "But you have to get out first, and you won't have reception for much longer."

"Flamin' fantastic," I said. "So we're gunna lose contact again?"

I should have saved my breath; the next thing I heard was the *beep beep beep* of the call dropping out.

"Flamin' fantastic," I said again. "Lost reception again."

Anxiously, the detective asked, "Do you know what to do?"

"Kinda. Maybe."

"What's wrong?"

"He gave me directions to get out," I said, slipping my phone back into my pocket. "Out of the house, anyway."

"And that's...bad?" Tuatu hazarded dubiously. "How?"

It wasn't that it was bad, exactly. It was more that I'd expected

Zero to say something terse and bossy, like, "Stay where you are. I'm coming."

"Just...dunno if that was really him," I said. "Don't know if we should follow the directions or not."

Detective Tuatu looked toward the rustling trees worriedly. "What are our options?"

"Well, either it was him and we should do as we're told, or it wasn't him and we're on our own anyway. Depends on whether you think it's worth the risk or not."

"Should we see if there's a door there?" he suggested. "That'll give us an idea of whether what he said is true or not, anyway."

"Yeah," I said slowly. There was something else bothering me, and I didn't know what it was. I didn't like that, but the trees were starting to sound like they were about to uproot and walk toward us, and I liked that idea a heck of a lot less. "C'mmon, let's get it over with."

It's not as reassuring holding onto someone when you're the one leading into danger, but Detective Tuatu's hand was still a bit of comfort. Not so much because I thought he'd be much good in a fight, but because I had to be brave and couldn't run away if he was depending on me. I'd still much rather have been holding onto Zero's hand, but if I couldn't be, at least I still knew what I needed to do.

Tuatu followed me gingerly between the trees, and it might have been the breeze that suddenly stirred around, but it almost looked like the weeping willows actually reached out for us as we passed, trailing fronds languidly through the air.

"Better get a wriggle on," I muttered, pulling him along a bit quicker. I'd just come to the unpleasant realisation that the wind wasn't causing the stirring of the willow fronds—the fronds were stirring up a sticky, slow breeze with their movement.

Detective Tuatu obeyed without hesitation, crowding on my heels as the glimmering, rocky surface came within touching distance.

I put my hand out to it, expecting to feel mossy, slick rock, and felt something soft and cobwebby that gave a bit beneath my palm instead. I prodded at it and my hand went through softly, silkily.

"Well, I wouldn't call it a door, but I s'pose Zero knows what he's talking about," I said. "Wait here. Gunna try it."

"What's the point of me waiting?" Tuatu asked, his voice dry. "If it's a trap, I might as well get trapped with you than left by myself in here. I'll likely die either way."

"Aren't you cheerful?" I muttered, but there wasn't much use talking about it, because he was right. I pushed right into the glimmery whiteness, and felt it press against my face for an instant before it allowed me through—body, hand, Tuatu and all.

I smelled rain and stone as soon as my nose broke the cobwebby surface, and maybe my training had been good for something after all; I was already looking around for needle-wielding goblins when Detective Tuatu began to exit.

There weren't any; we were in a cave sort of area that was very different from the place we'd come from.

"Hey!" I said in surprise. "It *is* the way out!"

Detective Tuatu threw an unimpressed look around. "The way out of *what*? It doesn't look much better out here. It doesn't look like an *out here*, either, if it comes to that."

"Yeah," I agreed, looking around at the glistening, rocky shadows around us. There was even less light here than there had been in the house behind us, but the darkness was of a different quality here. Instead of the stuffiness that felt like it could swallow us up, there was a cool, pleasant feel to the air. Like there was a cave opening up further, letting in fresh air to feed the greenery that crawled all over the rocks and made every crevasse and crack deep green.

I felt the breeze touch my face, fresh and cool, and smelled the distant scent of wet concrete. This wasn't a cave; this was an underpass! I said without hesitation, "This way."

I still wasn't entirely sure that it had been Zero on the phone, and I wanted to make sure that we got out of Between as soon as we could, whether or not he was waiting for us.

"What are you looking for?" asked Tuatu, as I pulled him along.

"Nothing," I said, but I didn't stop looking around me. It was too hard to explain that I was looking for things that weren't exactly the things they were pretending to be—or that they *were*, here. Somewhere nearby, in the human version of this area, I was certain there was an exit from the underpass. Maybe we could get out there, if I could see things clearly as they were in the human world instead of how they were here Between.

For instance, not too far behind us, there was an outcropping of rock that suggested the idea of a car bumper if you looked at it in the right way. I stopped, squinted, and opened my mouth to ask the detective if he thought it looked a bit like a car bumper, too, when something moved out in the murky distance of the craggy cave floor.

"I think there are people out there," said the detective, and I didn't blame him for the nervous sound to his voice.

I was flamin' scared myself, because I knew they weren't human.

First it was one head popping up over the rocks, a spot of light on its forehead that made a soft glow around it; then the rocks around us were filled with gleams of light; scruffy heads and hoods popping up from the crags.

"G'day," I said to the biped who had arrived first.

It tilted its head at me; it was only a small thing, about thigh-high on me, and it was vaguely human-esque if you had a preference for little tackers with big mouths and bulbous eyes. They were mucky little things, too. I couldn't tell if they were male or female, with the amount of mud they had slathered all over them. No wonder we hadn't seen them until they turned on their lights —they blended right into the cave surroundings.

I threw a quick look behind us to see if we could get back to the door if we needed to, but there were more of the little beggars behind us. A lot more.

"Pet," said Detective Tuatu at the same time, "There's more of them."

"Yep, saw that," I said, trying not to sound worried. Little lights were blinking into being all around us, and I didn't like the way we were being edged forward, even if the little tackers in front of us were smiling encouragingly.

It was like being towed along by a wave further into the ocean —somewhere you didn't know if you'd meet a beautiful reef or a shark.

"What are they?"

"Dunno," I said. It felt like I was saying that a lot today.

"They don't look dangerous, do they?"

I looked around at the mucky little tackers suspiciously. In my experience, stuff not looking dangerous and not actually *being* dangerous were two very different, potentially deadly things. "Goblins don't look real dangerous, either," I told him.

One of the little cave people poked me in the hip and made me jump.

"What?" I demanded.

It made an encouraging hand flap at me, urging me forward. It wasn't like we could go back, anyway, so I said reluctantly, "We might as well go with them for a bit. Keep 'em happy for the time being. We'll try to slip away when we get closer to the exit."

I tried to make a mental note of where I'd seen the bit of rock that could have been a car bumper, but I'd already lost it in the movement of muddy cave people, so I kept my eye out for anything that could be used as a weapon instead.

That was another bit of my training that was starting to come in handy, because I could already see a couple of stalagmites that looked like cricket bats if I looked at them in the right way, and I was pretty sure we'd be passing close by them very soon.

They were still looking enough like cricket bats when we passed, that I could reach out and grab them. I passed one to Tuatu, who looked first grateful then confused, and kept the other for myself.

The little tackers who were herding us gibbered at me a bit, and I wondered if there was something about hearing that could be influenced by Between, too; because it almost felt as though I understood them. Well, almost felt as though I *almost* understood them.

It was as if they were saying, "Rude, nasty rude!" at me, but in another language that I'd learned a couple of years ago and was just remembering now. I was pretty sure it was, "Rude, nasty rude!" they were saying at me, anyway; even though I didn't know exactly how I knew it. I kept a good grip on my bat anyway. There were too many of them, and I wanted to have a weapon. They were good cricket bats, too; light and a little bit flexible. I wondered if I'd pinched them from some rich kid's car as we passed through, and grinned a bit. Maybe Zero could help me put 'em back in the right place when this was all over—or maybe stuff made its way back to where it should be if you tossed it back Between.

I mean, I doubted it, but it wouldn't hurt to ask.

The cave started to grow a bit lighter around us as we walked. It wasn't lighter in a daylight kind of way, though, which was disappointing; it was lighter in an amber, flickery sort of way that suggested there was a fire up ahead.

Actually, it was a couple of fires.

We came around the curve of a cave wall, and there it was below us; a valley as big as a sports oval, with soft, mossy bits all through it. Mossy bits, logs, and very large fires.

"You lot wouldn't be so cold if you didn't go around with mud all over yourselves," I told them.

One of them shook a finger at me and said something that probably had a negative in it, then patted its stomach.

Oh, right. Each of the fires had a decent-sized cauldron sitting over it—they must be communal feeders or something. Not like JinYeong, then. I'd have to ask him if vampires ever had parties.

Come to think of it, I probably didn't want to know.

Beside me, the detective stopped walking. I wondered why, until I realised that I'd stopped walking, and that I still had him by the hand.

Good, good. I was doing a good job as protector.

The little tackers began to chitter again, and one of them poked me in the ribs. Dunno how it reached that high, but it made me jump again, so I glared at it and shook my finger in its face.

"Don't do that!"

Something yelled from across the valley, sharp and demanding. There was a wizened old prune standing by the biggest cauldron below, and as I looked, it waved the ladle at us in a vaguely threatening kind of way.

I swung my cricket bat a bit against the grass-like stuff beneath our feet and wondered if that was a rock formation behind the old prune, or if it was a *really* big tacker down there. The old prune turned around and bashed at the rock, and the sound echoed across the valley. When it finally stopped, there was an even louder *crack*. Something that definitely wasn't rock stood up. Dark, craggy, and as implacable as the cave walls around us, the creature towered, dwarfing the old prune, the fire, and even the hill behind it.

"That's not rock," said Tuatu, with the feverish sort of voice that seems to be trying to convince itself that what it sees isn't right. "That's not rock! That's a person—a troll?"

"Your guess is as good as mine," I said. For all I knew, it could have been a troll.

The old prune by the cauldron pointed the ladle at us and made a gibber that I *thought* might be something like, "Off you go, then!"

Behind us, the little tackers swarmed and *pushed*, and despite how small they were, I felt myself being forced forward a step from the sheer amount of them.

Detective Tuatu asked, "Are they—what are they planning on doing with us? I don't see any weapons."

"Dunno," I said. I didn't want to hurt anyone who wasn't trying to hurt me, but I hadn't yet met anything Between that *hadn't* been after my blood—except the plants, I suppose. And just because we couldn't see weapons, it didn't mean they didn't have 'em. Didn't mean they needed weapons, if it came to that.

I leaned back into the swarm, making a bit freer with my elbow than I'd had before, and swung the cricket bat to make a clearing behind us as well. I didn't want to be too rough with them—they were only small—but I didn't want to be pushed toward that big brute before I knew exactly what he wanted us for.

Detective Tuatu looked down uneasily at the cricket bat I'd given him, then around at the muttering swarm, and I knew he was thinking the same as me.

"I can't—if they're not trying to hurt us, I can't—"

"Yeah, I know," I said. "But I bet they're gunna try to hurt us."

"How do you know?"

"We're Between. Everything here wants to kill or maim humans. It's like a cultural thing."

"Oh. Where—where did the bats come from? Before?"

"Dunno," I said again. "They were already here. Sorta. And they're sort of not exactly bats. Well, here they're not *usually* bats —here they're usually stalagmites. I just convinced 'em they're bats because we needed bats."

"Makes perfect sense," said Tuatu. He was looking a bit sick again. "What are they saying?"

"I don't speak the language," I objected. "I just wander in every now and then and get out before someone tries to kill me."

But as before, there was something familiar about the gibbering. If I didn't listen to it too closely, it almost made sense—like the book titles in Zero's bookshelf, which were written in a strange script that only made sense when you weren't trying to decipher them.

I stopped listening so hard, concentrating on swinging my own cricket bat back and forth with one hand, and feeling the *flickflickflick* as the top of it lightly swatted grass. That was hard, because the big brute from the middle of the valley started walking toward us, loosening his shoulders as he came, and I didn't think he was doing that to limber up to shake our hands.

"Pet," said Detective Tuatu, the tip of his bat dropping to the ground.

"Shh!" I admonished him. "Trying to hear over here!"

The conversation around the cookpot rose in the air, a steady cackle of appreciative, tongue-smacking talk, above which bubbled the suggestion of *fatten it up a bit, no I like it tough, young and tender, ah human flesh!*

Ah heck.

And up the hill toward us, Big Brute kept walking, his ridiculously long stride eating up the space between us while the little chirpers behind us crowded in closer, cutting off escape from the back again.

Ah heck.

"Reckon they want to eat us," I said. He wasn't carrying a weapon, Big Brute, but looking at the size of him and looking at the size of us, I didn't think it was gunna matter too much.

Where was Zero?

I couldn't call him on the phone again—probably hadn't called him in the first place, if my suspicions were correct—and I was pretty sure that yelling for him wasn't gunna do us much good, either.

Only Athelas had said something about a tracker trace, hadn't he? And there had been that time, just a couple of nights ago, when I'd screamed for Zero and he'd shown up.

Coincidence? Maybe. But maybe not.

Tuatu's grip tightened convulsively on the handle of his bat. "They want to—they want to *eat* us?"

Big Brute stopped a few yards away from us and stooped for a stone as big as my head.

Behind us, a current of meaning rippled through the chirpers; *Tenderise it! smash it! soften it up!*

"Oh yeah," I said. "They're definitely gunna eat us. You still don't wanna fight?"

"Oh no," said Tuatu, lifting his bat with a look of fascinated horror. "I'll fight."

"Cool," I said. "And if it looks like we're gunna die, yell out for Zero."

I don't really remember how the fight started. There was a staticky sort of pause where I thought I might be really close to wetting my pants and things got muggy and prickly like a hot summer day, then I was screaming and swinging and maybe dying, with blood in my eyes and something liquid in my lungs that burned.

Big Brute swung and missed because I had been *there* and suddenly I wasn't there anymore, faster than it was possible for a human not to be there, and—

Heck yeah!

I still had my vampire reflexes!

Long story—nearly turned into a lycanthrope, had to swallow some vampire spit—don't worry about it. Important thing was, I still had my vampire reflexes!

Things slowed down a bit, even though my lungs still burned. Tuatu. Where was Tuatu?

I saw him, swinging and swearing, already bloody and battered; but as soon as I saw him, he went flying, knocked into the cave wall by an arm as huge and rocky as the wall he hit.

Things got very fast again, and somehow I was screaming and hitting again, bashing Big Brute's ear as hard as I could—how the flaming heck did I get up here?—then the world spun around me and hit me very hard.

Someone was groaning like they were dying; probably me. I saw the cave roof above me, fractured into a thousand pieces—or maybe I hit the ground so hard that my eyes broke, I dunno—and Big Brute's craggy face.

Face, then hand.

A hand that still held a rock as big as my head, now poised above me.

Ah heck. Where was my cricket bat?

I turned my head, blinking to clear my sight, and saw it just out of reach in the muddy, churned grass.

Ah heck.

Something else was missing. Where was Tuatu?

I looked for him, but saw only splotches of red flung in an arc through the muddy stuff on my cricket bat; I could see them really clearly, and somehow the cricket bat seemed more important than the rock poised above my head, ready to dash out my brains.

"Pet?" asked a whisper, a deep rumble in the ground, and the world became real and painful around me again.

"Zero!" I yelled. "*Zero!*"

The air did something weird that *twang*ed over my head, and Big Brute froze, rock raised. A dirty hand slapped over my mouth, big and smelly and human, and a voice muttered in my ear, "Shh, shh, ladies can't be noisy here."

I dug my head into the sandy ground, tilting back to see who it was, and a familiar bearded face made a bird's nest grin at me through the thicket on his face.

The old bearded bloke. It was the old bearded bloke who had escaped murder and fae in the house across the road from me—when there was still a house there. Mad, dirty, and homeless, he had been following me around since I was a kid but tended to go to ground when there were a few too many people trying to kill him. I still didn't know who he was and why he stuck around.

I definitely didn't know why he was here, now; or why he was shaking one dirty finger up at Big Brute, who would probably swat him into next month any second.

Only he didn't.

He stayed as he was, frozen, his eyes wary and very intent on the old mad bloke.

I gurgled a dry laugh into the old bloke's palm and tried to blink away the dark strands of hair that were loose from my ponytail. What's the bet he was their king or something?

I couldn't see it, but the one at the cookpot shrieked something, and Big Brute's hand wavered, undecided. The old bloke shook his finger again, and the hand that had been covering my mouth slipped around to my collar and hauled at me, my shirt hitching up beneath my arms.

"Hang on," I said. "Gotta get me friend."

"Already dead," said the old bloke. "Can see the bones."

A voice, deep with pain, said, "Not dead, just got a broken arm."

I climbed to my feet with the old bearded bloke tugging painfully at me, swaying and nauseous, and saw Detective Tuatu propped up against the rock wall he'd hit. His bat was in splinters, and that struck me as funny, so I laughed.

"Stop it, Pet!" said Tuatu. He tried to get to his feet by himself, but his arm was definitely broken and he couldn't use it to help himself up. "Are you all right?"

It also struck me as funny that he was worried about me when he looked like he did, but since he didn't seem to like me laughing, I just went over and helped him stand up.

"Told you to hold onto my hand," I said. Like it would have made a difference. But it felt good to scold someone for something.

That made Tuatu laugh, even though he looked like he might throw up, too.

"Oi," I said. "If I'm not allowed to laugh, why are you?"

"Come along, pets," the old mad bloke said, his crafty old eyes darting back and forth. "Can't wait here. Pets are good tucker here."

"We noticed," I said sourly. The hand I'd helped Tuatu up with was hurting more than it should be, and I was pretty sure one of my fingers was at an angle it shouldn't be at, too.

"Follow, follow, follow me!" the old bloke sang, and twirled away from the valley.

"Who's that?" demanded Tuatu. He sounded like he was trying not to lose his temper, so I suppose that was an improvement from him sounding like he was gunna chuck up from the pain.

"A friend," I said. "He's not gunna stab us with anything, anyway. I think."

"How did he stop that big beast?"

I shrugged, and gasped a bit when it hurt. "Dunno. Why don't you ask him? Oi. I think I've dislocated my collarbone or something."

"You've broken your finger, too," said Tuatu. "We'll have to find somewhere safe to stop and patch you up."

"That'll be some trick with your arm like that," I pointed out, pulling him in the direction that the old bloke was heading. He was our only lifeline at the moment—where was Zero, anyway?—and I didn't want to lose him. "Reckon we'd better look after you first. Bones aren't meant to stick out like that."

"It's fine," he said, but he was pretty punch drunk as he trailed after me.

I grinned back at him and felt a bit of warm wetness at the corner of my eyes. Blood, or tears? It didn't matter; I just had to look after Tuatu until Zero found us. He was about as pale as an Islander can get, which was mostly grey.

"Liar," I said. "Bit fragile, aren't you?"

"I broke it when I was a kid," he said, with a bit of indignation. "It's weakened now."

"Oh well," I said, inclined to be generous. "The brute went for you first, so I s'pose you did all right."

"Someone needs to teach you a few things about combat," the detective said. "You nearly bashed my brains out yourself."

"Did I?" I looked across at him, and he was serious. "Sorry 'bout that."

"I thought you said Zero was teaching you how to fight."

"He is. But this was my first real fight—last time I just sorta legged it through with a sword for Zero and those three did all the fighting. I figured I was gunna die so things got a bit fuzzy in there."

The detective gave me a bit of a weird look. "Things got fuzzy, did they? I don't suppose you were a berserker in a previous life, were you?"

"Prob'ly not. Heck. Where's the old beggar got to?"

"Either I'm going potty, or he went through one of the cave walls."

"How hard did you get hit?"

"Pretty hard. Not my head, though."

"Then he probably went through the wall. Where?"

"Over there. The bit with the ferns," said Tuatu. "I suppose we can assume that it wasn't Zero on the phone earlier?"

There was the faintest bit of resistance from his hand, like he didn't really want to go through another door but didn't want to pull too hard, in case he hurt me.

That was kinda irritating but also nice of him.

My brain recognised that.

My mouth didn't. It said, "Scared, huh?"

"A bit," Tuatu said evenly. "If that wasn't Zero, who was it? They sent us right into the middle of an ambush, and I don't really feel like going through any more doors."

"That's what I want to know, too," I said. "And I wanna know if Zero knows Betweeners know how to hack phones or whatever, cos I think that's something he ought to know. C'mmon."

The detective pulled back more strongly. "Pet, can we slow down and think about this?"

"Think about what? Big Brute back there, or the nasty old prune by the cookpot?"

"Good point," said Detective Tuatu, and started walking again.

He was breathing a bit heavily, which was worrying. He was also losing a lot of blood where the bone protruded from his arm, and that was more worrying. If he fainted, I didn't think the old bloke and I would be able to manage carrying him between the two of us. I didn't like the idea of leaving a blood trail behind us in Between, either. I remembered how urgent Zero had been about me not leaving blood trails through Between, and it bothered me to be letting Detective Tuatu leave his blood here now.

Maybe I could ask Zero to do something about that if I ever found him again.

"I'll have a look for a way out once we're away from this lot," I said, jerking my head back the way we'd come. "Reckon I saw one back there, but the little chirpers pushed us away from it."

"Oh well," said Tuatu, looking at the ferny bit of cave wall where the old bloke had disappeared. "I suppose we can only die, after all."

"That's the spirit," I said, and pulled us both through the door.

Sunshine glowed against my face, bright and sudden, warming the well-maintained topiary of a very big garden all around us. We were on a wide, pebbled path bordered by ivy-clad statues and manicured bushes; safe, sunshiny, and nothing deadly within reach of us.

Flamin' suspicious.

Detective Tuatu, looking as suspicious as I felt, limped into the garden beside me, and didn't complain when I pulled him right into the middle of the path.

"What's in this place, then?" he muttered. "Killer statues?"

"Probably," I said cheerfully. I glanced around us, careful to stick to the centre of the path and out of reach of anything that might like to grab either of us as I did my reccie, and grinned.

Right there. There were a couple of ivy vines down the path to our left, between two of the statues. They'd joined up with each other, as if they'd been blown together by a summer breeze and grown together since, but there was something a bit solid to the way they joined together, like etched vine leaves on the wooden seat of an old-fashioned swing set.

"Beauty!" I said happily. "C'mmon!"

Something pinched the shoulder of my shirt and tugged at it.

"There you are," I said. "'Bout time you showed up again!"

"Not that way, pets," said the old bloke, still tugging at me. "This way, this way!"

"I don't think so," I said. I wasn't going to ignore my instincts again. "There's a swing set here. Someone's playground or back-yard is right through here."

The old bloke glared at me, then blew a raspberry in my face.

I stepped back to avoid the spit, and something curled around my neck, jerking me back against a statue with an impact that expelled a yelp from me, jarring every broken bone in my body.

There might have been a few I hadn't found yet.

"Ah heck," I said.

Beside me, Tuatu coughed, and then groaned. "Pet," he said. "There's a vine around my neck."

"Mine, too. Arms?"

"Yeah."

"Oi," I said, turning my head back to the old bloke. "You better flaming—what the heck?"

He was gone.

Something sharp pricked my neck in a thousand places,

drawing blood, and a million similar needles punctured my arms and legs and torso, even through my jeans.

"Ah heck," I said again.

You remember I said that at least the plants Between weren't trying to kill me?

Scratch that. The plants here were out to get me, too.

CHAPTER TWO

"What's happening?" Detective Tuatu's voice sounded slurred.

Beggar me. The thorns must be sending some kind of drug through our systems. I could feel a faint sleepiness sinking into me, and through the panic it seemed good that Tuatu should fall asleep rather than be in as much pain as he must be in, with those vines gripping his broken arm so tightly.

"I reckon the plants want to eat us as well," I said. My voice didn't sound slurred—mostly it just sounded annoyed—so that was nice. A sourness in my stomach rose until I could taste it in my mouth, fighting against the sleepiness or maybe just burning it away.

Probably the vampire spit thing again.

"Great," said Tuatu hazily. "Just what I needed right now."

"Welcome to my life," I told him, and wriggled my shoulders cautiously against the vines. More of the needles pricked me, and I said aggrievedly, "Ow."

"Doesn't hurt."

"Nice for some," I muttered, and this time I threw myself forward as much as I could, bracing against the pain.

A million needles gripped me by the arms and sank deeper, a million points of agony that had a deadly, sleepy taint to them.

"Beggar me," I gasped, and yelled, "Zero! *Zero!*"

"Quiet, Pet," said a voice so welcome, I almost thought I'd imagined it.

Almost.

I couldn't have imagined the way Zero's voice rumbled through the air here Between, shivering through the thorny vines that encased me and Detective Tuatu and convincing them to loosen without a touch.

I looked up, and there he was; huge and welcome, his almost translucently white skin and hair a pale flame against the hedge behind him, his leather jacket unzipped. Funny, that. Zero usually zipped his jacket up when he was preparing to go Between. Must have been in a hurry when he left.

The last of the vines slithered away from me, and I tried to take a step toward him. Maybe I was more affected than I'd thought, or maybe the last couple of punctures had done more harm than I thought. My legs didn't catch me, but Zero did; gently, carefully, as if he knew exactly where all the broken bones were.

There was a slight slither beside us, and Detective Tuatu collapsed between grass and path in a tangle of limbs.

"Whoops," I said. "You should have caught him. He's not doing too well."

"He's alive," Zero said, and picked me up.

"Oi! Where are we going?"

"Home."

"Better get him, then," I protested, pointing at Tuatu with my undamaged hand.

Zero stopped in the centre of the path, and I could feel the reluctance fairly *radiating* from him.

"If you try to leave without him, I'll bite you," I warned.

A very big sigh slowly left Zero's huge chest, and he put me down in the middle of the path with one hand gripping my hoodie.

I batted at the hand. "I can stand up. He's the one who needs help."

It looked like Zero sighed again. Despite that, he left me on the path and took a step back toward Detective Tuatu. While he was doing that, I looked around covertly for the old mad bloke. He must have seen Zero before I did, which explained why he'd run for it. I didn't blame him for not wanting to be seen by any of my three psychos, but I couldn't help feeling a bit miffed at him for not making sure we were okay before he left.

At any rate, there was no sign of him, and I didn't want to keep looking, since Zero took only a moment to kneel before rising again with a bundle of detective in his arms instead of a bundle of Pet.

The detective's eyes fluttered open.

In amazement, I said, "Flaming heck, you're pretty tough, after all!"

Zero took a step down the path, and said brusquely, over his shoulder, "Hold onto my pocket. If you let go, I'll leave you behind."

I grabbed his pocket. "No, you won't."

"What are you doing Between by yourself?"

"I'm not by myself," I pointed out, tilting my chin at Detective Tuatu. "Got him."

"Pet," he said, very deep and rumbly.

I coughed. "I told you on the phone. Someone threw a body at us and then there were cops everywhere, and we didn't think they'd understand that we didn't kill the bloke."

"You didn't tell me anything on the phone."

"Yeah? Beggar me. That means the people here know how to hack phones."

"Phones don't work Between," Zero said briefly. "Not unless someone wants them to work."

"Figured," I said. "Anyway, we were being careful, but then some little chirpers ganged up and sicced a rock troll thing on us. Ohhh."

There must have been something in my voice that worried Zero, because he stopped for long enough to look back at me. "What?"

"What about the blood?"

"What blood?"

"Not me; the detective. He bled a *lot* back there when we were fighting the rock troll thing."

"His blood isn't important."

"Important to me," mumbled Tuatu.

He was still struggling to keep his eyes open—dunno why. It wasn't like he'd enjoyed his time Between, so far; I would have thought he was pretty happy to give in to oblivion.

"Why'd you make sure I didn't go bleeding Between, then?" I demanded. "Every time I get a bit of a cut, you're always nagging at me not to leave it around the place."

"I said *his* blood isn't important."

"That's rude."

"He got himself involved."

"So did I," I pointed out. "Actually, I'm always getting myself involved, so if anyone should be—"

"Be quiet, Pet," said Zero, and started walking again.

"Yeah, but he saved my life, and—"

Tuatu snorted, then fainted.

"Where's Athelas and his magic healing hands when they're needed?" I grumbled.

"Is that why he's injured? He was protecting you?"

"Yeah."

"All right," Zero said. He didn't say anything else, but I was pretty sure I felt something stirring the not-quite-human air around us.

"Are you healing him?"

"I don't have that talent," said Zero. "I can take away pain, but not heal."

"Oh. Oi, if my call didn't get through to you, how did you know where to find me? Was it that tracker thing Athelas mentioned before?"

"Yes." Zero continued on in silence for several more strides before he said over his shoulder, "You don't have to yell as loudly as you did. Just keep calling. You don't need to deafen me."

"Oh," I said again. "Sorry."

There were a few minutes of silence. Zero strode along as if we were out for a walk instead of making our way home from Between, and the world flickered from alien to almost-recognisable around us as we went.

Then, just as I was pretty sure we were about to come back into the human world properly, Zero asked, "Broken bones?"

"Yeah. He broke his arm and I think he—"

"Not him. You."

"Finger. Maybe my collarbone, too, and a couple of ribs."

"JinYeong will look after them."

"JinYeong?" I protested. "Why can't Athelas do it?"

"Athelas is at work."

"What, still? I'll wait for him."

"At the moment," said Zero very deliberately, "I am taking away a good portion of your pain. If you don't do as you're told, I will release it again."

"That's you?" Oh well, it was probably a good thing; I thought I'd been going into shock. "Can you teach me how to do that?"

"No. You need magic to do it."

I made a face at a sunflower we passed. I might have been imagining it, but I think it made a face back at me. I looked away hurriedly before I could hear it say something, too.

"Oh yeah," I added. "And that's another thing. Back there I could understand those little chirpers. Well, not exactly understand 'em, but pretty nearly. Is there a bit of Between in my head or something?"

For the briefest moment, I had the idea that Zero was completely, utterly shocked. It didn't show on his face—nothing much ever showed on his face—but there was a kind of crackling feeling to the air that I was pretty sure I wasn't imagining, and just the barest suggestion of a missed step somewhere in his stride.

"We'll be back in the human world in a moment," he said, ignoring the question. "Try not to stumble too much. And try not to make so much noise when you walk. I'll be doing my best to make you unnoticeable, but if you're going to blunder around like that, I won't be able to do it."

"I've got broken bones!" I said indignantly. "And I'm not making *that* much noise!"

"You didn't break your legs," Zero said. "You sound like a cow in a mud flat."

An odd filtering of light briefly passed over him and maybe it spread to the garden, or maybe I started to be able to see things in the human way again, because instead of flowers and hedges, I began to see the walls of an alley on either side of us; an alley painted with flowers and bushes and fake chairs.

"What are you gunna do with the detective?" I asked.

There was a slight pause. I could imagine why; Zero was probably tossing up the pros and cons of either the hospital or our house. Hospital pros: We could just drop the detective there without too many problems, and Zero didn't have to think about him again. Cons? The detective might start talking about us, or Between, while he was out of it—or on pain meds.

House cons: Zero would have another human in the house, and another human to look after. Zero didn't like having humans under his protection. He said it was because he didn't want the bother, but I was pretty sure that what he was really worried about was getting fond of them.

I probably didn't explain it properly, but Zero's not human. Not exactly, anyway. He's part human, part fae. Maybe I should explain that now, since I didn't really explain about Between—all the layers stuff.

We all live together; me, two fae, and a vampire, in my parents' old house.

'Cos I'm not *Pet* exactly. I *am* a pet.

Zero, Athelas, and JinYeong? Two fae and a pouty vampire— my owners.

It's not that hard; all I have to do is cook, clean, and try not to die. And if I'm a very good pet, one day my parents' house will be mine again. Zero promised.

"Gunna take him to the hospital?" I prompted Zero, now.

"No," he said, even if he said it reluctantly. "JinYeong can do some work on him too."

"What sort of work?"

I was suspicious; the last time JinYeong had been enlisted to help me, I ended up having to swallow vampire spit. I was pretty sure Detective Tuatu would prefer the hospital, even if it would take longer for his wounds to heal.

"A bite; nothing more."

"Didn't that knock him out, last time?" I asked.

"It also healed his wounds by the time he woke."

"Vampire spit; gotta love it," I said. "Oi! Hang on! How's he going to fix me, then? I'm not drinking vampire spit again! Zero. Zero!"

"Quiet, Pet," said Zero, with the certain ice in his voice that I couldn't disobey. "People are beginning to look at us."

"How come we're coming out here, then?" I asked. "Don't we usually go straight home?"

"We were being followed," Zero said. "I'd rather not bring strays home with us."

"Good idea," I said, in heartfelt agreement. I added, more quietly, "I'm not drinking vampire spit again."

Zero didn't answer me. He didn't talk all the rest of the way home, either. I didn't mind; we didn't have far to walk, but even though I didn't hurt as much as I had while we were Between, my body seemed to feel as though it *should* be hurting, and there was a strange lethargy to my walk.

By the time I saw the double-story, off-white patch of street that was our house, it was an effort to pick up each foot, and I stumped grimly after Zero with all the joy of a terrier about to visit the vet.

I was so tired that I didn't even see that someone was sitting on the poky little veranda until they stood and strolled toward the balustrade.

Slender, suited, and faintly smirking. Pointed chin with a mouth that always seemed to be pouting, and perfectly styled hair. Skin the colour of milky coffee and dark, dangerous eyes that were slitted as he watched us.

Ah, great. It was the vampire.

I stomped up the stairs after Zero, wondering if the steps were meant to feel like they were jarring me on the inside like I was spring loaded.

To JinYeong, Zero said, "Look after the pet. It's got some broken bones; maybe more. Come and take care of the detective afterward."

One of JinYeong's eyebrows went up. He pursed his mouth and looked at me sidewise, then sighed and pinched my ear between two long fingers.

"*Durowa, Petteu,*" he said, and pulled me through the wall and into the house.

Normally, I would have threatened him a bit—or at least resisted being dragged around the place by my ear—but I was so tired I just plopped down on the couch and glared at him.

That eyebrow went up again. "*Wae?*"

"Don't wanna swallow your spit again," I mumbled.

JinYeong snorted softly. I wasn't sure if it was an offended snort, or an amused one. "*Pilyo obseo.*"

I had to think about that for far too long. Then, yawning, I asked, "You mean there's no need for me to swallow your spit? Good. What do we do, then?"

Very deliberately, JinYeong opened his teeth and put them back together with a faint, almost porcelain click.

"You're gunna *bite* me?"

JinYeong's eyes, liquid and darkly amused, rested on me. "*Ne.*"

"Ah, man," I grumbled. "Well, I s'pose it's better than drinking your spit, anyway. Hurry up and get it over with, then."

He leaned forward, ducking his head for my neck, and I swatted at him.

"Gross! Not there!"

This time, JinYeong was definitely offended. He lifted his head to glare at me, and when I pushed my wrist toward him, he looked at it like it was something the neighbourhood cat had left on his doorstep.

"What? You don't like wrists? You bit Tuatu on the wrist last time."

JinYeong pushed my wrist away with one finger and leaned in again. I thought he was going to ignore me and bite my neck anyway, and I was trying to decide how angry I could be bothered to be when he hooked his finger into the short sleeve of my t-shirt to make a bare patch of skin on my shoulder, and bit me there instead.

It hurt, but not as much as my broken finger had hurt when I first discovered it. I said sulkily, "Ow."

JinYeong looked up through his lashes but didn't otherwise move, his mouth warm and cold at the same time. I tried not to move too much—I hadn't expected it to take longer than it had taken with Detective Tuatu that time: A single bite, a single second, then oblivion—and although my broken ribs didn't exactly *hurt* at the moment, they felt weird and out of place.

"How come I'm not falling asleep?" I asked.

Dunno who I was asking—Athelas wasn't there, and he was the one who usually answered me. Zero mostly didn't, and even if JinYeong did, nine times out of ten, I couldn't understand him anyway.

"Oh, that's right," I added, to the same general audience of myself. "I've already got vampire saliva running around my body. That's probably it."

JinYeong made a small mumble of noise that I took for agreement. I felt a bit sleepy, but not the kind of knockout sleepy I'd experienced when I ingested his saliva. Maybe I would ask Athelas about it when he got back from work.

"You gunna be much longer?" I asked JinYeong, peering down at him. I was beginning to suspect that he was more concerned about drinking my blood than helping me to heal, even if I couldn't see any blood around his lips.

A moment later, JinYeong drew back. I grimaced involuntarily; if it had hurt when he first bit me, it hurt much more as the teeth came out.

I said "Ow!" again, sadly as he pulled back, and there was a slightly wet chuckle from JinYeong. He leaned forward once more, eyes slit, and licked the wound he'd made. That was gross, but the blood stopped welling, and it stopped hurting straight away, so I only really said "Yuck," out of habit.

JinYeong sat back with red lips and heavy lids, looking far too satisfied.

"Oi!" I said resentfully. "Were you drinking my blood?"

JinYeong gave me a bloody, sharp-edged grin.

From behind me, Zero said, "The blood would have come out whether or not he drank it. It might as well be used."

"It was being used where it was."

"Bites on the shoulder hurt more than ones to the neck," he told me. To JinYeong, he said, "Tend to the detective. I'll take him home when he's fallen asleep."

"*Ye, hyung*," purred Jin Yeong.

He was flaming happy. Oversized mosquito.

I turned around to ask Zero, "Should the detective be going home? Reckon there's some people out to get him."

I had put a dryad at the detective's house, though. It was a small plant that wasn't always a plant, and lived to protect—that should mean something, right? He'd be safe.

"The detective will have to look after himself," said Zero. He wasn't looking at me; he was looking through his desk. He definitely didn't want to discuss this with me; but more than that, I got the feeling that he was concerned about something else.

I couldn't help saying, "He can't look after himself if he's unconscious," but I didn't want to push it. I was *pretty* certain the dryad would be good enough protection for most things, and it was better than nothing.

It wasn't like I'd be able to change Zero's mind, anyway. The only reason he'd helped Detective Tuatu with his previous case was because I'd gotten involved and my three psychos had been responsible for my involvement. Getting me out of trouble had involved getting Detective Tuatu out of trouble, so things had worked out. I didn't have that kind of leverage this time.

"When's Athelas getting home, anyway?" I asked. "He's at work a lot lately, isn't he? What's he trying to find out?"

"Don't bother Athelas with questions when he gets home," Zero warned me, and followed Jin Yeong back upstairs.

Jin Yeong came back down later, but Zero didn't. I would have wondered what was happening up there, but I felt the slight sideways tug to the fabric of the house as Zero left. He must have been taking Tuatu home.

I would have complained to the uninterested Jin Yeong about that, but I didn't feel as energetic as I would normally have felt about it. I mean, I know I was injured, but it wasn't like the injuries weren't being fixed. It was as though my mind still thought I was injured and in pain, leaving me utterly disinclined to do anything but hunch up on the sofa with the vague uneasiness of someone who's forgotten something important, like turning off the stove.

Besides, Jin Yeong was inclined to pace around the living room, and that was off-putting. Why was he so restless?

Oh yeah. That's right. I'd booby trapped the house before I left yesterday. They weren't proper booby traps—they were vampire booby traps. Stuff that obsessive-compulsive, numbers-loving, finicky vampires would be bothered by on a very fundamental level. Stuff like a single curtain ring missing from a set, the pictures around the house being a few millimetres higher on one side than the other—maybe a *very* tiny drop of someone else's perfume in a certain irritating vampire's wardrobe.

I grinned. Jin Yeong looked at me suspiciously and went away again with an annoyed "*Aish!*" but he came back as soon as he heard the jug boiling for coffee.

ATHELAS HADN'T COME HOME BY DINNER TIME, AND NEITHER had Zero, which was rude. Jin Yeong came back downstairs to pace, and that was annoying enough to make me pull out my phone and try to call Athelas. I didn't want to be eating dinner with only the vampire for company.

Enough was enough.

Jin Yeong paused from his pacing long enough to look quizzically at me as I put the phone to my ear. I stuck my tongue out at him to tell him to mind his own business, and he flicked his eyes toward the ceiling and went on with his pacing.

The phone rang for far too long, but just as I was beginning to think I wasn't going to get any answer, there was a slight beep, and I heard someone pick up the line.

"Athelas?"

Nothing, just a murmur in the background.

I said again, "Athelas? You coming home for tea?"

"Ah!" sighed a voice that definitely wasn't Athelas'. "Very good!"

"Oh, heck no!" I said, and hung up. I threw my phone on the coffee table and complained to JinYeong, "Think my phone's still hacked after Between. Some weirdo was just whispering in my ear. Flaming creepy!"

One of JinYeong's brows went up. He picked up my phone from the coffee table and looked it over, but he mustn't have been able to see anything wrong with it, because he threw it back down on the coffee table a few moments later.

"*Pab hae,*" he said to me.

"Whatever," I muttered, but I got up to make us something to eat, anyway. I was hungry, too, or I might have pretended not to understand.

I went back to the couch after dinner, lying down to take up all the space so that JinYeong couldn't sit down as well, and somehow or other I fell asleep while I was waiting for Zero and Athelas to get home.

I fell into a confused dream of voices asking my name and prodding at me, that devolved further until I was back with the muddy little tackers poking at me again, and woke up just as confused, to see Zero stepping down into the living room.

He stopped when he saw me, and asked, "Why are you sleeping here?"

"Just happened," I mumbled. I felt weird.

Actually, I felt great. Why was that? I was pretty sure I'd been nearly half killed yesterday.

That's right. Vampire spit.

I looked down at the hand that had had the broken finger, and it was straight and unbroken. It wasn't even a little bit bruised anymore; nothing like the mess it had been yesterday. I wriggled it cautiously and it bent without a pang, so I used it to poke myself in the ribs.

Nothing there, either.

I felt for my collarbone, and while I was doing that, I asked Zero sleepily, "Where were you?"

"Taking a walk," Zero said briefly.

That woke me up a bit more. "Yeah, but where were you walking *to*?"

I mean, he wasn't gunna tell me, but I wanted him to know that I knew he wasn't telling me stuff. I wanted to *make* him not tell me, instead of talking past me.

"Go back to sleep, Pet."

"Can't," I said. "My owner just came home at—hang on, what is it? Three in the morning? Yeah, my owner just came home at three in the morning. We pets can't ever get back to sleep after that. We're too excited."

I looked him up and down, searching for a certain tell that was, contradictorily, both bright and shadowy, and saw it there on his forehead.

"You've been getting all lordly Between, haven't you?" I demanded. That was the bright shadow of a crown that banded across his forehead. I'd seen it once or twice before.

"Pet—"

"And where's Athelas? Did he not come home again? He's working a bit hard, isn't he?"

"I wasn't being lordly Between," said Zero, after a pause. "I was accessing my birthright."

"Isn't that dangerous for you?" I asked. If he was going to distract me from inconvenient questions about Athelas—and I would have to come back to that question later, too—by answering other questions that were a bit less inconvenient, I was gunna take full advantage. "Accessing your birthright when you're Between? Got the impression you were trying to avoid some people."

Zero looked at me for a very long time before he said, "Only if I'm too slow."

"You were cleaning up the detective's blood, weren't you?" I said accusingly.

"If you're not going to sleep, get me coffee."

"All right," I said, and got up. "But you were Between, cleaning up blood, weren't you?"

"It's just as well I did," Zero said. "Why didn't you tell me you'd left blood there yourself?"

"Me? But—oh!" I said guiltily. "Forgot about the thorns."

"I already took care of that when I came to get you," said Zero.

"Yeah? What blood, then?"

The scent of JinYeong's cologne wafted into the room a moment or two before he did. "*Ko*," he said. "*Coppi isseo?*"

"Just about to make it. What do you mean, nose?" I felt my nose carefully, and there was a crustiness there that flaked away in rusty brown bits that might once have been red. "Oi! When did my nose start bleeding?"

He answered me with something I was pretty sure was *When you broke it*.

"That's funny," I said. "I don't remember that breaking."

Zero said, very coldly, "You didn't clean up the pet after you healed it?"

JinYeong shrugged and said something about an order.

"Let me guess," I said. "He says you didn't tell him to clean me up, just to heal me."

JinYeong grinned.

"I've scrubbed the blood from Between, at any rate," said Zero. "Is the pet still affected?"

"*Ne.*"

"Affected by what? Oh, vampire spit? Yeah, that's still going on. It came in pretty handy, actually."

There was a slight snort from JinYeong, and a short, dismissive sentence.

"What?" I demanded. "We did all right! You try fighting a rock troll!"

JinYeong said a couple more sentences in Korean that I was pretty sure claimed he *had*, in fact, fought rock trolls; three of them at once.

It was my turn to snort. I did it much more loudly than he had, scattering more bits of flaky red, and scoffed, "'*Course* you did!"

"*Ibwa, Petteu!*"

Look here, Pet.

"Can't," I said smugly, skipping away into the kitchen. "Gotta make coffee. Boss says."

He followed me into the kitchen anyway, and sat elegantly on the other side of the kitchen island as I boiled the jug and got out the coffee beans, resting his chin on the palm of his hand.

"What?" I demanded. "It's no good glaring at me."

"*Isseo, matchi?*" he said, eyes narrow. *There's something, isn't there?*

Heck yeah, there was. He had to have noticed some of the things I'd done around the place, even if he didn't know he'd noticed 'em. If I'd done a good enough job, it would have been grating at him for the last couple of days.

"Dunno what you're talking about," I said.

"*Ittda,*" muttered JinYeong, this time to himself. "*Hwakshilhae.*"

I turned around to put the coffee beans in the grinder and grinned at the cracked tile above the sink. I wondered which thing it was that was bothering him. Probably the curtains; they were the most obvious.

While the coffee was grinding, I washed my face in the sink. When the water ran clear instead of rusty brown, I wiped my face on the inside of my shirt and called out to Zero, "How's the detective?"

"Sleeping," came Zero's voice. "He'll be recovered when he wakes up."

"Any cops around his place?" I turned around with the ground beans, still wiping at my face with one hunched shoulder, and found JinYeong watching me with narrow eyes. I mouthed *what?* at him and kept going with the coffee.

"One or two," Zero said, stepping up into the kitchen. "They didn't see me arrive. Come here, Pet."

I threw him a wary look but did as I was told. First he looked at my nose, then my formerly broken finger; then he got me to do a few reaches and stretches—probably checking on the ribs and stuff.

"Good as new!" I told him happily.

JinYeong looked smug at that, annoying little mosquito. He said something at the ceiling in a soft, satisfied sort of a way, and that was annoying, too; but since he'd actually fixed me, I didn't like to be too grumpy about it.

"Don't go to see the detective for a while," Zero said to me, and sat down beside JinYeong.

"Why?" I argued. "He's injured—"

"He'll be healed by the time he wakes up."

"—and there's someone out there trying to frame him."

"Exactly," said Zero, as someone knocked at the door.

"Yeah, but—"

"You are not," said Zero, his voice much colder, "to go and see the detective until I tell you otherwise."

Again, someone knocked at the door.

"Anyone bothered about that?" I asked.

"Ignore it," Zero said. "Humans don't answer the door at this time of day. They usually don't knock on other people's doors, either."

"Yeah," I said. "But I reckon we should answer this time."

Zero leaned his forearms on the kitchen island. "Why?"

"'Cos I reckon the knocking is coming from the linen closet."

CHAPTER THREE

Jin Yeong's head came up swiftly. "*Hyeong, eotteokaeyo?*"

"I don't know," Zero said slowly. "Whoever it is might have—never mind. There's no use worrying about that right now. They can't get in unless I let them in."

"You gunna let 'em in?"

It took him a moment to answer, and that worried me. I didn't often see Zero hesitate.

"Yes," he said. "But not just yet. They may not know exactly where we are."

"Who's *they?*"

"I don't know," he said, but there was hesitation in his eyes as well.

"Yeah, but you've got a pretty good idea, don't you?"

"While they're here, try not to notice things," he said.

"Things like what?"

"Between things. You're just a pet: A very human pet."

"*Nae kkoya,*" said Jin Yeong, as if he was agreeing.

"What, I'm supposed to pretend I belong to him?"

"You do belong to him. You belong to all of us."

"Yeah, but—"

"Don't argue with me, Pet," said Zero, with finality. "Don't argue with them, either. Don't talk to them at all if you can help it. Jin Yeong—"

"*Kurae, kurae, nan halgaeyo.*"

Zero didn't look convinced that Jin Yeong either understood, or would behave himself, but he nodded. "Very well. The room may change around you—don't mind it. Everything will be where you need it to be, it will simply look a little different. The view from the windows might also be different."

I couldn't help grinning. "Are we moving house?"

"Something like that," said Zero. "They've got a fix on one of the doors from Between, but there's no need to let them have the human location. We can always get rid of that door later if need be."

"That gunna help?"

"If we do well this morning, perhaps."

The knocking came again, this time more loudly, and someone said distantly, "My lord, please allow us in. We're here officially."

The house around us flickered. Jin Yeong grabbed a wall, but I didn't realise what was happening in time, and when the house shivered and became more an idea of a house than a solid object, I fell over.

Zero's huge hand grabbed me by the collar just as it looked like I was going to sink through the floor, and reefed me back up through the carpet.

"I told you to not see things when they got here, not before," he said. "Use your eyes."

I looked around, and the house shifted before my eyes. For a moment it was the house I'd lived in for years, then it was another house; much smaller and neater.

"Don't do that," I muttered, and it flickered once more.

When things stopped moving, it almost looked like my old house around me again, and I wasn't sinking through the carpet.

"Jin Yeong?"

"*Quaenchanayo*," said JinYeong, and disappeared into the kitchen.

Pity I hadn't thought to do the same. I edged toward the two support beams that were behind the couches, and said, "What, we're ready? That was quick."

Zero said, "Be sure to keep quiet as much as possible, Pet."

"Yeah, got it," I said, and gave him the thumbs up. I felt a bit sick in the stomach, actually. The house moving around us shouldn't have worried me too much—after the times I'd been Between, it shouldn't have felt much different—but there *was* something different about it.

Maybe that was the difference between magic and Between. I would have to ask Athelas about it when he *finally* got home. And thinking of Athelas, it was definitely weird that he hadn't shown up in the last couple of days. Zero didn't look worried, but Zero didn't ever really look *anything*.

I was so busy thinking about Athelas that I was taken by surprise when Zero opened the linen closet and two gold-armoured fae shouldered their way through the door frame and into the living room.

One was male, his colouring as golden as his armour, the other female, her hair raven dark and oiled in braids. The male took the lead, very nearly oblivious to the female who strode after him, which made me think she was his lieutenant—if those were the kind of ranks fae held in their forces, anyway.

These people—were these people part of that group Zero called Enforcers? Was that the 'gold' they were always talking about?

Another thought struck me, and I grimaced. They'd come from Between, right into the house. I'd never seen that happen before. I mean, Zero and the others came straight into the house from Between, but we'd never had visitors that way—not unless you counted the old mad bloke, and he wasn't Behindkind. He already knew where the house was, anyway, and he was human, so he'd used human ways of sneaking in.

Oh boy. What's the bet this was my fault? What's the bet someone had tracked me and Tuatu through Between? Was that what Zero had been about to say earlier?

I grimaced and edged just a bit behind one of the support beams. Dead cert. It couldn't be a coincidence that someone had found the house right after me and Tuatu were wandering around Between by ourselves.

Hang on, though. How would they know I belonged to Zero?

Maybe it wasn't my fault.

Zero waited until they were in the room properly, and until the golden fae shifted uncomfortably, before he asked, "For what reason have you tracked me down?"

Jin Yeong chose that moment to saunter back into the living room from the kitchen, raising an insolent brow at the two fae as he passed them to stand by Zero.

That reminded me that I was pretty close to hiding behind the wooden beam, and I shuffled a bit closer to Zero as well.

The golden fae said in a rich, plummy voice, "What is that *thing* doing with you?"

Okay, that was rude.

I glared at the fae, crossing my arms, but held my tongue. Zero had said not to talk if I could avoid it. I was not gunna talk.

It wasn't until I saw Jin Yeong baring his teeth at the golden fae that I realised I wasn't the one being talked about, after all. He said something snarly and bloody, prowling a few steps back toward the fae, and Zero held out one arm to stop him.

"Don't stop it," said the golden fae, his top lip curling back in disgust. "I'll be happy to put it out of its misery once and for all."

"*Hyeong,*" said Jin Yeong, a laugh trembling on his voice and his eyes bright with death. "*Ah, hyeong, jinjja andwaeyo?*"

"Sit down, Jin Yeong," Zero said.

Jin Yeong, very elegantly, very deliberately, sat down on our usual couch and crossed one leg over the other, watching the golden fae through his lashes. His mouth was pursed mockingly as usual, but I could see the bloody darkness to his eyes.

"I really don't know why you make such things a part of your unit," the golden fae said.

I nearly grinned. For once, I wasn't the one who was being treated like I wasn't there—or like I was something someone had scraped off their boot after a walk through the back paddock. It was nice for a change.

Hang on, though.

Who did this prissy little fae think he was, to come into our house and make remarks about Jin Yeong?

"Who's this galah?" I demanded.

The fae looked down the bridge of his nose at me, a slight, well-bred frown between his straight golden brows. "What is *that*?" he asked, in a pained voice. It sounded like he'd been trying not to notice me as much as he could and regretted that he couldn't do so any longer.

"I'm a pet," I said, and champed my teeth at him. "I bite, too, so watch it."

I mean, Jin Yeong is an annoying little git, but he's *our* annoying little git, and no one should be allowed to bother him except us.

"It's our pet," said Zero briefly. "Ignore it. Coffee, Pet."

"And refreshments," said the fae sharply.

I was pretty sure I wasn't imagining the way the female fae's eyes flicked briefly toward the ceiling. I met her eyes by accident as she smoothed out her expression again, and for the very smallest amount of time I saw a gleam of amusement to them.

If it comes right down to it, I'd rather have my masters than hers, anyway.

I took myself off into the kitchen to see what I had around. Good thing I'd been shopping yesterday. And that I already had a few things ready in the fridge.

Good thing there was a decent blood supply, too. I grinned and took out one of the bags. I'd been meaning to try something —might as well do that today.

I wasn't grinning when I came back out with a tray of *hors d'oeuvres* and coffee, though. That would have been stupid. Athelas wasn't here to have tea, but I brought out a pot as well; I figured the female fae would probably like it, and it wasn't like she'd done anything to annoy me.

I was right; she went right for the pot while the golden fae went for a cup of coffee and the *hors d'oeuvres*. She might even have tipped her head slightly at me in thanks, and that was more than my three psychos usually did, either. I gave her a bit of a grin and pushed the butter shortbreads toward her. Athelas always likes those, too.

Plus I was pretty sure she wouldn't like the other stuff I'd brought out.

Zero took his usual biscuits, too. He asked the golden fae, "Why are the Enforcers suddenly interested in my unit again?"

Rats. I'd missed stuff while I was in the kitchen. I should have been listening.

"The Enforcers are always interested in your unit," said the golden fae. "Particularly when it seems as though it's beginning to mimic a unit you once formed with—"

"This unit is different," Zero said harshly.

"Is it?" The golden fae reached for a butter shortbread, then drew his hand back and took one of the darker snacks on the tray —one of the savoury ones with mince and a few other things in them.

In his seat, Jin Yeong suddenly leaned forward, his eyes flickering from the *hors d'oeuvres* to the golden fae, and then up at me. I blinked back at him expressionlessly, and he sat back again.

"That's a shame," said the golden fae. "I was sent to give you permission to start such a unit once again—on the strict understanding that it won't be officially acknowledged."

Zero, his voice quiet and dangerous, asked, "What makes it different from the last one, in that case?"

"They won't countenance it, but they won't obstruct it, either. Not this time. Things are becoming messy Between, and the human world needs closer policing."

"Why not make a proper unit—or units, in that case?"

The golden fae sipped his coffee. "Even someone as far away from Behind politics as yourself must realise that Behindkind don't appreciate humans being protected at the expense of Behindkind."

"More than anyone," said Zero, with the same kind of emphasis as the other fae, "I know exactly how much Behindkind don't appreciate humans being protected at the expense of Behindkind."

"Thus it happens that I come to see you," said the golden fae, and finally bit into the savoury snack.

I counted to about three before he spat it out, retching against the back of his hand. Behind him, the female fae went very stone-like, her face as still as a statue's. I was pretty sure she was trying hard not to laugh.

"Oh yeah," I said, to the retching fae. "That's one of JinYeong's. You probably shouldn't eat those. They're a bit fresh."

He got himself under control, face red and eyes watering. "There's fresh blood in it!"

"That's what I said. JinYeong likes his refreshments with a bit of blood in them. You want the ones that are on the other side of the plate."

"I am no longer hungry!" snapped the fae.

"Pet," said Zero, and although his voice was quiet, it wasn't *dangerous* quiet. Actually, I wasn't sure exactly what tone it had to it. "Take these refreshments back into the kitchen. Leave the coffee. *Stay* in the kitchen."

"Yes, boss," I said cheerfully. I gathered up everything that was edible—plus the golden fae's cup, which he put back on the tray with an expression of disgust—and took myself off into the kitchen again.

I mean, I could still eavesdrop from the kitchen, and at least there I didn't have to look at the golden fae's smug little face.

I heard his nasty plummy voice say, "Is it safe to be keeping that where it can see so much?"

"The pet is useful to me," Zero said, his voice flat and unanswerable.

"I suppose you can always dispose of it when it has reached the end of its usefulness," the golden fae said, but he sounded dissatisfied.

"I'm more use than you are," I muttered to myself. "At least I can cook. At least I can tell the difference between cooked and uncooked pastries."

"As for your offer—"

I held my breath. Take it, Zero. Take the offer. We could look after humans who are being hurt by Behindkind.

"—we're declining it."

I let out a small, bitter huff of air. That would have been too much to ask, I suppose. Maybe he could be convinced. Maybe he just needed to be reminded of his human side. Maybe—

"Perhaps you feel like you can't make a decision at once," said the golden fae, a disagreeable ally.

"I've made my decision."

"I've been instructed to revisit you in a month's time to hear your final answer."

"I've given you my final answer."

"Even so," said the golden fae, his voice straining to remain polite. "I will return again in a month's time to hear your final answer."

I grinned at the wrong scenery outside the window. I might not like Zero's answer to the proposition being offered, but I was pretty happy about how much it annoyed the fae. I was also fairly certain that when the fae came back to meet us again, he wouldn't find it as easy as he thought to get back.

There was a faint rustling from the living room, and I caught the play of shadows against the wall. I wondered if Zero knew the shadows were set off by foliage on the breeze, caught in street-light from the real windows instead of the ones that looked like they were there. It was all fake daylight out there, and I wouldn't put it past the fae to realise the light and shadows weren't quite in the right place.

Should I go in there and make a distraction?

Bad idea, said a voice inside me that had an edge of Zero's voice to it. Luckily, Zero herded the two fae back toward the linen cupboard before I had the chance to do more than take a few steps back toward the living room.

Neither of them looked in my direction as they passed the kitchen, which was probably just as well since I was supposed to be being unnoticeable. I mean, I hadn't done that great of a job, but no one had actually tried to kill me today, so that was a win.

I took some mince out of the freezer for dinner, feeling pleased with myself. There was still going to be a bit of a battle when it came to convincing Zero to take what he'd been offered, I had no doubt about that, but in general, life felt vaguely promising.

Down the hall, the door to the linen cupboard closed with a distinct snap, and the play of light and shadow from the windows fluttered. I looked toward the closest window and saw the normal view; mostly darkness with a bit of tree and shrub lit by the street-lights. Things felt a bit colder, too, but that could have been the shadow falling across the floor from the direction of the living room.

Zero stood in the doorway.

I smiled hopefully at him, and the smallest of lines formed between his brows, like he was in pain. He opened his mouth to speak, but nothing came out.

With the air of a man who gives up on everything, he vanished from the door.

I would have followed him out, but in his wake came Jin Yeong, prowling into the room to lean elegantly against the kitchen island.

I looked at him suspiciously. "What?"

Jin Yeong narrowed his eyes at me. "*Noh mwohya?*"

"What?" I demanded again.

His eyes flicked away, mouth pursed in discontent, and I saw his gaze fall on the plate of remaining snacks. His face brightened, and he reached for one of the ones the golden fae had spat out in disgust earlier.

"Wouldn't eat that one, 'f' I was you," I advised.

Suspiciously, Jin Yeong asked something I was pretty sure was *blood snack, yes?*

"Nah," I told him. "That's one with holy water."

He flicked it back down with a hiss, then looked at me and reached for it again. "*Anin ko,*" he said.

I don't think so.

I grinned at him. "Wanna bet on it?"

He stopped with his hand halfway there, eyes on me. He was almost completely certain there was nothing bad in it. But with me grinning at him, he couldn't be sure, and there was no way he wanted to give me the satisfaction of spitting it out in front of me.

I blinked innocently at him, and that did it.

Jin Yeong said, "*Aish!*" and turned on his heel, stalking away into the living room.

"Sure you don't want it?" I called after him. "Made fresh today!"

He threw himself into our couch, taking up the whole thing by way of revenge, and regarded the ceiling coolly as if that's what he had been going to do with his morning, anyway. I put away the piece he'd been about to pick up for later. It didn't have holy water in it. I mean, I don't have a death wish or anything.

I followed him out into the living room again, since the house had stopped being another house and was back to being itself. At least I wouldn't have to worry about shadows being in weird places or my foot going through the carpet again.

"You lot going to be looking after humans now?" I asked. I knew he wasn't, but maybe if I could—

"No," said Zero. "We are not forming the kind of unit that protects humans."

Hopefully, I suggested, "Not officially?"

"Not at all."

"Oh," I said sadly.

"Pet—"

"Yeah, I know. You're big important fae, and you don't have time to make sure burbling humanity isn't taken advantage of."

"*Ne*," said Jin Yeong.

"Protecting humans is a useless venture," said Zero brusquely. "One is saved, and ten die. They run headlong into danger and disregard common sense, and they die on a breath. There's no sensible way to take care of them."

"I haven't died yet," I reminded him.

Zero looked at me for a silent moment, then said, "I told you to stay unnoticed."

"I'm not the one who was nearly puking on the carpet," I said. "It was that galah. I was flamin' quiet."

"*Jal haesso, Petteu*," said Jin Yeong, and patted me on the head as he sauntered past on his way to the bathroom.

"What, is he going out?" I asked. "What for?"

"He's looking for some information for me," Zero said. "Don't change the subject. Insulting fae Enforcers and giving them blood to eat is *not* staying unnoticed. You're fortunate he thought you're an idiot."

"There's a change," I muttered. Imagine that. Fae thinking I was an idiot.

Zero didn't reply, and maybe that made me a bit too confident. It felt as though, even though he was chiding me, he wasn't exactly *angry* about the golden fae.

"What about Detective Tuatu?" I asked. "He's gunna need some help. Someone's trying to frame him for murder, and I don't reckon they're going to stop just because it didn't work the first time."

"Pet," said Zero. "You're a stray. Don't bring home strays of your own."

"I'm not a stray," I said, with dignity. "This is *my* house."

"Not yet," he said. "And if you make more trouble than you're worth, I'll erase your memories and leave you out on the street to follow someone else home."

"Detective Tuatu's not a stray, either," I said, because I couldn't say what I really wanted to say. Not if I wanted to stay here in my house.

Then I went back to the kitchen, with hot, tight eyes, and did the washing up.

Just have to last a few more months, I told myself. Or maybe it would be a year or two. Who cared if Zero was cold and horrible, so long as I got my house in the end? Who cared what the fae thought, anyway? I'd have my house, and myself, and quietness again.

I wondered if the old mad bloke had ever thought that. I wondered what he'd been like before the fae made him mad. Probably like me, trying to doggy paddle at the edges of water that was too vast and violent and incomprehensible to survive in. It was probably why he went mad.

I waited until I heard the shower turning on for a second time before I wandered back out into the living room and sat on my couch. I'd already felt Jin Yeong leaving the house while I was in the kitchen, with the faint tug of reality being pulled aside, so I let myself lounge out a bit into his space, staring up at the ceiling and wondering about stuff in general.

Stuff like the way my hearing was getting better—or maybe just growing in a different direction—and the fact that if I wanted to keep tabs on how Detective Tuatu was doing, I'd have to be pretty sneaky about it.

I glanced across at my phone, still sitting on the coffee table, and wondered if I dared call him on it. Not until Zero had a look at it, probably. Not, I realised belatedly, at this time of day, either.

When the shower turned off and Zero emerged, I could have asked him to look at the phone. Instead, I pretended to be asleep. And yeah, I know it was childish of me, but there was a raw patch at the back of my throat, or maybe it was further down in my chest, and I didn't want to talk to anyone.

Zero didn't notice. At least, I don't think he did. I only knew he'd walked past me because I saw the flicker of darkness through my eyelids as he passed in front of the light, and when I opened my eyes just a crack, he was nowhere to be seen. He'd probably gone to bed for the few hours' sleep he usually takes.

I should have done the same thing, but I didn't; I fell asleep on the couch again. It wasn't that I was waiting for Athelas. I wasn't. But I'd made tea while Zero was in the shower, and if Athelas didn't come home in time, I'd have to empty the pot before the leaves got all stuck to the pot, right?

I fell asleep instead, and maybe it was a cold morning, because I found myself walking down cold, white corridors. Kinda like hospital corridors, but shinier, and no smell of disin-fectant.

What the heck? How did I get here?

I looked around me for some kind of sign or lettering—or even doors—but there was nothing. Just...corridor. Really shiny, white corridor.

I was dreaming, right? Had to be.

But the floor felt hard beneath the soles of my sneakers, and when I nudged the toe of one of them against the tiles, it was grippy, too.

"Flamin' fantastic," I said sourly. "Just what I need."

If it was a dream, it was still too flaming real for comfort. I had a tendency to die in dreams that felt too real, and dying was just a bit too real as well.

I turned around a couple of times, trying to find the best way to go, but it was just a corridor. And I mean, it was *just* a corridor: Ceiling, floor, walls along the side that continued to infinity, for all I knew. It was corridor and nothing else.

Had to be a dream, right? But Between was pretty weird, too; and Behind was even weirder. If there was anywhere in the world —worlds? Layers?—where there could be a place that was nothing but corridor, Between or Behind would be that place.

I started walking again; there wasn't much else I could do. If I was dreaming, I didn't know the right way to wake myself up, and if I wasn't dreaming, I had to try and get out some way. There wasn't much of a feel of Between about the place, either. It didn't have that sense of stuff hiding just below the surface, or of things just unseen. You know, that kinda crawling feeling that stuff is moving in the corners of your eyes whenever you look away; the one that makes you hunch your shoulders and scratch your cheek.

Maybe this was what it felt like to go mad.

I squinted at the far end of the hall. There was something huge and rectangular hanging there—a blueprint that was probably of the building I was in, with a big button sticker on it that I could just make out to read *you are here*. It had a title on it, too, but it was too small to read.

Right. That's where I was going. End of the hall. Maybe I could figure out where I was, and if this was a dream. If it was a dream it probably didn't matter where I was, but if it wasn't—hang on. Too confusing. Whatever this was, I wanted to know where I was.

So I kept walking.

I walked for a *long* time. Maybe an hour or two. The hallway never got any shorter in front of me, but it never got any longer behind me, either. I would have given up sooner, but it wasn't like I had anywhere to be, and if it comes to a choice between a boring dream and a nightmare, I'll take the boring dream every time. *If* it was a dream. The floor still felt pretty real beneath my feet, and the cool air made the inside of my nose too dry.

I stopped eventually and sat down with my back against one of the hallway walls. It was solid against my back, too, and very cold; opposite me was one exactly the same. White, smooth, and cold. Just a wall.

Hang on, though. Was it really a wall?

I looked at it suspiciously.

It looked like a wall. But then, stuff that looked like itself in the human world was very often different depending on how I could see it Between, so that was no guarantee it was really a wall. Actually, I was getting to the point where I didn't know if walls were really walls, or whether they were actually hedges, or whatever they were Between and Behind, and I just couldn't see them properly.

If it only depends on your point of view, what's actually the truth?

I stared at the wall, wondering about that, until it occurred to me that no matter whether I got an answer to that particular question or not, it wouldn't help me right now, so I went back to basics. I narrowed my focus on that wall, trying to see it differently—trying to see it as anything else other than a wall—and for a split second there was a flicker to it, like an old VHS that had been watched one too many times.

"Not a wall, then," I said. I'd wasted a couple of hours walking. If this was real, maybe Zero would have noticed my absence at the house by now. If it was a dream, all I'd done was bore myself for a couple of hours. I didn't ever remember a dream being this long, though. I was pretty sure I would have remembered something as long and boring as walking for two hours.

I turned my head sideways and gazed at the wall that wasn't a wall, and after a while it seemed like it might not be so shiny and hard as it had been. Or perhaps as if in its other form, its Between form, it wasn't really something solid at all.

"Looks like mist," I said to myself, ignoring the question of whether Between and Behind existed in dreams. I'd never dreamed them before, but my dreams weren't exactly the measure of normality before now, either. I reached out to touch the sudden cloudiness, and there was a sensation of cool dampness beneath my fingers.

At first it was a springy sort of cool dampness, but when I said persuasively to it, "You're actually mist, you know," it became ethereally cool and damp, and my hand passed right through.

I stepped through it quickly before it could change its mind—before I could think about what I might meet once past it, too. Lucky for me, it wasn't anything dangerous; just a white, bare room with nothing but some sort of modern art at the centre of it. There were no doors, and no windows.

Great. First I was in a hallway with no end, and now I was in a room with no doors.

Someone sighed. It was a familiar sigh, and I was already looking around when Athelas' voice said, "Ah, you're back again."

It wasn't modern art in the centre of the room. It was Athelas.

And when I say he was in the centre of the room, I mean the *centre*. Not just in the centre of the floor, but in the centre of the space itself, suspended in mid-air by nothing like a magician's assistant, his back to the floor and his chest to the ceiling. His head dipped toward the floor as if he were unconscious despite the sigh and the speech, and even his legs dangled a little lower than his torso.

I took a step toward him, swallowing, and wondered how it was that he was hanging from nothing. It wasn't nothing, though;

as I moved closer, there was a kind of glitter to the space beneath him, filaments dancing on the air behind him.

No, not behind him—*through* him. Filaments of glass or spiderweb, piercing him in a million different places from beneath and emerging on the other side as if they suspended him from the ceiling.

Oh man.

I really hoped this was a dream.

"What—" I stopped, and swallowed again, because I thought I might throw up. "What happened to you, Athelas?"

Athelas' head lolled to the side until he was looking at me through the strands around him, eyes cold and shadowed. "What are you doing here again?"

"What do you mean, again? This is the first time. Actually, I'm not even sure I'm here. I think maybe I'm dreaming."

Athelas gave a groaning sort of laugh and said, "I should have killed you when I had the chance."

It took my breath away, because I could hear in his voice that he really did regret it—at least halfway.

"That's flamin' rude!" I said resentfully. "I make you tea and everything!"

That made Athelas laugh again, and I wished he hadn't, because it sounded painful.

"They've done a much better job on you this time," he said.

He was looking at me now, and I wished he wouldn't do that, either. He didn't even blink; just stared at me through slit eyes of a grey that was too light and depthless to belong to a human. I'd seen him look at other Behindkind that way, but never me.

"Don't glare at me," I said, and my voice didn't shake. I was *pretty* sure it was a dream. Like, sixty percent. "I didn't do this to you."

He pulled in a rough breath, and that scared me, too.

"Ah, they've certainly put some effort," he murmured. "Shall I kill you, I wonder?"

I was pretty sure he was talking to himself and not me, and I didn't like getting too close to him while he wasn't paying attention to me—he looked like he was just on edge enough to hurt me if I surprised him. So I said, "I'm gunna try to get you down from there."

Athelas laughed under his breath, looking at me through slit eyes. "I'll kill you," he said.

"What the heck is your problem?" I demanded. "What are you gunna kill me for? I'm trying to help you!"

"Really?"

"What does it look like I'm doing?" I wanted to call him something nasty, but I was afraid that if I did, he really would try to kill me. Anyway, I don't think human insults really work on Behindkind. Maybe I can ask Jin Yeong about Behindkind insults —he probably knows enough of 'em.

"Who knows?" said Athelas, and he laughed again.

It had a sticky sound to it, and I wondered exactly where those filaments were passing through his body. Nowhere good, by the sounds of it.

"Well, I'm trying to help," I told him, stepping carefully around all the filaments. I didn't want to think what they'd do to him if I accidentally touched one of them. "What are these things?"

"A very textbook way to go about information gathering," Athelas said, turning his head back to the ceiling. "How disappointing. Your methods were just beginning to seem more interesting. If you think to disarm me by asking questions to which you already know the answers, you'll find yourself very much mistaken."

"Fine," I said. "Don't be helpful. You're the one who's in a pickle, you know. I could just leave you here."

His head whipped around so quickly that it made me jump.

"They are moonlight," he said, and laughed again. "They came for me by moonlight, and now hell bars the way."

"That's the opposite of helpful," I said. To myself, I muttered, "Don't know why fae can't just say what they mean."

"Life is so boring when everyone says what they mean."

"Yeah? How're you finding life at the moment, then?"

Athelas looked back up at the ceiling, and I was instantly regretful. Even if it was a dream, that was a horrible thing to say to him.

"Sorry," I said gruffly. "I shouldn't have said that."

"So difficult, isn't it, Pet? Minding one's tongue."

"Some days more than others," I said, making another circle around him. The filaments might have been moonlight, for all I could see how they worked, or how on earth I was supposed to get him out of them. It made me think of a less fiery but significantly more torturous Brunhildan funeral pyre. "We're not gunna have any Valkyries shrieking at us when we get you off those things, are we?"

"So ignorant," sighed Athelas. "Didn't I tell you they're moonlight? Valkyries would have killed me at once—this rig is not meant for death, but torture."

"I know," I said, and there was a snubbed sound to my voice.

"Dear me, are you crying? I'm sure she wouldn't have done that."

"No," I said, and cleared my throat. I was probably going to have to touch those things. I needed to know how strong they were, and how much connection they had with Athelas.

Again, those grey eyes came to bear on me, light and almost unbearable. He said, "It's not very original of you."

I wiped my eyes so I could see the filaments more clearly. I didn't want to touch them too roughly. "You actually think I'm not Pet, don't you?"

If he thought I wasn't Pet, who did he think I was?

Ah heck. He thought I was one of his torturers. Dead cert. No wonder he'd said he would kill me!

"Didn't I say that this rig is for torture?"

"Who the heck am I, then?" I demanded, wiping away a fresh swell of salt-water from my eyes. "If I'm not myself, I wanna know. I usually dream as myself."

I put out a hand to the filaments, and my fingers glittered with salt-water just like the filaments glittered with moonlight. When I touched one, the lightest breath of contact, Athelas groaned deep and harsh.

I snatched my hand away. "Right," I said, and there was a cold wetness all down my cheeks. "This is gunna take a while."

"Take your time, Pet," he gasped, and laughed. "I'll wait on your convenience."

"Stop laughing," I said, pushing away tears. "It's weird and scary."

"If you don't want me to laugh, you should work on your interrogation tactics," said Athelas. "You were much better at this the first time—at the first, I really believed you were the Pet. Killing you helped with that."

"What do you mean, killing me?"

Athelas smiled at me, all steel and ice. "I'm sure you remember as well as I. You died quite swiftly, but I don't think it was painless."

"But you said before that you *wished* you'd killed me, not that you'd done it!"

"Indeed."

It made no sense. But it didn't stop me saying resentfully, "Why'd you kill me? What did I ever do to you?"

"Why should I not?"

"If you believed it was me, why kill me?" Something sour and acidy ate away at my stomach.

"You seem to be under the mistaken impression that I care for the pet," Athelas said. "You are, of course, free to carry on your interrogation in any way that seems good to you. I'm a captive audience, after all."

For some reason, that made me smile. Athelas was even

lecturing his torturers—the fae really did believe themselves superior to everyone. "You saying it's torture to talk to me?"

Athelas closed his eyes. "Of a sort, I suppose. You'll notice I did not refer to it as effective torture."

"Are those threads really moonlight?"

"It's good policy for a torturer to know his or her own equipment," said Athelas, without opening his eyes. "There's nothing more terrifying than a torturer who knows what he's capable of."

"If I try to take them out, will they all hurt you as much as they do now?"

"Oh, at least that much! There's nothing like moonlight for piercing where it shouldn't pierce. Just ask your little shifter friend."

"I thought you could heal," I said. "Can't you heal yourself?"

The ghost of a smile passed over Athelas' face. "You have a certain knack, don't you? Such an innocent way of putting your finger on sore spots! I wonder how they knew about that?"

A horrible thought seared my stomach and burned its way up my throat. "Do you mean you're healing all the time, and those things—those things are—they're—"

"Always healing, always injured. A really very charming method of torture; something I would deign to use, myself. Did I not say a torturer should know his own equipment? You are unconvincingly ignorant."

For a couple of minutes, I thought I might actually be sick. I crouched close to the floor with my legs pressing into my stomach and chest, one palm flat against the cold floor, and concentrated on breathing.

When I looked up again, Athelas was still smiling at me with his head in that same, uncomfortable twist; a curious smile that was something more like a smile I was used to seeing from him.

"Yes, that would bother the pet. Shall I tell you some other things that would bother her? We'll play a game—two lies and a truth. You decide which is true and which is false. Convince me with that borrowed face that you really are the pet, and perhaps you'll get some information out of it."

"Just wait until I get you back home," I told him. "I'll put some of JinYeong's blood in your tea or something. *And* I won't buy the expensive tea you like! I'll go back to giving you supermarket tea, and you'll just have to make do! Why can't you speak without making a riddle of everything?"

"You—she—" he stopped, and seemed surprised. "Dear me. I seem to be having some difficulty. I believe I know how Zero feels at last."

I wasn't sure I wanted to know, but I asked anyway. "What are you talking about?"

"How did you get to know that about her?" Athelas' head turned again, and this time his grey eyes were steel. "Did you get her? I'd swear you couldn't get through my lord, so you must have taken her by stealth."

"Nobody got me!" I said. "I'm right here. You. Can. See. Me."

"Yes," said Athelas, and he turned his face away. "Leave now, while you can."

"After I've rescued you."

There was no way I was going to leave him suspended in moonlight that pierced him through every time he healed; not if I could do anything about it. I went back to the threads, hoping that I could see them as something else, or convince them to be something else.

"I really wouldn't bother," said Athelas. "I'll only kill you."

I didn't look up into his eyes again. I was too afraid of what I would see there. So I kept going on the threads of moonlight, trying to see them as something different, or feel them as something different. They were Between stuff, after all. There had to be a way of seeing them differently to make them be something different.

Athelas would have to understand if I rescued him, wouldn't he? He'd have to understand that I was me, and that I wasn't pretending to be anything. I had a very strong feeling that things I did in this dream—if it was a dream—might be able to have some impact on real life, just like things done Between could impact Behind or the human world. And if that was the case, freeing Athelas in a dream might also help free him in real life.

I wanted to do what I could, no matter how much Athelas mocked, or laughed, or cut with his words. None of my three psychos were very good at using words for anything other than bare bones communication or elaborate mocking, but we were linked until they finished their business and until I got my house back. I wasn't going to let any of them die if I could help it. They were *my* psychos.

So I reached for the strands of moonlight again, steeling myself against the shuddering gasp from Athelas as I touched them, and felt them, hard and resistant, between my fingers.

Moonlight, my eye. They were something a lot more substantial than that.

"You're moonlight," I said to them. "Why aren't you acting like it?"

Hang on. *Hang* on.

Moonlight was just reflected sunlight, right? And sunlight could be waves or particles.

"You should stop moving so much," I said to the solid strands of moonlight. "Why do you want to work so hard? There's no need to be making yourself a wave as well as a particle. Why don't you try just being particles?"

The moonlight glittered, and it seemed to me that it grew just a little bit less solid. I reached out a finger to stroke one of the strands, lightly and painlessly, and my finger passed right through it, sending a shower of glittering particles to the shining floor beneath us. The blue, bloody patch in Athelas' shoulder, where it had pierced just a minute ago, welled with the heaviness of blood and sank a little.

Athelas opened his eyes for the first time in a very long while, and said raggedly, "Interesting. Is it really to be a rescue?"

"That's the point," I said. I nearly added, *You ungrateful, twisty Behindkind, you!* but I'd said something unforgivably awful to him already.

"Of course," said Athelas, his eyes a glitter of steel before they closed again. He turned his head back toward the ceiling. "I almost forgot. Do let me know when you're finished, won't you?"

I would have had to bite my tongue again if I hadn't seen how parchment pale his face looked; how deep the lines beside his eyes had become. Whatever Athelas might say, or laugh, he was in a crazy amount of pain; and if pets snap when they're in pain, Behindkind are capable of worse.

Maybe the lower parts of the moonlight had been supporting Athelas more than the upper part of them had been suspending him, because as the last of them disintegrated from beneath his upper body, he sank slowly against me, the fullness of his weight bearing down on my shoulders bit by bit. I caught him as he drifted downward, and the filaments from above shredded into particles of light, drifting down after him until he rested on the cold white floor in a nimbus of sparkling moonlight.

Blood leaked from him in round-edged waves and haloed his body, and I hesitated for just a second. He'd said he was going to kill me. Not just once, but three or four times now.

But I couldn't just leave him there; and it wasn't like he could hurt me now, anyway. He couldn't even sit up. There was blood seeping from him everywhere, deep blue and sticky, and his eyes were nearly shut, with just a slit of glittering grey to them to show he was still alive—still, barely, conscious.

I dragged him, bloody and supine, over to one of the walls, and propped him there. He fell against me, too heavy to support his own weight, and for a brief moment cold, grey eyes met mine, close and unclouded and utterly alien.

Then there was a hand around my neck—just a single hand, long fingers pinning me to the wall with inhuman strength.

Ah heck.

Athelas was healing a *lot* quicker than I'd expected.

"Athelas," I said, my voice strained. "Please don't kill me."

"Too late," he whispered.

Pressure, around my neck. Pressure, and suffocation; then, more quickly than I would have thought, darkness.

CHAPTER FOUR

I WOKE, GASPING, AND I COULD BREATHE. I OPENED MY EYES thankfully, and the first thing I saw was Jin Yeong, sitting on the coffee table again, watching me.

I threw the cushion at him.

"What the heck!"

Jin Yeong ducked, and the pillow sailed over his head, ruffling his hair.

"*Ya, Petteu!*"

"Don't throw things at Jin Yeong," said Zero.

Good grief, how had I missed Zero sitting there on the coffee table beside Jin Yeong? It was probably the nasty sharp gleam to the vampire's eyes—he was still watching me, and that made me uncomfortable.

"What?" I demanded. "Why are you both watching me sleep? It's weird."

"What were you dreaming about?" Zero asked. "Stop waving your arms around, Pet."

"I'm *trying* to get up! My head's gone weird."

"It's the vampire saliva starting to wear off. You'll live. What did you dream about?"

"Athelas, if you really gotta know."

Zero frowned. "What about Athelas?"

"He killed me," I said shortly, wrapping my arms around my knees. There was a sick, wobbly feeling inside me. I'd always known Athelas could kill me at a moment's notice if he wanted to, but I suppose I hadn't really expected him to do it. "Which was rude because I was trying to help him."

"Is that why you were crying?"

"I wasn't crying," I said automatically, ignoring the tear the rolled down my cheek. There was still water welling up there; my eyes felt wobbly and slick, too.

Jin Yeong reached out a finger and stole the tear.

"Oi!"

He brandished it in my face. "*Igon mwohya?*"

"What is it with you and personal space lately?" I said sourly, hunching my shoulder to wipe away the salty drop on the other cheek before he could pinch that, too.

He said something short and toothy, that whispered a meaning of *bite me* in my head though I didn't know the words he used.

I turned to Zero with wide eyes. "Did the vampire just say *Bite me?*"

Jin Yeong grinned.

"Don't bite the vampire."

I gave Jin Yeong a dirty look. "Heck no. I'd probably catch something nasty."

That stopped him grinning.

Zero, his expression put-upon, asked, very clearly, "What exactly did you dream, Pet?"

"Hang on—how come I understood him?" I asked. I didn't want to talk about Athelas. I didn't want to talk about the painful way he'd laughed, or the strands of moonlight piercing his body, or the way his hand had curled around my neck at the last and killed me. "I don't know those words in Korean. I don't even think that was a literal translation to make, but I still understood it."

It didn't occur to me until Zero said, "Athelas isn't here," that I realised I was actually waiting for Athelas to explain. That made my chin do a very weird wobbling sort of thing.

He'd *killed* me. Why was I still listening for his voice?

"Yeah," I said. "I know that."

There was silence for a few moments, until Jin Yeong's derisive sniff of laughter broke it.

Zero said, "I asked you a question, Pet."

"Yeah, but how come I could understand the vampire when—"

Jin Yeong hissed again, this time in annoyance. "*Vampire bureuji ma. Oppalago burreo.*"

"I'm not calling you *Oppa*!" I snapped. "You're flaming old! I should be calling you *Ahjussi*!"

Jin Yeong was still opening and closing his mouth in shock when Zero said icily, "Pet, if you can't keep to the same subject for more than ten seconds at a time, I'll leave you and Jin Yeong to fight it out between the two of you. *Answer my question.*"

I desperately wanted to complain that Jin Yeong had started it, but Zero's eyes were absolutely icy, and I didn't dare. I didn't dare to ask him about Jin Yeong again, either; or to keep stalling about Athelas.

I said, "Dreamt I was in a corridor. Nothing there but walls and floor. Walked for ages but it didn't go anywhere, so I went through the wall instead."

"And then?"

"And then I was in a room. Athelas was there, too; somebody strung him up with clear stuff in the middle of the room—he said it was moonlight. He thought I was someone else and said he was going to kill me but I figured if I could get him out of the moonlight stuff, he'd realise it was me."

Zero didn't look at me, and his voice was quiet when he asked, "Did he?"

"Nah. Got him out, then he killed me and I woke up."

"You woke up," said Zero. He didn't say it in any particular way; just said it, which was weird, because of course I woke up. He'd seen me wake up. But he'd said it as if perhaps he was surprised I'd woken up.

I sat up straighter in alarm. "What? I'm not supposed to wake up if he kills me in a dream?"

"It depends on the dream," Zero said, sitting back with folded arms. "Since you're not dead, it seems unlikely that your dream was the kind of dream that will be useful to us. Tell me if you have it again."

"If it's not the sort to be useful, how come you want to know?"

"Because if you have it again, it *is* the sort that will be useful," said Zero sharply. "And because if it's the useful sort, I want to know why you aren't dead."

"You lot really need to learn how to say things in a nicer way," I complained. "You're not supposed to ask people why they didn't die."

"Should I have congratulated you?" asked Zero.

The ice was gone from his eyes, and I got the impression that he was a bit amused, so I said, "Yeah."

"Congratulations on not dying," he said. "Make sure to tell me if you dream the same dream again."

"Okay," I said. There was a bit more warmth in me than there had been earlier. I asked him, "You want coffee?"

"Yes."

"Biscuits?"

"Yes."

"Oh yeah. And can you check out my phone? Jin Yeong says it's okay, but someone else was talking on it when me and Tuatu were Between, pretending to be you."

Zero took the phone and looked it over, front and back. "I told you earlier: phones don't get reception Between. There was no need to attach anything to your phone—you were simply given another form of reception."

I thought about that, and said, "Yeah, but it happened later, too; when I tried to call Athelas."

"Did it?"

"Yeah."

"The reception you had Between was suspect, but there's nothing wrong with it now."

"Oh. Is it okay if I do a bit of shopping today? We won't have anything to make pancakes with if I don't."

Zero thought about that for longer than it should have taken, and I was very careful not to grin. I was pretty sure Zero loved pancakes about as much as I loved coffee, even if he would never say so, and I was also pretty sure that he was caught between upholding his ban on me going to see the detective, and his desire for pancakes.

At last, he said. "All right."

"And since I'm gunna be out—"

"You're not going to see the detective."

"Yeah, but—"

"I don't want you near the detective at the moment. It's too...complicated."

"How come it's okay for me to go to the supermarket alone, but not to Tuatu?" I demanded. "I've been attacked three times at the supermarket—I've never been attacked at his place!"

"You're not going to the supermarket alone," said Zero. "I'm going, too."

"Oh. Well, couldn't you come to Tuatu's house, too?"

"*Pet*," said Zero, between his teeth.

JinYeong, still sitting on the coffee table, laughed sarcastically to himself, and I thought I caught a murmur of meaning to what he said. Not enough to understand it, but enough to know he was probably being rude about me.

I waited for a bit, but Zero didn't get any chattier, and JinYeong only waved me away to the kitchen. He was probably still ticked off at me.

Suited me. I went to the kitchen to make coffee, and called the detective. If I couldn't see him, I at least wanted to make sure he was alive.

The line picked up, and there was the sound of wary silence. Good sign, I s'pose.

"Oi," I said, filling the jug.

There was silence for a beat longer, then a sigh. "Pet. Why are you calling?"

"Making sure you're still alive," I said, grinning. It was good to know he was still alive. Some days, it felt like I was surrounded by death—an irresistible force that mowed down anyone who stood too near to me.

I dunno. Maybe I've seen too many bodies in my lifetime. Seeing my parents' bodies would have been enough, but since the psychos had moved in two months ago, I'd seen more bodies than most gravediggers.

"I'm still alive."

I set the jug to boiling and looked around for the mugs. Great. No one had done the washing up. I mean, I was the one who was meant to do it, but it was still annoying.

I asked, "Your bones heal?"

"Yes. Actually—"

"Vampire spit."

"What?"

"Vampire spit. It's like the sticky plaster of the fae world, apparently."

"I was healed in an impossibly quick amount of time by *vampire spit*?"

"Yep."

"That's disgusting."

"Thank you!" I said. "None of those three understand how gross it is. Probably because they don't have to use it—actually, they *can't* use it, so..."

"Pet? What's wrong?"

"Nothing wrong," I said slowly. "Just wondering something."

"What?"

"Why Jin Yeong hasn't tried to kill Zero yet."

"Is that something you're expecting?"

"Dunno," I said. If I got technical about it, Jin Yeong had already made several feints at ridding the world of Zero—but if I really thought about it, feints were all they were. Things had gotten very close to a fight more than once, but although Zero had been wary, he had never been completely defensive. Perhaps Zero, as much as I now did, understood that if Jin Yeong had really been serious about killing him, there were much easier ways about it than an outright fight.

It was only a little while since I'd learned how dangerous vampire and lycanthrope saliva was to Behindkind like Zero.

I said, "Just wondering why Jin Yeong hasn't gone in for poisonings yet."

"Did the vampire bite me?"

"Yeah," I said. I dug vindictively into the coffee with a teaspoon, and briefly considered putting something nasty into Jin Yeong's cup. "You're lucky. You were already unconscious."

"Yeah," said Tuatu. He didn't sound convinced. "Pet, is the quiet one around?"

"Athelas? Nope. Why? You wanna talk to him?"

"Yes."

"I wouldn't, if I were you," I said, with conviction. Detective Tuatu wasn't anything like knowledgeable enough to be dealing safely with Athelas, and he'd already slipped up when they first met. Pity I hadn't got to him first to tell him not to agree that he owed anything to Athelas. "What do you want to talk to him about?"

"That body—"

"Your friend, was it?"

"Yes. I've just been paid a visit by Internal Affairs; they want to know why we were texting and why I didn't meet him the night we were supposed to meet."

"Awkward."

"Yes. I couldn't tell them we *had* met that night—"

"Well, technically you didn't," I said. There was silence on the other end of the line. "Sorry," I said. "But you really didn't, and it's probably better if you don't tell them you were there that night."

Detective Tuatu sounded slightly amused. "Thank you, Pet; I'm not as naïve as you seem to think."

I ignored that. "You get arrested?"

"Nope. Not even officially under investigation—yet. They wanted me to help with their enquiries."

Good. The dryad must be doing its job.

"All right," I said. "Be careful. And if you see Athelas at the cop shop, tell him I've been trying to call, all right?"

Tuatu's voice sharpened. "You haven't seen him since that day?"

"Yeah. Why?"

"Neither have I. I thought he'd stopped doing whatever it was he was doing—that's why I asked you if he was there. I have some questions for him. You haven't seen him at *all*?"

"Yeah," I said again, and there was another layer to the feeling of worry that had begun to creep over me. Athelas was Athelas, but still...

"Do you think it's got something to do with—"

"Whoever's trying to frame you for murder? Yeah. I wouldn't leave the house for a few days, if I were you. Don't reckon it's safe."

He didn't promise anything, just asked, "What about you?"

"Me? I got Zero. I'm fine," I said. "Worry about yourself. Oi. Gotta go: The coffee's ready."

"All right," he said. "But don't go doing anything stupid, Pet. Whatever you did last time to convince them to help out—just don't."

"Yeah, yeah," I said, and hung up.

When I came back into the living room with the coffee and biscuits, Zero was less laconic, but not by much.

"Do you dream like that often?" he asked, as he took his coffee. Maybe he was trying to stop me bringing up Tuatu again.

"Nah," I said. It had been at least eight or nine years since I'd had this sort of dream. "I usually get nightmares. Just one, though, so maybe that doesn't count."

Zero sipped his coffee. "You wouldn't call what you had a nightmare?"

That made me stop and think. Long enough to make Jin Yeong get up with an impatient sound between his teeth and take his own coffee from me.

At last, I said uncertainly, "I don't think so. It wasn't...scary enough, I suppose."

"Being killed by Athelas wasn't scary enough for you?"

"Dunno, maybe my brain was pretty sure it was a dream all along. It was nasty, but it wasn't as scary as the nightmare. And I could do stuff in it—walk around, get into the next area. Like a video game."

"But you've had nothing like it before?"

I shrugged. "Maybe when I was younger. I didn't have anyone to dream about for the last little bit. I only dream about people I know."

"I see," said Zero, but he didn't sound satisfied. He was frowning, too, but I didn't think that was at me in particular. More like he was worried, maybe.

And yeah, maybe I wasn't telling him everything, but I didn't particularly want to talk about the kind of dreams I'd had when I was younger. They usually involved horrible things happening to people I loved, and that was worse than dreaming about horrible things happening to my psychos, even if I was personally involved in the horrible things that were happening to Athelas.

There was something about being personally involved that

made it, I dunno, *better* than having to watch it unfold without being about to do anything about it. Yeah, Athelas had killed me, but it was still better than waking up sobbing because I hadn't been able to do anything about the deaths of people I loved.

After lunch, I went to the supermarket without thinking about it—without checking first with Zero, either. I remembered when I was halfway there, but since I was pretty sure Zero had only said he was going to come with me to reinforce that I wasn't to go and see Tuatu, I didn't bother to turn around. It hadn't been *that* long since I'd been shopping, and I could have lasted longer without coming again, but I'd kinda thought I might be able to spend a bit of time looking for my werewolf friend Daniel if I came out alone—even if Zero wouldn't let me go see Tuatu.

He was recuperating, too, which just goes to show you what happens when people get too close to me.

I was just thinking about that gloomily when a very big, very white hand reached over my shoulder and grabbed the handle of the trolley I'd been about to pull out.

"Flaming heck!" I said, jumping.

It didn't show on his face, but I know he was laughing. "You should pay more attention when you're out alone. I could have hit you over the head before you knew I was here."

I glared at him. "Yeah? What about the security cameras in here?"

"Security cameras are easily taken care of," said Zero, shuffling me out of the way. "Pay attention when you're out alone."

"Fair enough," I said, trotting after him. "You worried about me? 'Zat why you followed me?"

"I didn't follow you," Zero said, steering toward the wrong aisle. "I came directly from Between."

I grabbed the trolley and towed him toward the rice aisle instead. "Yeah, whatever."

"How long will this take?"

"What, the shopping?"

"Yes."

"Dunno, half an hour. Hey, reckon I'll go to the library afterward."

I looked up and found that Zero's cold blue eyes were resting thoughtfully on me. "I'll come with you," he said. "How long will that take?"

"You only came out with me to make sure I don't go off to visit Detective Tuatu, didn't you?" I said accusingly. I'd thought as much—there was no need for me to be going to the library right now.

Zero looked down at me but didn't answer. He steered the trolley toward the next aisle, passing the rice aisle.

"Okay, so if we can't visit Detective Tuatu, can we go see Daniel?" I asked, giving up on the right aisle. We needed more biscuits, anyway.

"Why do you want to see the lycanthrope?"

"Wanna make sure he's healing all right."

"He's recovering well."

"Yeah, but I want to *see* him recovering well."

"You've still got some vampire saliva in your system," said Zero. There was a bit of a burr to his voice—or maybe a buzz. Like the sound was just a bit off. "It's not wise while he's still in his wolf form."

Oh yeah. Zero was probably making sure no one could overhear us talking about stuff like vampires.

I frowned. "What, you reckon he'd bite me or something?"

"No," Zero said. "It's more likely that you'd bite him."

"What? Jin Yeong didn't!"

Shortly, Zero said, "Jin Yeong has had many years to learn how to control his instincts."

"Yeah? Is that why he's so flamin' sulky all the time?"

Zero cleared his throat and turned down the aisle.

"It's no good," I told him. "I already saw you smile."

"I didn't smile."

"Yeah you did. Who thought it was a good idea to turn someone like Jin Yeong, anyway?"

"It was my decision," said Zero, and continued down the aisle and right past the biscuits like he hadn't just dropped a bombshell.

I grabbed the biscuits and chased after him. "What? You turned him? How? You're not a vampire! You're not, are you?"

"Keep your voice down a little, Pet," said Zero. "I'm not a vampire. Jin Yeong is the result of Behindkind trying to interfere in human concerns."

"You mean trying to help humans?"

"It's interference. It never ends well, and rarely ends in anything other than disaster."

"Okay, well, I can see why you don't want to help humans if you end up with vampires like Jin Yeong, but you helped me."

"I didn't help," Zero said. "We have a bargain. An even exchange. Your service for our protection until a certain set of circumstances play out."

"Yeah, but you've saved my life heaps of times, and you're training me, so—"

"It's an even exchange," he repeated, voice hard. "Don't begin to read too much into bargains with the fae, Pet. Humans who read too much into fae bargains tend to die young."

"Pretty sure humans around fae die pretty young in general," I muttered.

It wasn't meant for Zero to hear, but he said grimly, "Exactly. Help from the fae very rarely helps the humans involved."

"Okay, that makes a lot more sense," I said.

Zero, looking as though he thought he might regret asking, asked warily, "What makes more sense?"

"If you're trying to protect humans by keeping out of their way, you should just say so. I don't get why you have to talk in riddles all the time."

"I don't care what happens to humans."

"Yeah?" I said. "'Cos you keep pretending you don't care what happens to them, but I'm pretty sure you've just been trying to protect them in a different way."

Zero's icy blue eyes met mine and then turned away. "No," he said. "I was explaining it in a way that might appeal to you. I do not care what happens to humans."

"All right, if you say so," I said, seizing the side of the trolley to pull it across the top of two aisles. We needed flour next. I'd told Zero I would make him pancakes. "How did it happen, anyway? Jin Yeong, I mean?"

"I found him in the mountains in South Korea during the Korean war," said Zero. "His entire corps had been slaughtered by vampires, and one of them stayed to play with Jin Yeong. He was... more of a handful than the vampire expected. They were both dying when I got there, on either side of the room, and neither of them knew what to do about it."

"Why'd you say it was your decision, then?" I asked. "Didn't he just, I dunno, *turn* into one when he died?"

"No," Zero said. "A vampire's bite isn't the only thing needed to turn a human into a vampire. Vampire blood is also needed."

"Weird," I muttered to myself. "Figure he was just hatched or something. Hang on—is that why you lot kept telling me not to bite him?"

"Yes."

"You could have just told me that's why. It's not like it's something I thought about."

Zero glanced back at me. "You didn't think of it?"

"Nah. I'm not a vampire; why would I have a burning urge to bite someone?"

"Ingesting vampire saliva usually has that effect on humans. If they're able to bite a vampire within the time they're influenced, the cycle continues on to create a new vampire. If it's Behindkind the infected person bites—"

"Wait, if I'd bitten you then, it could've killed you? Just like if JinYeong or Daniel bit you?"

"Yes."

I drew in a breath between my teeth. "And you just kept me around the house when you thought I might go biting you? After I turned halfway into a lycanthrope and nearly did bite you?"

"I told you not to bite me."

"Yeah, I remember." It had seemed weird at the time, but now that I knew why—actually, no, it was even weirder. "But if it's an instinctive thing—"

"You didn't bite me."

"No, 'cos I'm not an emotionally unstable vampire."

"Athelas spoke of testing you; causing you to ingest more potent levels of saliva to gauge your resistance to the side-effects of it."

"More potent—*what* sort of more potent levels? JinYeong already licked his finger and shoved it down my throat!"

"If JinYeong kissed you to prolong the time of exposure—"

"*What?* No. *Heck* no."

Zero's blue eyes were just a bit paler, and I was pretty sure that was a sign of amusement. He only said, "Athelas didn't think you would like the idea, so I didn't bring it up with you."

I couldn't help grinning. "Pretty sure JinYeong wouldn't like it much, either."

"Athelas didn't mention that, but he did say that in the interests of scientific research—"

"Heck no. Not even for scientific research."

"There are," said Zero thoughtfully, "a very great number of things that need to be scientifically researched when it comes to you."

"Oi! I'm not a lab rat, you know."

"No," Zero said, but there was a considering sort of tone to his voice that worried me. "You're not. That also is very interesting."

. . .

ZERO AND JINYEONG WERE BOTH GONE THE NEXT MORNING, which was flaming rude when I'd woken up in the mood to cook. Making a big, cooked breakfast would have settled that, I was pretty sure. Maybe it would also have settled the uneasy, restless feeling of discomfort that I had this morning.

"Fine," I said to the empty house. "If bad stuff happens, it's not my fault."

I hadn't agreed not to go see Daniel, just Tuatu. I hadn't even agreed not to call Tuatu again, so I could do that if I wanted to. I could do whatever I wanted to do. I could *definitely* go out this morning, anyway.

I would be very careful to stay away from Between, men in green pants, and blokes who looked like moths with a blank for a face. Zero couldn't complain if I was being careful, after all.

That decided, I made myself coffee and ate biscuits, muttering. I didn't know where to find Daniel, which was annoying; if I'd still had the lycanthrope abilities I'd had when I was close to turning wolf, I would have been able to find him. It put a bit of a damper on my plans for going out and Doing Stuff By Myself, but it occurred to me that at least I could go find Athelas at the police station and see with my own eyes that he was still whole and healthy, instead of stranded in the middle of a room by fibres of moonlight.

That would be nice, I thought doubtfully. Well, not exactly nice; but I wanted to see the Athelas who was real—not the one who had killed me in a dream. And despite the fact that Zero seemed determined to be off-hand about Athelas' prolonged absence and my dream, I didn't feel comfortable at all.

Mind you, would I really know if Zero was uncomfortable about it? I thought about that doubtfully as I tied the laces on my sneakers. He was pretty flaming hard to read at the best of times, and I'd only just started to be able to pick it when he was amused at something. Sometimes, anyway. Would I really know if he was worried? Would he let me know if he was worried?

Yeah, probably not.

He'd asked me about the dream—*and* he'd said to tell him if I dreamed it again. Zero didn't do stuff for no reason. So maybe he really was worried after all, even if he was talking as though he wasn't. Or maybe Zero just knew more about it than me and JinYeong, and wasn't telling. That was also pretty likely.

In any case, I was going to see what I could sniff out about Athelas. And if Athelas was okay, and there was nothing to worry about, then I was going to see if I could find Daniel. Maybe I'd try and find Daniel even if Athelas wasn't okay—Daniel hadn't killed me, after all.

I took it easy on the walk there. It was starting to get a bit hotter these days now that summer was really here. As hot as it ever gets in Tassie, anyway. The sun really bites here, but there isn't usually much in the way of humidity. The sun's enough to get you too hot, though, and I didn't seem to have a hat that wasn't webbed up with about ten years' worth of spiders. I can face the stuff that comes through Between from Behind, but I can't handle spiders. I'd rather just set fire to the stuff. Hopefully JinYeong never finds that out.

I was still a bit too hot by the time I got to the cop shop, but after I'd washed away the sweat at the tap outside Maccas and dried my face on my shirt, I was pretty normal looking. I must have been, because the cop that offered to take me to Detective Tuatu's desk was cheerful and didn't ask what I had in my pockets.

He left me at Detective Tuatu's desk, too, which was pretty handy as well as really trusting for a cop. I hadn't expected things to be that easy. I sat there for a little while, looking around at everyone who was moving around the floor, then got up and wandered in the direction of the toilet sign—and, more importantly, the stairwell. I was pretty sure it was the seventh floor where Athelas had been working undercover in Upper Management, and the stairwell was sure to lead there sooner or later.

The thing was to move slow but not too slow. Don't bounce. Don't draw attention to yourself. I'd managed to creep up on my psychos once or twice, after all. I mean, that was when I'd had a bit of Between to help soften my footsteps, but I'd still done it.

I looked around reflexively for a bit of Between to soften my steps, fortunately reminded of past successes, but there was no sign of anything more than the white coolness of laminate and fake marble around me as I climbed the stairs.

Mind you, no one from downstairs yelled at me to come down.

And when I finally got to the seventh floor, no one yelled at me to get lost. There wasn't even a suspicious look levelled at me, which was nice. Of course, things would probably get a bit harder once I opened the door at the top of the staircase and actually came into contact with humans again.

Humans, or something else.

I swallowed, my throat suddenly very dry. Oh yeah. What was I going to do if there were things like the Moth Man up here? Sandman, Zero had called him. I couldn't look at a Sandman's face without feeling like I was going to lose myself, but if I didn't look at them, they'd probably know I wasn't meant to be here.

I grinned a sickly kind of grin at the steps beneath me. It was probably the first time I would be glad to see a flicker of Between to my surroundings, instead of wary and a bit scared.

Well, the second time, anyway.

The first time it had happened had been here in this station. I'd been in an interview room, and I'd been so glad to see Between cracking through the wall like sun-damaged glaze, my three psychos coming to get me.

Without meaning to do it, I set my chin.

"Don't worry, Athelas," I muttered. "I'm coming for you."

Sort of, anyway. At the first sight of any Behindkind, I was probably gunna run for it and yell for Zero.

I put my hand on the door that said *push*, and pushed.

I dunno, I think I expected it be locked or something. Even if it had just been a restricted area of the cop shop, I kinda expected it to need something extra to get through. Maybe a swipe card or a pin pad or something.

I didn't, though. The door just said *push* so I pushed, and it swung open, too.

The room opened wide and tidily partitioned in front of me; a series of gridded cubicles on the left, partitioned to the shoulder, and a small, windowed office to the right that had no one sitting at the window where they should have been sitting. Air conditioning swirled softly, a flutter of disrupted paper in the background, but there was no other noise. No one else there. No one to stare, no one to display confused curiosity about why there was a skinny teenager walking in by herself. Just...no one and nothing but the air conditioning.

"What is it, Christmas?" I muttered. The difference between this floor and the one below was chillingly stark. I would have preferred to brave the stares of anyone wondering why I was there than walk into a white graveyard.

Knowing my life, it was likely there really were dead bodies hanging around. I didn't look too closely at the cubicles just in case there were bodies in them, and hurried toward the far end of the room, where a line of printers guarded the turning into a hallway.

I didn't know where I was going, but I kept going for the hallway. There was no stopping now—not when someone might appear any minute. Wherever it was I was looking for Athelas, it wouldn't be here in all the low-walled cubicles, surrounded by printers.

Nope, Athelas would have made sure he had his own office. Dead cert.

I passed by the printers, turning left, and found myself walking down a white hallway, unpleasantly reminiscent of my dream the other night. I tried not to shudder. It was just a hall-way; nothing but a hallway. There were a lot of hallways that were white and cool and felt like they went on forever.

Funny, though. I stopped part way down the hallway, staring at the far end. Lots of hallways were long and white and cold, but did a whole lot of them have the same blueprint at the end of them? The one with the button sticker that helpfully said *you are here*?

Yeah, nah. There was no way this wasn't the same one I'd dreamed.

I looked around nervously as I walked, but this hallway didn't stretch forever like the one I'd dreamed, and the blueprint actu-ally got closer as I walked toward it. Had I been here before? I didn't think so, but how else could I have dreamed about it? At least this time I was actually getting somewhere when I walked, and that helped me to squash away the horrible feeling that I could find a moonlight-pierced Athelas somewhere around the place.

It didn't help with the feeling that something had definitely gone wrong with Athelas.

I kept walking right until the end of the hall, and it let me get there, which was nice. I stopped in front of the blueprint after a quick look around to make sure there was no one watching me. The title was just the street address of the cop shop, and the words, *Hobart Police Station*. It would have been handy to see that in my dream. I'd have to remember to tell Zero that without letting on I'd seen it in real life.

Funny, though. I could have sworn the *you are here* sticker was in a bit of a different place than I'd seen it in my dream.

I looked at it a bit closer, but if it was different, it wasn't different enough for me to remember how. I left it behind with a lingering look over my shoulder, turning to the left rather than the right just because although I'm more left handed than right handed, I felt that if a nebulous *someone* didn't know that and was expecting me to go one way, it would be to the right.

Never said I'm not paranoid, did I?

It occurred to me some time after I turned the corner that I'd also turned left to get into this corridor. If I kept going, I should get back into the main room with the cubicles, shouldn't I? My eyes slid past the couple of doors in the new corridor, but instead of the window I should have been able to see on the left at the end, or the protruding tail-end of a printer or two, I saw only another left-hand turn.

Oh, and the blueprint again, with the *you are here* sticker maybe just a bit higher than it had been last time I saw it. And this time, there was no right-hand turn opposite the left-hand turning.

There was definitely something dodgy going on here. I left the doors for later and went on toward the left hand turn in the hallway, trying to remember everything I'd learned about widdershins, and wondering if it was something that was a *thing* Between. I certainly couldn't see anything else that was Between around here, but maybe widdershins was a kind of manual hack to get into Between instead of the easy way.

S'pose that was just another thing to add to the things I wanted to ask Athelas when I found him. Whether it was actually possible to make a manual way into Between that didn't involve, well, pushing into Between.

I poked my head around the edge of the hallway, and sure enough; there at the end of it was another left-hand turn. No right hand turn to take instead, either, and exactly two doors in that corridor. I looked back over my shoulder, then down the hall again. Yep. Pretty much the same position, too. Maybe they were different levels of the same rooms.

Well, I'd come this far; might as well see if it kept going on in left-hand turns like a weird, impossible corkscrew, or if I would manage to find the main room again at the end of one of the turns. I took the left-hand turn with a last look over my shoulder, trotting toward the newest iteration of the police station blueprint, and passed the two newly familiar doors, one on the right hand and the other on the left. When I got to the blueprint, there was another left-hand turn; another two doors in the new hallway.

I narrowed my eyes at it, then turned around and jogged back the way I'd come. Yeah, so maybe it was a way into Between, and maybe the different hallways were different levels of the same room each time. Question was, which one did I want? Which one was Athelas most likely to be in? I didn't know, but I did know that I wanted to make sure I could get back out before I went much further in.

I counted six right hand turns before I stopped, dizzy and a bit breathless.

Hang on.

Hang on. Where had the other room gone?

Oh yeah. I was definitely Between—or at least partway there.

The question was, *why?* I had to assume that most—if not *all* —fae could slip Between and Behind without too many issues; so why was there a floor in the police station that had a widdershins hallway that should have ended up where it started but didn't?

And more importantly, how the heck was I supposed to get out again?

"Widdershins," I said aloud. "It's got something to do with widdershins."

Pity no one had ever taught me anything about widdershins in school.

I pinched my phone out of my pocket and opened the web browser. It wouldn't load, and I stared at it for far too long before it occurred to me why that was. Ah heck. I'd used up all my data already. This is why I needed an Athelas. He might be tricky to deal with, but at least he didn't run out of data or battery.

I could phone a friend, though, couldn't I? There was reception here, which was a hopeful sign, unlike last time when I was properly Between. At least the phone was behaving itself like normal.

Obviously, I couldn't call Zero. Well, not until there was no other way out, anyway. That was just asking for trouble. And I didn't know Jin Yeong's number—or if he even had a phone—but there was always Detective Tuatu. Even if he didn't know what I needed to know, at least he could search for it on the internet.

I grinned, and called the detective. "Oi," I said, by way of greeting.

"What?" he asked cautiously. "I've got enough house plants and I'm better now."

Rude! The dryad wasn't a house plant, it was protection. I ignored his ingratitude and asked, "Know anything about widdershins?"

"What?"

"You know, widdershins?"

"My grandmother said never to go that way."

I pursed my lips and looked around me. "Oh. Whoops."

"Whoops, what?" demanded the detective. "Where are you?"

"Between a couple of floors, I reckon," I said. His voice was tight and concerned, and since Detective Tuatu tended to run into danger when he was concerned, I added, "Relax. Sit back down. I'm fine. What else did your grandmother say about widdershins?"

"Never go that way!"

"You said that."

"Go back as soon as possible."

"What else?"

"Pet, where are you?"

"Told ya. Between floors somewhere. Not exactly Between, though, I reckon. Not yet. Did your grandma tell you something about how to get out of somewhere when you've gone widdershins?"

"Deiseil!" he said, and I heard the surprise in his voice. Whatever else he'd learned from his grandmother, it was buried really deeply. I had some suspicions about his grandmother, and all of them were toward the Behind side of the world. He added, "She said you have to go deiseil to fix it. You have to look for the sun."

"Don't reckon that's gunna help. I'm inside."

There was another silence from the other end of the phone, and I couldn't help grinning. He was trying really hard.

Then Detective Tuatu said, "Does it have to be a real sun?"

Sun? Hang on a bit. There was a sun on the right-hand door of every iteration of the hallway—part of the logo on each placard, I'd thought, but now I wasn't so sure. I looked at the left-hand door and instead of a sun there was a moon.

"Ohhhhh!" I said, deeply satisfied. "Ah man, that's clever! Thanks! Catch ya next time!"

I hung up, and he rang up again a second later, making me jump.

"Pet—"

"Don't call me," I said. "I'm supposed to be sneaking. I'll bring ya something nice as a thank you later on."

I hung up again, hoping no one had heard it bingle, and put my hand on the door handle of the sun door. It wasn't like things could get worse, after all. I could only get properly Between instead of halfway there, and I'd been Between before.

It wasn't like I could get Behind from here.

Wait. Was it?

I'd think about that later when I knew I could get out, I decided. I turned the door handle and stepped into the room without stopping to think about it again. The door shut behind me with a small, definite bump that pushed me another step forward into the room. Printers at my right; gridded cubicles dead ahead; doorway leading downstairs to my left.

I was back in the main room.

Grinning, I slid my phone back into my pocket. This was

good. This was very good. Now that I knew I could get back out, I would be able to have a proper look down the widdershins hallway. I took one step toward the hallway again and heard a noise that turned my blood cold.

The door to the little receptionists' office was opening.

I dropped into a crouch within the nearest cubicle without thinking about it, my heart beating fast.

Ah heck. There was somebody coming.

CHAPTER FIVE

I SMELT HIM BEFORE I SAW HIM; THAT WHIFF OF COLOGNE sweeping forward with the breeze of the opening door. What the heck?

Why was Jin Yeong here?

And if Jin Yeong was here, did that mean Zero was, too?

Oh boy.

I heard Jin Yeong take a step forward into the room, then a second one that froze just as his foot hit the carpeted floor.

Ah heck. If I could smell him without the use of my rapidly waning, vampire-saliva-induced abilities, Jin Yeong could definitely smell me in the room with his fully-fledged abilities. Well, the particularly *non*-smell that was apparently me, anyway.

I stood up. "You following me or something?"

Jin Yeong made an annoyed sound through his teeth, and slapped the door shut behind him.

"What are you doing here?" Might as well try to brazen it out.

"*Mwoh hanun kkoya?*" He glared at me, turning the question back on me.

"Same thing as you, probably," I said. "Trying to find out why we haven't seen Athelas in the last couple of days. Oi. Don't tell Zero you saw me, and I won't tell him I saw you."

Jin Yeong gave me a flat look and said something in Korean that carried in it the meaning of "I'm *meant* to be here."

"Yeah?" I tipped up my chin at him, but he only raised an eyebrow. "I'll make you some more of those blood snacks if you don't tell. Without holy water."

His other brow went up. Jin Yeong considered, tilted his head, and said deliberately, "*Ne.*"

"Good," I said. "What'd you find? There wasn't even someone at the proper reception desk, which is pretty bad for—oh."

I looked Jin Yeong over and saw the faintest speck of blood on his cuff.

"Did you vamp the receptionist?" I said accusingly.

Jin Yeong's lips pressed together in a smug, satisfied smile. "*Ne.*"

"What did you do with her?"

He made the faintest of head-tips toward the office.

"She's still in there?"

"*Ne.*"

"You didn't kill her, did you?"

That only earned me a small, upward flick of the eyes that as far as I was concerned, could either have meant of course he had, or of course he hadn't.

I sent a suspicious look in his direction, but said, "Right. What are we gunna do, then?"

"*Uri aniya. Nanun.*"

I stuck my tongue out at him.

"*Petteu—*"

"I'm here already," I said, and grinned at him. "You don't know what I might get up to if you let me run around by myself. I'm not going home yet."

Jin Yeong sighed, and said something that suggested, *Search the office—then onwards.*

"Onwards, where?" I muttered, and caught a brief grin from him. He was looking too smug, so I added, "The widdershins part?"

I was surprised to see a faintly impressed look to Jin Yeong's face, despite his usual *moue*. That was weird and a bit off-putting, so I wrinkled my nose and looked away—and right at the slumped body of a human worker, sprawled over his desk.

"What the heck!" I complained. "Did you do that?"

One of Jin Yeong's eyebrows twitched up, but he didn't reply. He didn't need to; I could see the twin spots of blood on the bloke's collar.

"Hang on, you got here first?" He must have been in the office, vamping the receptionist, when I went through widdershins. "Your nose isn't working too well at the moment, is it?"

That earned me a glare, which was more comforting than the approval. Jin Yeong said something in Korean that included the words, *here, unexpected* and *Pet*.

"That's the point," I told him. "You're s'posed to expect the unexpected. What are you looking for?"

Jin Yeong went into a swift, elaborate spate of speech that held absolutely no meaning for me. I was pretty sure he was doing that on purpose, somehow, because I couldn't even understand the little bit I'd begun to understand every now and then.

"You're doing that on purpose," I said, and went to check on the receptionist without him. She was still breathing, and she didn't look like she'd lost too much blood, either; there were two tiny points of red on her neck where Jin Yeong had been having a quick drink, but her breathing was regular.

Just like she was sleeping.

"You say Zero sent you here?" I called softly to Jin Yeong. Considering Zero had been steadily refusing to admit to me that anything had gone wrong with Athelas, that was a flamin' cheek. He really was concerned.

"*Ne*," he said. He was flipping through the desk drawers closer to him, and he wasn't trying to be very quiet about it, either. That worried me a bit.

Not because he might get us caught, but because if someone came to find out about any suspicious noises, JinYeong might catch *them*, and I didn't yet know if JinYeong was the sort to kill humans without thinking about it any more than the Behind-kind he routinely killed.

I had my doubts. I was also pretty sure that this floor especially catered to humans.

"How come?"

JinYeong shrugged, but I was pretty sure it wasn't an *I don't know* kind of shrug. It was more likely one of the *How is it your business and why should I tell you?* kind of shrugs.

I stuck out my tongue at him and wiggled the receptionist's computer mouse to see what she still had up on the monitor.

The screen came to life in a glow of blue light, and I grinned. "Heck yeah!"

She must have been in the middle of doing the employee clockings, because there were about three different windows open. By the looks of it, one was the sign-on clock record, one was the pay screen, and the other was some sort of reconciling software.

Pretty useful for me, because now I would be able to see when Athelas had last signed in. I didn't know what last name Athelas might be going by, but I was betting it would be Butler, or Steward, or something like that.

Yep, there it was; top of the second screen I paged through: *A. Butler.* There were clockings in army time for the first couple days of the week, then nothing for the last three days. I gazed at it, frowning, for a bit too long, and JinYeong came to see what I was looking at, his face sharp and interested.

"Nothing big," I said, pointing at the line, "but I don't reckon Athelas has been here for the last couple days."

"*Ah*," said JinYeong. "*Kurae. Johah.*"

"How's that good?"

I almost heard him say, "Now we have a timeline," but the Korean he was speaking muddled the meaning of it.

"Maybe someone got him on the way to work," I suggested. "They haven't been paying him since he stopped signing in. Maybe they don't know, either.

"*Kaneunghae*," muttered JinYeong, but he didn't look convinced, and I wasn't convinced, either.

"Yeah," I agreed. "Or they've been fiddling the books to cover up when he really went missing, and they know where he is. Only I reckon it's all humans around here. I can't even see a bit of Between for someone to accidentally walk through. Not if you don't count the widdershins hall."

Actually, nothing looked dangerous up here. Dangerous for your average criminal, maybe. For Behindkind, I couldn't imagine so.

"Can't see why Athelas went undercover at all," I said. "It's all humans and paperwork. If someone from here was trying to set up the detective as a murderer, I don't reckon they would have done it by throwing a body at us from Between."

JinYeong shrugged, the shape of his mouth not quite matching the meaning of his words as he said something like, "Behindkind have many friends."

"Yeah? I don't think they're as friendly as that, but I s'pose you know what you're talking about. The question is, where's Athelas? Did someone get him on his way to work, or after he got here?"

JinYeong shrugged and wandered back into the main room, but it wasn't long before I heard him prowling toward the printers. I nipped out of the office and trotted after him like a good little pet. I didn't want to be left behind here with all the vamped humans; they were too pale and limp for comfort, even though I knew they were still breathing. I was also half-afraid someone official would come up here while they were still asleep and discover them in their vampy-chilled state. If someone discovered them, I preferred to be with Jin Yeong rather than by myself.

And then there *was* someone—someone at the door, anyway. The soft slap of a hand hitting the *push* plate on the door outside and the faint squeak as it began to swing inwards. I heard it in one split-second; the next, a swift cloud of cologne with very sharp fingers whisked me into the closest cubicle and underneath the desk.

Squashed into a space that was too small for me to comfortably sit if I were by myself, and *definitely* too small to be sharing with a glittery-eyed vampire, I hugged my legs to my chest and turned slightly away from Jin Yeong—only to be halted by his left leg, which was considerably longer than mine, and could only fit beneath the desk by stretching out around me and propping against the cubicle wall. He seemed to be sitting on the other leg, which I suppose was considerate of him. I glared at him anyway, and he snarled silently at me.

We were both uncomfortable. Perfect. And if anyone heading down the hallway looked back, they'd still probably see us until they were more than halfway down it.

Even better.

"Where is everyone?" asked someone's voice. There was a chill to it that curled around my ears like nails down a chalkboard. "There should be some workers here—humans."

"Lunch time," said a voice that sounded like a normal voice. "They'll be back later. Did you need to see one of them?"

"Not one of these ones," the first voice said dismissively. "I simply wished to be sure that nothing had gone wrong. Our other location had a small scare a couple of nights ago with a few missing staff."

An edge of grey came into sight around the wall of the cubicle that left us semi-exposed, and I gripped a fold of my jeans in my fist. It wasn't until a flicker of movement drew my attention to the finger Jin Yeong had put over his lips, his eyes pinioning me, that I realised it was his trouser leg I was clinging to instead of mine. I would have let go if I could, but I couldn't; that edge of grey separated from the cubicle wall and became the fuzzy, difficult to see shape that was distinctly that of the Sandman, the back of his head smudged into indecipherability.

I couldn't have said why—it wasn't like I could see his face properly—but I was sure it was the same one who had tried to accost me outside the supermarket a couple of weeks ago. Beside him was a human in business trousers and shirt. He was probably trying to walk carefully but it just looked like he needed the toilet.

Maybe he did. Was he afraid he was going to be killed? I would have been, if I was him. That cold, chalkboardy voice was terrifying enough, but I had seen the Sandman's real face, and I knew exactly how terrifying that could be.

To my relief, the two kept walking slowly up the hallway toward the blueprint; I willed the Sandman not to look around, and somehow, he didn't.

The human, all blue business shirt and dipping bald patch at the back of his head, surprised me by having the brass face to say, "Nothing goes wrong here."

There was a cool, grating silence, and I saw the Sandman's head turn toward the human and away from us. He said, "I am here because there *was* a problem. I had to help fix that problem."

Beside me, Jin Yeong sat forward, crowding me. I poked him in the ribs and scowled at him. *Shove over!* I mouthed.

Jin Yeong very slowly leaned closer and made a small, deliberate snap of teeth at me. Of course I stuck my tongue out at him, then hunched my shoulders and turned away. His leg was still in the way, but I could elbow that, too, if I needed to.

"The problem is solved," said the human, and his voice shook as they disappeared from my sight.

"It will be," said the Sandman. "But there are some tools needed to complete the job."

Wait. Was he—were they talking about Athelas?

I turned my head again, and my eyes met JinYeong's. He was listening intently; he'd already come to the same conclusion.

"You've already given us so much," said the human.

"It is necessary," the Sandman said, his voice muted by the length of the hallway.

I leaned forward, trying to hear, and cold fingers closed around my wrist. JinYeong's teeth were bared when I glanced at him; his leg pressed warningly against me, and I realised that I had leaned too far forward in my attempts to hear. I could again see the Sandman and his human companion, which meant they would be able to see me if they looked around.

I hunched back under the desk as they approached the end of the hallway, and as the sound of their passage faded, I tried very hard not to wriggle. I felt hemmed in by JinYeong; his leg pressing against me on one side, fingers around my wrist, his eyes and teeth glittering far too close on the other side. Why the heck did he wear so much perfume? All I could smell was JinYeong; around me, in my hair, in my nose.

I wriggled violently, elbowing JinYeong in the movement, and huffed back against the back of the cubicle to get away from his leg. There was a very small movement of the partition behind me, and JinYeong's teeth gleamed in a silent snarl.

"*Petteu,*" he hissed in my ear. "*Choshimhae!*"

"You flamin' *choshimhae!*" I whispered. "Why do you stink so much!"

"*Nemsae obseo!*"

"Shh!"

"*Ah!*" he muttered beneath this breath, and I grinned.

There was a final stirring at the end of the hallway—and if I was guessing about it, I would have guessed that it was toward the widdershins side—and the moment it ceased, I started wriggling out from under the desk. There was an annoyed mutter from JinYeong, but I ignored it. He was probably just complaining about someone finding his pong unliveable, anyway.

When we were out, I saw him briefly waver in a movement toward the widdershins hallway, but he controlled it.

"*Nawa, Petteu*," he said softly.

"What about him?" I jerked a thumb at the hallway. If the Sandman knew something about Athelas, we should be following him.

Through his teeth, Jin Yeong said the same thing he had said before; but this time the meaning hissed into my mind, hot and clear, "Come *out*, Pet!"

"No need to yell!" I muttered, but I followed him toward the door. "What about them? The humans?"

"They'll wake up soon, comfortably."

Well, that was nice, anyway. Safely on the other side of the door, with a conscious look over my shoulder, I said, still quietly, "Reckon he was talking about Athelas?"

Jin Yeong shrugged; said, "Could be, could be not," so that I understood it.

"If he was, doesn't that mean Athelas is still there in the building? That's the hall I dreamed about."

"It's Sandman," said Jin Yeong, still understandable, for a wonder. He pinched my collar between his fingers and pulled me down the stairs. "Then of course it's dreams."

"That thing gives people bad dreams as well as having a flamin' terrifying face?"

"*Mwoh, bisutae*," he agreed.

"So he could have just given me dreams about that hallway without it meaning anything?"

"*Ani. Imi isseo.*"

To my delight, that was almost understandable. If I was right, Jin Yeong was saying that there was a meaning, but the meaning wasn't necessarily that Athelas was stuck in the police station.

"Why's he giving me dreams, anyway? I don't know him; how come he's shoving nasty dreams in my head?"

"*Nado molla*," JinYeong said. He sounded annoyed, but I didn't think he was annoyed with me so much as himself, for not being able to understand what was happening.

Once we got outside, I was going to nick off by myself and have a go at trying to find Daniel, but JinYeong must have been expecting me to do something like that, because when we got out of the station, he grabbed me by the collar again before I could leg it and pulled me through a rippling of heat haze that wasn't exactly heat haze.

I grumbled and tried to shake off his hand, but there was no moving those slender fingers. For an annoyingly pretty bloke, JinYeong was even more annoyingly strong. He pulled me right into Between with him, though our shadows didn't follow us, and we walked between the road and the shadow of the fence on an *almost* bitumen path that shimmered with something warm and living. A few birds flew away as our bodiless shadows flitted past out in the real world; I heard them distantly, and almost saw them, but there were little fluttering animals on the shadowy, Between version of the wooden fence that stopped me seeing anything except them.

"What are those?" I asked, brightening straight away. They were clockwork, I was pretty sure; all tiny bolts and bright patches of colour painted on metal plates, with feathers sticking out of weird places that would never let these things fly. "Are they birds?"

"*Manjiji ma, Petteu*," said JinYeong warningly.

"Wasn't gunna touch it!" I said, pulling my hand back.

"*Igodo manjiji ma*," he added, pointing at another bright thing that had caught my attention. His finger shifted, pointing without hesitation another three times. "*Igo, igo, igodo manjiji ma.*"

"Wasn't gunna touch any of them," I muttered. He had pointed at all the interesting things ahead of us: A couple more variations of the metal birds, and what looked like it might have been a small clockwork safe. I pointed at the safe. "All right, what's that, then?"

Jin Yeong murmured something that had the meaning of *"It's none of your concern,"* which was rude. I mean, it was true, and anything that looked like a safe, left out in public, was definitely not something I wanted to be messing with, but still.

"Is that visible in the real world?" I asked him.

Jin Yeong sighed and said something I was pretty sure was, "This *is* the real world."

"Well, the human world, then?"

"*Ne.*"

"What are you gunna do about it, then?" I demanded.

"*Amudun obseo,*" he said shortly, but as we passed it, he gave it a short, solid kick that set it tumbling backwards and somehow *more* than backwards. Backwards in Between, maybe—where backwards was actually deeper into Between.

"So *that's* how you do it!" I said in satisfaction, startling Jin Yeong.

"*Hajima,*" he told me.

"Would I go messing with stuff like that?" I asked him solemnly, but I grinned all the way home.

I stopped grinning when we got home, though: Zero still wasn't there.

"Flaming rude," I said, and sat down on the couch.

Jin Yeong threw a pillow at me and said lazily, "*Pab hae,*" which meant he wanted to eat.

I nearly pretended not to understand him, but I was still feeling the urge to cook, so there was no point in cutting off my nose to spite my face. I didn't want him to feel too comfortable about things, though, so I just looked at him for a bit before asking, "How come I can understand you more these days?"

He shrugged. "*Nan molla.*"

I don't know.

"Fibber," I accused.

One of Jin Yeong's brows went up.

"It's the same thing where Zero and Athelas can understand you, isn't it? 'Cos I'm pretty sure that speaking Korean is something different from that."

Jin Yeong's lips pursed in dissatisfaction. Oh yeah. I was definitely right.

"Ohhh!" I said slowly. "It's all about hearing, isn't it? 'Cos I'm good at hearing stuff I shouldn't hear."

"*Ani*," said Jin Yeong, unconvincingly.

"It is."

"*Anin ko.*"

"Pft," I said, and advised, "You need to work on your poker face."

"You," said Jin Yeong, very clearly, though he spoke in Korean, "need to—"

He stopped, and I grinned at him. "Yeah? What do I need to do?"

"*Ah!*" snarled Jin Yeong, and stomped off to his room.

I'd almost forgotten what I'd done in his room until he swept back in, looking annoyed and uncomfortable. That's right. There was still a drop of Athelas' perfume lingering in his room. Didn't look like he'd figured out what it was, but it was still affecting him. He hadn't found the other stuff, either. I gave him a sarcastic look as he passed through the living room again, and he was annoyed by that, too; though he couldn't protest it. The whole house seemed to annoy him at the moment, though I was pretty sure he still didn't know what was bothering him, let alone what I'd done around the house. But it was getting to him, all right.

I made stew for dinner. I had all the stuff for it, and if Zero was gunna be coming home late, it was something I could leave in the crockpot to stay warm until he got to it. I'd just put the glass lid back on top of the crockpot after a taste test when something hard and wooden hit me in the head, then dropped onto the kitchen bench with a clatter.

It was a curtain ring.

I looked up innocently into Jin Yeong's glaring face as he prowled across the kitchen toward me. "What?"

"*Hajima!*"

"If you want me to understand, you're gunna have to speak English," I said.

Jin Yeong narrowed his eyes at me. "Bad. *Petteu!*" he said, with great distinctness. "*Ilon kol hajima.*"

"Stuff like what? Why are you throwing curtain rings at me?"

Jin Yeong, his teeth showing sharp tips through the softness of his lips, leaned very close and said, "*Choshimhae, Petteu.*"

"All right, all right, blood breath," I grumbled. "I'll put the rings back. Took you long enough."

His voice followed me as I went upstairs to get the rest of the curtain rings. "*Do itdda, matchi? Matchi!*"

"Heck yeah, there's more," I muttered to myself, grinning. "Just you wait."

Zero arrived home late. I jerked upright where I'd been trying not to fall asleep on the couch, alerted by the tug of Between, and trotted off to the kitchen to boil the jug and put a bowl of stew on the table before I actually caught sight of him.

I heard a faint whisper of sound as he stepped up into the kitchen, and looked around. He was there by the island, dishevelled and a bit bloody, and there was a burn across one cheek that had burned off a few of his frosted white eyelashes and half the eyebrow.

"Heck!" I said, dropping the coffee tin. "What happened to you?"

"Has Athelas returned?" There was a tightness to his voice that wasn't annoyance or pain.

"Nope," I said. I ducked under the kitchen island for the first aid kit I kept there: Zero healed quicker than I did, but without Athelas, he'd probably still need a bit of patching up.

He must have been hoping against hope, because he only nodded and sat down, and he didn't try to push me away when I gave him his coffee and started dabbing at his face with the antiseptic, either.

Strike a light. He *must* be concerned about Athelas.

"Don't know much about burns," I said. "Can't look it up, either; no data left on my phone."

"Just clean and cover it," he said.

"Haven't heard from Detective Tuatu since this morning, either," I told him, touching tiny bits of balm to the burn on his cheek. I was pretty sure I was hurting him, but I didn't know how to be any gentler, so I just kept going. "Tried to call him half an hour ago."

"The detective can look after himself."

"You reckon?"

"Have you considered," said Zero, closing his eyes briefly, "that the detective simply doesn't want to speak with you?"

"Yeah." I covered the burn and collected all the blue-tinted swabs I'd used to clean it. "But he always answers anyway, even if he doesn't want to talk."

"Don't attempt to convince me to help the detective," Zero said, abruptly rising from the stool. He hadn't touched his dinner, just his coffee, and now he stood with his back to me, looking out into the living room.

"Not gunna," I said, packing the first aid kit away. "But it's a bit funny, isn't it?"

Over his shoulder, Zero asked, "What's funny?"

"Athelas went back undercover the other morning, just before me and Detective Tuatu found that body. Right before someone framed Tuatu. And Athelas hasn't been home in three days now."

"I'm aware."

"Something's happened to him, hasn't it?"

"Yes."

"Didn't think there was anything that could get Athelas. What are we gunna do?"

Zero's shoulders stiffened. "*We* are not going to do anything. It's my own affair. I should never have allowed him to remain with me in the first place—I knew the risks. I'll look for him tonight."

"Again." I would have bet my last buck that he'd been searching for Athelas all day. Somewhere Between or Behind, by the look of him; there was blood on him that wasn't blue.

Still, it surprised me when he said, "Again," in agreement.

"At the police station?" There was so much I wanted to say—so much I wanted to tell him—but I couldn't do it without giving away that I'd been there, too. I would have to wait for Jin Yeong to give his report.

"No," Zero said. "Jin Yeong looked there today—he would already have told me if Athelas was there."

Well, if Jin Yeong didn't have a phone, they must have some way of talking to each other that I didn't know about. I decided to winkle that out later, and asked, "Where, then?"

"I don't know."

"What are we gunna do?"

He still didn't turn around. I dunno; maybe he really didn't want me to see his face.

"Pet—"

I don't reckon he knew how defeated he looked with his back to me, shoulders dropped. Just now, he didn't look like a high and mighty fae who could crush the world of humans with a look. He looked like a human who had lost a friend and didn't know what to do or where to turn.

"You didn't want Athelas here anyway," I said.

"Yes."

"And he's always doing slippery little things around you that you probably wouldn't approve of."

Zero sighed; a huge, emptying sound. "Yes."

"Yeah," I said, more to myself than him. "I thought so."

I climbed on the stool he'd vacated and launched myself onto his back, legs dangling. It was a bit further from the floor than I'd realised.

Zero didn't even bother to brace himself for my weight, but he looked over his shoulder at me, perplexed. "What are you doing?"

"I'm hugging you," I said, with my arms clutched around his neck. "Didn't your parents ever hug you? Thought one of 'em was human?"

"Stop it."

Sometimes I'm not a very obedient pet. I locked my arms before he could start to unwind them and did the same with my legs around his waist. "Nope," I said. "You're getting a hug whether you want it or not. It's good for the soul."

"I'm fae," Zero said. He sounded perplexed, too. Every now and then he does, when he's talking to me. Maybe it's because he's not used to dealing with humans much. "I don't have a soul. Pet, let go."

"I don't think that's right," I argued, clinging tighter around his neck to leave no cracks where he could work his fingers in to pull my arms apart. It wouldn't last long—there was no contest in strength between us when it came to me and Zero—but I was pretty sure that the human side of Zero was still there, and still needed comfort every now and then, even if he wouldn't admit it. "And I'm not sure Athelas is right about you, either."

"*Ah mwohya!*" complained JinYeong, as he padded into the room. "*Petteu, wae irae?*"

"Just cos you're a dead cold fish doesn't mean everyone is," I told him, tucking my head in close to avoid Zero's tugging fingers.

JinYeong glared at me. "Throw it out, *hyeong*," he said, and he must have meant me to understand it, because I didn't have any trouble with the meaning. To Zero, he spoke rapidly and incomprehensibly except for the odd word or two I understood. As he did so, Zero sat down almost automatically, forgetting to tug at my arms, and I loosened my grip until I could drop onto the stool beside him instead of hugging his neck. I was pretty sure JinYeong was giving Zero a run-down of how things had gone at the police station today, and I wanted to listen carefully to make sure my name wasn't mentioned.

JinYeong saw me paying attention and showed me the tiniest edge of tooth in a smirk. I glared at him around Zero's shoulder. Little rat. He better not give me away.

He didn't, though; or not as far as I could tell. I would have to go shopping for some stuff to make him snacks tomorrow—I'd actually half-thought he'd give me away despite his promise not to. *Especially* when he found the missing curtain rings. He must really want those blood snacks.

When they were finished discussing it, JinYeong in incomprehensible Korean, and Zero in scarcely more comprehensible sentence fragments, Zero said to me, "JinYeong tells me a Sandman has been at the station. If you happen to see one again, call me at once. Don't attempt to talk to it."

"No worries," I said. "Wasn't gunna try to talk to it."

He hesitated, then said reluctantly, "Give me the detective's number."

I couldn't help the grin that spread on my face. "You're helping him?"

"No," Zero said shortly. "He'll be helping me. If the two incidents are related, he has information that could help me find who or what is keeping Athelas."

"You going out again now?"

JinYeong must have been visited by the same thought, because he grabbed a bowl and filled it with stew. He'd already eaten, but he was probably planning on going out again with Zero, and they usually came back pretty tired after going out. Reckon killing people does that to you.

"Yes," said Zero. "Call me if you have another dream."

They left me there with two empty bowls and too many questions, while Between snapped and sang, then grew quiet. I huffed a sigh and turned off the crockpot, then washed up the dishes. Looked like I was being excluded from the investigation again. Nothing new there—you don't take the pet along when you're investigating the disappearance of your friend, do you?

Mind you, most pets don't have a phone and friends in the police force, so if I really wanted to know what was going on, was there anything stopping me? I mean, apart from Zero, if he caught me.

Maybe I was safer trying to find Daniel. At least it was something I *could* do, instead of sitting around and waiting for an Athelas who wasn't coming home and couldn't be helped by the pet. Supermarket tomorrow, then, I decided, sniffing a bit. There were still Jin Yeong's blood snacks to make.

CHAPTER SIX

I SHOULD HAVE GUESSED I'D DREAM ABOUT ATHELAS AGAIN
when I fell asleep that night. Should have guessed I'd find myself
back in that hallway, after trudging down so many versions of the
real thing. But somehow it was still a nasty shock to find myself
there, chilled and stuck with no way forward and no way back.

I tried walking the hallway again for a while, hoping not to
have to go back to where I knew Athelas was waiting—hoping to
find something that would be useful when I inevitably got there.
Just like the first time, there was nothing there; no way of getting
out of the hallway by going forward or back, and no way of
getting any closer to the blueprint that was always just out of
reach down the hall, the *you are here* sticker a sarcastic reminder of
my inability to get myself out of this dream or this hall.

Nor were there any sun or moon doors.

"Fine," I said, my voice a small, scared growl. "I'll just go find
Athelas again!"

It took me about fifteen minutes after I said it, to actually
push through the wall construct and do it, though. And when I
did, and the moonlight room opened before me, dread pricked at
my stomach.

Ah heck. Around me was the same room, windowless and white, the same glimmers of moonlight dancing on the cold air—in the middle of the room, the same Athelas who had killed me, pierced through by that moonlight.

Athelas turned his head languidly, and there were deep bruises beneath his eyes.

"Welcome back," he said. There was the smallest smile on his lips.

I didn't like it much, so I said, "You *killed* me."

"And yet, here you are back again! Strange, is it not?"

"That's one way to put it."

"You shouldn't have come back," he said, and the malice in his eyes made me shiver. He could hardly do more than turn his head and stare at me, but it was still horrible. "I'll only kill you again."

Even though I knew it wasn't really me he was talking to, it still made me shiver.

"Didn't have a choice," I said shortly. "I went to sleep, and here I was again. It's not like it's any fun being killed by you, you know. And you don't exactly have people lining up to help you, either."

Athelas laughed, and if his laughter had been frightening yesterday, today it was horrible. "Nonsense. I have you. What could be more fitting?"

"Yeah, but you don't think I'm *me*."

"Exactly so."

"That makes no sense."

"Does it not? Allow me to offer some advice, in that case: If you're trying to convince a subject that they're facing someone they know, you should really adjust their memories of the last time you tried to do so."

I looked up at him. "Yeah, I'll remember that. You mean someone with my face tried this again before I got here today?"

"If you prefer to express it thus," murmured Athelas.

"I flamin' do!" I said in annoyance. "Oi. If I try to rescue you this time, are you going to kill me again?"

"Of course," he said. He sounded far more tired than I remembered him sounding last time. "Don't think I won't."

What the heck had they done to him while I was awake, to make him so grey and tired?

"What happened?" I asked. I could feel warmth growing behind my eyes again, and blinked it away. This Athelas wasn't exactly the Athelas I was used to; here and now, he would only mock me for tears. "What did they do to you?"

"You were there," Athelas said. "Don't you remember? They gave you to me to kill."

"If you didn't want to kill me, why do it?" I said exasperatedly. That was no reason for him to be as grey as ash, was it? He hadn't hesitated when he killed me, so it couldn't have meant too much to him. Even if he didn't think I was me, there should have been some hesitation, shouldn't there?

"I've regretted not killing the pet as soon as I met her for some time now," said Athelas. "No, *don't* take another step toward me. I've already told you I'll kill you. I don't think the pet is quite as stupid as you're playing her to be."

"I nearly rescued you yesterday," I said. It was hard to make myself take another step toward him, because it seemed like I could still feel the bruising around my neck, even if it wasn't visible to the mirror. "If you hadn't killed me, you could have been—"

"If you hadn't been wearing that face, perhaps I wouldn't have killed you," said Athelas. "I've no love for the pet. I won't be rescued by it, even if it's just a ploy—even if there's no one else to rescue me."

"There's Zero," I said, ignoring the hurt his words caused. "I told you, he's coming for you. He's just gotta figure out where you are, so if you can start being helpful and tell us where you actually are—"

"An interesting tactic," murmured Athelas. "Having seen I'm perfectly willing to slaughter the pet, you're now proffering false hopes?"

"They won't be false if you stop waffling and tell me where you are!" I snapped, a bit more tartly than I meant to. "We already went to the station to try and find you—me and JinYeong, and you weren't there. Just don't tell Zero, 'cos he doesn't know I was there."

A smile passed over Athelas' face. "Goodness me. You almost sounded as if you could be the pet."

"It's because I *am*," I muttered; but I muttered it to myself. Athelas obviously couldn't understand. How the heck was I supposed to convince him I was actually the pet?

I took one more step toward him, but I felt sick. I really didn't want to do this. I didn't want to go over there and try to free him when I knew exactly what he'd do as soon as he got the chance.

"Dear me," said Athelas. His voice was only a thread, but it was a mocking thread. "Don't tell me that you're hesitating? That's really not very Pet-like of you."

I pointed at him. "You killed me last time. Of course I'm going to hesitate. If you're bored, you could try talking."

"How novel."

"Yeah, yeah, I'm a bad interrogator or whatever. If you don't think I'm the pet, at least tell me something you expect them to know, whoever *they* are."

"They?" murmured Athelas. "Very well. As for *them*, I'm not entirely sure myself who *they* are. I can see their footprints through Behind and Between, and I saw their influence at the Waystation. If I was to guess, I would say they're a very well put-together rebellion."

"Rebellion against what?"

"The Family, one presumes. A bit more of a bloody rebellion than Zero's, too, if one considers the retaliation when the Family found out about the Waystation. It's not me that any of you should fear—it's the Family."

"What's it got to do with me, then?"

Athelas' eyes flickered away, and he sighed. "Why should it have anything to do with you? You're merely a pet. You're kept to give some measure of pleasantness around the house."

I frowned. "I don't think so. I don't think that's why Zero keeps me around, and I don't think that's what you think, either."

"Think as you please. A pet is a pet. What else can it be?"

"Dunno," I said. "But I'm pretty sure there's something else. You lot wouldn't keep me around if I wasn't some use."

"That's very jaded of you, Pet. So. Very. Unlike you."

"Don't tell me what's unlike me," I told him. "You're just a fae. You don't know about humans. You don't know about me, either."

A faint smile passed over his face. "Are you ready to give up?"

"Nope," I said. "But while you're being so talkative, you might as well tell me why you lot decided to keep me. Zero wouldn't have kept me if you didn't suggest it first."

"Aren't you underrating yourself? There are many cases of fae seeking temporary comfort in the arms of humans, after all."

I stared at him. "That's rubbish! It's nothing like that with Zero."

"Is it not? Perhaps you'll have to make up your own theory, in that case."

"You know what the really annoying thing is?" I asked him. "It's that even if you did think it was me, you couldn't be more flamin' hard to understand! What kind of twisty people did you grow up with, anyway?"

"The fae," he said. "What else do you expect? Well, Pet?"

"So you're still gunna call me *Pet*?"

"Merely for the sake of ease," he said. "And as I assume the real Pet is dead, I might as well call you by that name as any other. It will be a reminder to me in future to take care of vermin instead of allowing such to live."

I glared at him, and that made it a bit easier to take the last few steps toward the base of the solid moonlight that pierced him. "You're just full of nice things to say today, aren't you?"

"Oh, are we beginning again?" asked Athelas. "I don't think it's very wise of you."

"Haven't decided yet," I told him.

"It's of no use—I won't allow you to rescue me."

"Fine, give me proper answers when I ask you questions, then!" I said, in exasperation.

Athelas laughed. "Even less finesse! Why should I answer those questions? You don't listen to the answers."

"All right," I said. "If I can't rescue you, and you won't answer those questions about me, you can flamin' answer some other ones."

"Can I?"

"Yeah. I want to know if walls are really walls."

"This is certainly very pet-like. Perhaps you could expand on what you mean."

"Well, when I'm in the human world, things mostly look like they should to humans. Sometimes I can see stuff that looks different, but mostly it's human. When I'm Between, there's a lot more that looks different, and when I'm Behind, it's all different again. Which one is the truth? 'Cos if it's just the way you look at stuff, one of 'em has to be the truth, doesn't it? I mean, is the freezer aisle in the grocery store actually the freezer aisle, or is it a hallway in an ice castle?"

"It is both."

"Yeah," I argued, "but if it depends on the way I see things, doesn't that mean the way I see things changes them?"

"No," said Athelas. "That's something different again. That is something that gets humans killed. Your only talent is sometimes seeing things as they are on a different plane. You don't change them, and your sight only affects yourself—your own perceptions."

I thought about that for some time longer before I said, slowly, "I don't think so."

Athelas looked away. "Do you not? I wonder why you asked me, then."

"I mean, I mostly think that's right, but sometimes I change stuff. It's not just how I see it. I sort of *tell* it to change and it does."

"Humans can't force things to reveal their Between and Behind appearance," said Athelas, his eyes flicking back over to me. "Nor can they force a thing to be something it was never meant to be on any plane. If you could do that sort of thing, you would be a very different pet indeed."

That was weird. He *knew*—oh yeah. Athelas was treating me as though I was someone pretending to be Pet, and not Pet. So that meant whoever he thought I was didn't know about the things I could do.

More importantly, it meant that Athelas was trying very hard to make sure that whoever he thought I was remained ignorant of my abilities. What was so important about me being able to make things reveal their other, Between selves?

"Hang on," I said, remembering what else he'd said. "You mean there are some people—some Behindkind—who can make a thing be a different thing? Something that isn't normally Between or Behind?"

"Do you think that playing ignorance will make me believe that you're actually the Pet?"

"Sorta," I said. It wasn't so much that I thought ignorance would convince him—it was more that I'd hoped he would be able to tell that I was me.

How was I supposed to convince him that I was me when he was certain I was dead?

I circled him warily a few times before it sank in that there *was* no way to convince him. I would just have to free him again as best I could and hope I could persuade him not to kill me again. It's not like I was actually gunna die, after all.

"What are you crying about now?" asked Athelas wearily. "Stop it."

"I'm not crying," I said. "I'm snivelling. There's a difference."

"Is there?"

"Yeah. You wouldn't understand. You're just Behindkind."

There was a small hiss of laughter—or maybe it was pain—from Athelas. "Perhaps not," he said. "But I understand that you're stalling, for what that's worth."

"Trying to figure out a way to get you free without you being able to kill me."

"There isn't one," said Athelas.

"I'll make sure I release your hands last this time, anyway," I said. That way, he wouldn't be able to use them to strangle me.

"Do you really think that will help?"

"Dunno," I said. "But it's better than being killed."

"Shall I tell you a secret?"

"That'd be something new," I said suspiciously.

"I've been alone for two days since I killed you—do you really think I don't have a weapon by now?"

"If you've been alone, where did the weapon come from?" I pointed out. At the same time, it *was* Athelas. More suspiciously still, I asked, "What weapon?"

A brief smile came over Athelas' lips and left them oddly rigid. "A knife."

"Okay, so you got a knife from somewhere, even though no one has visited you, *and* you managed to get one that isn't steel?"

"You seem unconvinced. Never mind. I'll show it to you later."

"No thanks," I said. "I've already got one. Oi."

"Yes, P—yes?"

"What's the point of all this?"

"The point of what?"

"You, in this room. You said torture before. How come I'm torture?"

Athelas looked at me through his lashes. "I misspoke," he said. "You are a form of information gathering. The moonlight could more rightly be called torture—the entire affair smacks of mismanagement."

"Are you really gunna hang there and critique the blokes who're torturing you? What if they decide to do something worse?"

"There's nothing worse they can do to me," said Athelas. "I already know their limits. You should tell them to release me now, while there's still a chance for them to die quickly."

"Pretty sure that wouldn't make anyone let you go," I said, but I still felt chilled.

"Very well," said Athelas, and there was a dreadful edge of ice to his voice when he said, "I shall enjoy tearing you each apart, piece by piece, slowly."

"You never get any less creepy," I said, but I couldn't put it off any longer. I started working away at the moonlight again. "Don't kill me this time."

"I've already told you—"

"I know," I said. "But just don't."

If Athelas yesterday had been able to withstand all but the roughest of my ministrations, today each touch of moonlight drew a gasp from him, and when I got to the middle ones that needed a firm pinch to convince them to disintegrate instead of the feather-touch the outer ones needed, he actually groaned.

I couldn't help it; I stopped.

"Maybe I can get Zero," I said, more to myself than him. There were tears streaming down my cheeks now. I didn't try to stop them because I knew I couldn't; and because I knew Athelas would only sneer at me for that, too.

"Very good," gasped Athelas. "Do try. I look forward to seeing if this place is able to make any reasonable facsimile of my lord."

I was pretty sure I didn't understand what he'd said, but I hazarded, "You mean you don't think he can get in?"

"How cleverly you misunderstand."

"What the heck is wrong with you?" I demanded. I was heart-sick and shivering, and it shouldn't have made me lash out at him, but I didn't seem to be able to help myself. "You're strung up on moonlight, hidden away in a little room, and I'm trying to help you!"

"Are you really? I'm quite certain you're trying to help yourself, but that's a matter of perspective, I suppose."

"Zero's been looking for you for the last two days," I said. I didn't mean to sound accusing, either, but it came out that way. "He's been really worried."

"My lord is always worried," said Athelas. "But considering he moved heaven and earth to separate himself from me, I'm not entirely certain why you think he'll be looking for me."

I stared at him. "What are you talking about? We've all been living together for the last couple months; of course he's worried about you!"

For the first time, his eyes really focused on me, and I felt that he saw me, the Pet, and not a person-wearing-Pet's-face.

"Athelas," I said, hope blossoming in me. "Do you see me?"

"I see," he said, on a sigh, and his head dropped as if it were too weary to hold itself up. "Then free me."

I went back to the moonlight, ruthless in my hope, and pinched off each of the threads with my teeth gritted against the sound of Athelas' pain. They disintegrated one by one, allowing Athelas' legs to drop to the ground first in a gentle waft; then his shoulders. I supported them until the last of the moonlight was undone and I could feel him pushing against me with one hand.

That was good. He had his balance.

The hand on my shoulder didn't leave, though; and I reached out to grab his elbow, worried that he was going to fall. When I looked up at his face, he was watching me, a curious smile on his lips.

"Thank you," Athelas said, his voice a shard of ice. "It is much more convenient killing you when my limbs are free."

"What?" I fell over, scrabbling to get away, and Athelas laughed.

Step by step he approached, leaving a trail of half-formed, slurred footprints in blue blood, and I frantically pushed myself up. I was too late; he was on me in a second, pinning me to the floor with one hand, a cool prick of metal sending something warm trickling across my neck.

"I was wrong," said that voice of ice, in my ear. "You haven't killed the Pet—you still have it alive somewhere. Much easier to *prod* a human into giving away secrets than it is to prod Behind-kind, isn't it?"

I didn't know how, but I'd lost him again. For just a few minutes, it really had seemed like he saw me for the Pet again. My hand reached out, quivered, then reached out again to touch him; a futile gesture.

Cold and hot met in a stab of pain in my neck, red blood gushing to meet blue. My head dropped sideways and far away on the floor was my hand, with a splash of blood on it that burned. How did it get so far away, I wondered; and as I wondered, I died.

"AWAKE OR NOT?" SAID A VOICE IN KOREAN.

Something poked me in the cheek—JinYeong's finger, probably. For a very brief moment, I thought about biting that pretty little finger and seeing if I could draw someone else's blood, but that reminded me just in time that with JinYeong's saliva still somewhere in my system, it would be very dangerous for me to draw *his* blood.

"I believe so," said Zero's voice. "Make coffee."

At first I thought he was talking to me, and tried to make my sluggish limbs move, but JinYeong's voice said, "*Ne, hyeong,*" with some sullenness, and his presence retreated.

I opened my eyes, since my limbs were too difficult to manage, and a big, white hand levered me up into a sitting position.

"Ow," I said, my voice as rough as though I really had just been stabbed in the neck. It didn't hurt, but there was a pain somewhere that seemed to be assuaged by saying it, so I said it again.

"It will fade," Zero said.

"That's good," I said, because there didn't seem to be anything else to say. "You blokes just get home?"

"We've been back for an hour or so."

"Find anything?"

"A few friends of the Family who might have known if something was going to happen."

"They know of anything?"

There was silence, and the jug boiled away in the kitchen. "No," said Zero at last. "Nothing to do with the Family, at any rate. They knew Athelas was likely to be with me, but nothing more."

Funny that he was answering my questions. Nice, for a change. I asked him, "That what they said, or what you think?"

"It's what they said. At this moment, I have no reason to doubt them."

There was a soft noise of contempt from JinYeong as he stepped down into the room with two mugs of coffee. I didn't know whether he was being contemptuous about the Behind-kind's information, or about Zero's trust in it, so I just stared at him.

Why was he so flamin' pretty, anyway?

JinYeong narrowed his eyes at me and gave Zero a cup of coffee. "*Wae?*" he demanded.

"You're too flamin' pretty," I said. My voice sounded choked. "Don't know why someone doesn't punch you in the face."

Jin Yeong, looking offended, thrust the second cup of coffee at me. A small slop of it hit my hand, burning where a splash of my blood had burned earlier, and I sniffled very hard to stop even hotter tears from spilling over as well.

"*Ah, wae irae?*" muttered Jin Yeong, hunching back into his side of the couch.

Something hit me softly in the side of the face, and a blood red, silken handkerchief fell into my lap. I dabbed at my hand and pushed it back at Jin Yeong, who took it by one corner as if it were soiled beyond recovery.

"You dreamed of Athelas again," said Zero.

Even more than last time, I didn't want to talk about it. I said baldly, "Yes."

"Did he kill you again?"

"Yeah. He still thinks I'm someone else with my face. Reckon he's in the police station."

"I see," said Zero. "Jin Yeong didn't find him there—are you sure?"

"That's what it looks like. He was still threaded through with moonlight, even though I let him out last time. How come he couldn't get away himself?"

"If it's moonlight, that isn't how it works. You can continue to be imprisoned in moonlight even if you appear to be free."

"That's flamin' nice."

"He's the one who told you it was moonlight, was it not?"

"Reckon he's lying to me?"

"Athelas is almost certainly lying to you about most things," Zero said. "If he thinks you're one of his torturers, he would be a fool not to do so. Whether or not being imprisoned in moonlight is one of the things he is lying about remains to be seen."

"*Cajok aniramyeon, wae salajyeossoyo?*"

"Bet there's other people who want him dead other than the

Family, or whatever," I said, even though the question wasn't aimed at me.

"Yes," agreed Zero. "There are many people who would like him dead—however, the people who would want him tortured are very few. It's a course of action that carries with it many risks and very few rewards. There is also the matter of what information they're seeking."

"And why use my face for it?" I asked. Zero looked at me frowningly, and I added, "From what he said, someone was there before the first time I appeared, using my face, and then again after he killed me the first time. He killed them, too."

"That is something I would very much like to know the answer to," he said.

I looked down into my half-empty coffee cup. "I wanna know why I'm dreaming about him."

"*Nan mariya*," agreed Jin Yeong. "*Wae?*"

"'Cos if there's someone out there who wants me for something, it means they know a heck of a lot about me as well as you guys. The way Athelas is talking...the way he..."

"Drink your coffee, Pet," said Zero abruptly.

I blinked, finding some hotness behind my eyes, and said, "It was definitely the police station we were in. How come Athelas wasn't there when...when Jin Yeong visited, then?"

"Jin Yeong tells me there are several layers to the station, leading Between," said Zero. "It could be that, though Jin Yeong thinks not—or it could be just that whoever is keeping Athelas is trying to give us false information through you. It's possible they want us to be looking there."

"Still means they know a flamin' lot about us," I muttered. "It's worrying Athelas, too, I think."

"I believe we can presume that the reason your face is being used is the same reason that you have been allowed to dream. It would possibly be as well if you expected someone to be listening in on your conversations with Athelas."

"Wait, so he was right? I'm being used as leverage to get answers from him, just in a different way than he thinks?"

"It's likely," said Zero, a line deepening between his brows. "At any rate, you should behave as though there is someone listening at all times."

"Yeah, of course," I said, as if I'd already been doing that. What had I said to Athelas these two times? There was a sinking in my stomach; I'd said a *lot*. "Oi."

"What?"

"Is it possible that I'm just getting through by mistake? No Sandman or whatever sending me there, just an accident."

"No," Zero said, and he must have been worried enough about Athelas to be preoccupied, because it wasn't strictly necessary for him to say, "But it's not possible for you to be having the kind of dreams you're having, either."

"Right. So it's not possible, but there's a lot of not possible things happening, so maybe that's another one of them."

"For that to be so, there would have to be some connection between yourself and Athelas. And in that case, it would be more likely for you to dream of JinYeong, since the connection you have with him is a physical one."

"No thanks," I said. And because I still wanted to say it, even though I felt like rubbish, I mumbled, "Got enough nightmares already."

Maybe I didn't get the delivery right. JinYeong sent me a sultry grin, his eyelids dropped low, and blew me a kiss.

"Ew," I said. I looked away, and found I didn't have any more coffee to drink. Of Zero, I asked, "How do we leverage this?"

"There's no necessity to leverage it," he said. "JinYeong and I will follow up some lines of inquiry from your detective friend today; we'll no doubt be able to find Athelas from that."

"Yeah, maybe," I said. "But even if you can, I'm gunna dream like this again, right? So we should have a plan on what to do when it happens."

"There's no need for a plan," said Zero, his voice icy. "We'll find him quickly. If you dream again, try not to talk too much, and don't release Athelas. If you don't release him, he shouldn't be able to hurt you."

"Yeeeah," I said slowly. I wasn't as sure about that as Zero seemed to be. But then, Zero hadn't seen a contained, unarmed Fae produce a knife out of nowhere, either. "You blokes gunna sleep at all?"

"There's no need," Zero said. "Prepare something we can eat as we go, Pet. We leave in fifteen minutes."

CHAPTER SEVEN

IT WASN'T THAT I WANTED TO GO OUT AND FOLLOW ZERO Between or Behind, or wherever he was going. I definitely didn't want to be trotting alongside Jin Yeong, either; he was weird and unpredictable. I mean, he was always weird and unpredictable, but he seemed a bit more weird and unpredictable lately. I had the feeling that as much as Jin Yeong showed his hackles at Athelas, and Athelas gently needled Jin Yeong, they both didn't like anything happening to the other. Jin Yeong definitely didn't, anyway. I still wasn't sure about Athelas.

So it wasn't that I wanted to go out and follow them. But as closed off as Zero was, there was still a kind of warmth to his huge presence—the feeling of safety, maybe—that made me feel cold in its absence. And even if I hadn't exactly welcomed Jin Yeong, I would have been glad for his slightly stormy presence around the house. I might even have cooked him something nice to eat that wasn't part of a bribe to keep quiet.

"Bad pet!" I muttered to myself, boiling the jug again. I would definitely need the caffeine today. I was too tired for how much sleep I had gotten last night, and I didn't want to risk falling asleep while Zero and JinYeong were out. "Athelas is missing. They gotta find him first."

But I found I couldn't bear to stay around the house by myself, either. I tried for a couple of hours, drinking far too much coffee in an attempt to stay awake and keep off thoughts I didn't want to have, before I knew it was no good. Then I hopped off my stool at the kitchen island, where I'd been trying, with a caffeine-induced restlessness, to pluck random things out of Between, and decided it was enough.

I'd go and find Daniel. Or maybe I would talk to Detective Tuatu, who knew? I just didn't want to stay where I was. Didn't want to do the kind of busy nothing I had been doing.

I left the house with another cup of coffee in a travel mug, barely warm through the layers of plastic, and headed off down the street without a very clear idea of where I was going. I let myself drift in the direction of the grocery store I'd worked at briefly, and tried to call Detective Tuatu again.

To my relief, he picked up after the second ring.

"Pet?"

"Oh good," I said. "You're alive."

"I was just about to call you."

"There's a change for the books! You all right?"

"I'm fine," he said. "Don't worry about me. Your friends came to see me last night."

"I'm talking about before that. You didn't answer when I called."

"That's what I was going to call you about. I had some other visitors—or at least, they tried to come in. Pet, what exactly is that plant you gave me?"

"Why? Something weird happen?"

"Not any weirder than what usually happens to me when I'm with you, but yeah, sure. It was weird."

Grinning in my anticipation, I asked, "Did the dr—the um, plant get really big?"

Maybe my grin came through over the phone. Tuatu's voice was annoyed when he said, "What did you give me?"

"Stopped someone unpleasant from getting into your house, did it?"

A silence, then a sigh. "Yes."

"Well, what are you whinging about, then?"

"I'm not whinging—"

"How big did it get?" I wished I'd been there to see it; I'd been pretty sure it would do something like that if there was a physical threat, but I hadn't known for sure.

Another silence, then I had the impression that Tuatu was grinning, too. There was a slight difference to his voice; warmth, or ruefulness, maybe. Then he said, "It got *so big*, Pet! It covered all the windows and the door. But it was still the same size at the same time, so I don't know if I dreamed it or not."

"It's a dryad. It's for protection," I told him. I probably should have told him earlier, but he'd only just come into the world where Between and Behind were things that were possible, and he'd been trying so hard to survive that I didn't want to burden him any more than he was already burdened. "Protection and wisdom. Reckon if you're not sure about something, you should ask it a few questions."

"Will it *talk* to me?"

"Nah, don't think so. But I reckon you'll get the answers you need if you ask the right questions."

"It doesn't come from this world, does it?"

"Far as I know," I began cautiously, "it's kinda this world, kinda that world. I found it Between. Reckon it'll be useful to you."

There was another one of those silences, which I'd begun to think of as the detective's way of figuring out what he wanted to say, before he said, "Thank you."

"No worries. Just be careful when you're away from the house;

it doesn't work if you're not with it. Make sure you keep wearing that pendant of yours, too."

"You said that before. I've got a bit of advice for you, too."

"Yeah? What is it? *Don't leave the state?*"

"Don't go back to the police station."

I pulled my phone away from my ear and stared at it as if it was the detective himself. "How'd you know I was there?"

"Think you're the only one with spies?"

"You've still got a couple friends in the cop shop!" I said, realising it in a sparkle of hope. Best news I'd heard in ages. "Proper ones!"

"Upper Management isn't a place you should be poking your nose around. People disappear up there all the time; the whole station knows it, but no one wants to talk about it because it's too crazy."

"Yeah, reckon it's not too safe for humans," I said; though the problem really was that Upper Management was *exactly* calibrated for humans. Exactly for humans. Only for humans. A sort of cheat code for humans to be able to get Between and access the things there. And that was a worrying thought to think; that there were potentially a whole lot more humans who knew about Between and Behind than just me. Not to mention the fact that if I was right, the Behindkind who were really behind whatever was going on at the police station, weren't necessarily actually *at* the police station.

"How are you doing, anyway?"

His voice sounded wary. "What do you mean?"

"Your friend that died—he wasn't a close friend?"

"Close enough. It's been a while since I talked to him, but close enough."

"Yeah, so are you okay?"

"I'll be happier when I find the people that did it."

"What did Zero say about that?"

"Nothing," said the detective, more sharply. "And I can look after it myself."

"All right, all right," I grumbled. "I was just trying to help."

"I told you not to help."

"Whatever. Just make sure that if my psychos get info out of you, you get something back. That's how it works with them. Don't let 'em cheat you."

"I'll remember that," said the detective.

Hopefully he would, too. He'd already mortgaged himself to Athelas a bit too much for my comfort. I asked, "You gunna be arrested, or not?"

"I get the feeling they're working on it. I'll have to be careful from now on—they couldn't pin the body on me directly, but they're not above planting evidence."

"At least they're human," I said. "Well, pretty much all the ones at the station are, anyway."

"They're all human?" asked Tuatu. "I thought—I just guessed that it had to be something more than that, if one of you was there undercover."

"Yeah," I said. "Reckon I'll have to talk to Zero about that. We were expecting to find a lot of fae at the station—well, Athelas was, anyway."

"Was he?" asked Detective Tuatu, and I got the impression he was frowning.

"How do you mean?"

"Well, if you know the place is full of humans instead of fae, why didn't Athelas? And if he knew, why did he stay?"

That, I thought, was a flaming good question. "Dunno," I said. "But maybe that's something I have to talk to Zero about, too. Right, I'm off; be careful today."

"You too," he said, and hung up.

I found myself outside the grocery store, which was pretty handy, because while I'd been talking to Detective Tuatu I had come to a conclusion in the back of my mind. That conclusion was that if I wanted to find out where Daniel was, and Zero wouldn't tell me for safety reasons, the best place to find out where he was, would be at the grocery store where he worked. I hadn't met any of the other lycanthropes other than the one who was trying to kill me, but I was certain it was the best place to find another one of Daniel's pack. There'd been enough of them around to make trouble in the area for a while now.

I went around the back instead of through the store, heading for the smoking area. It was nearly smoko time, which meant there would be a good cross-section of the store coming out soon. If I couldn't find a werewolf there, at least I could ask some questions. The speck of vampire spit running through my system must have been still pretty strong, because the whole back dock and smoking area smelled like dog to me. I didn't remember it smelling like that when I worked here.

I hadn't been hopped up on vampire spit when I worked here, either, mind you. The smell of the place made me want to hunch my shoulders up, which reminded me of my talk with Zero about vampire spit and biting people—or Behindkind. I hadn't thought I'd have a problem with it. I hadn't bitten JinYeong, and he was about the most annoying person I knew. I hadn't expected just the smell of lycanthropes to set me so much on edge.

I'd just reached the turning into the alley that was the smoking area when one of the workers loped past me and across the parking lot out the back. He had the same type of look to him that I'd often seen on Daniel, and to a certain extent on JinYeong; wild and frustrated, and just barely contained. Either this kid was being bothered by his boss, or he was feeling cooped up in the store.

I made a slight adjustment to my plans and nipped off after him, abandoning the smoking area. He was exactly the sort of possible-werewolf I'd come to find. He didn't smell more like dog than anything else around the store, but I hadn't expected him to;

even Jin Yeong hadn't been able to tell for sure when they weren't actually in the wolf state.

More importantly, he was carrying a takeaway bag of food, and if my nose wasn't good enough to be sure whether or not he was a lycanthrope, it was definitely good enough to smell the steak sandwiches that were in the bag. This kid was going off to feed someone who wasn't himself, and I was betting on that someone being Daniel.

Lucky for me, I'd been getting some practise following people lately. I hadn't been much good at it, but I was getting better. Hopefully I'd be good enough to keep out of sight of one long-legged puppy dog with a very distinctive smell of steak clinging to him.

I shoved the empty coffee mug and my hands in my pockets and sauntered after the smell of steak. Flamin' nice to be able to fall back a bit further if I wanted to; if I lost sight of the bloke, I could just follow the smell. I took care with my footsteps anyway. I couldn't do the cool *look away* spell thing that Zero did to stop people seeing him, but there was enough of Between around Hobart that I could make my footsteps quieter if I really concentrated on it, and that had to help a bit.

It must have worked, or maybe I'd just gotten a lot better at following people, because the bloke didn't see me. He didn't have far to go, either; just a couple of streets up and across until we were heading toward North Hobart again. Then we took a right that dipped toward the Brooker Highway, with older houses on both sides of the street, and the kid and his steak sandwiches vanished into one on the left.

"Gotcha," I muttered. It was possible the kid was just going home for lunch, but I still preferred to think that Daniel was up in the house somewhere. Zero had said he was in a hospital, and it didn't much look like a hospital, but things around Zero didn't usually look like what they actually were. Umbrellas that were really swords, for example.

There was a slight touch of Between to the place, too. Not so much in the feeling of it—maybe it was something about the way it looked. I didn't know what it was, but I was pretty sure I would be able to use it to get in without anyone noticing me.

Only problem was, I wasn't allowed to go Between without Zero or one of the others. Zero had also been pretty dour about me seeing Daniel, and while I didn't think I was going to get the sudden urge to bite Daniel, if Zero found out about what I was doing, I wanted to at least tell him that I'd been careful. It wouldn't stop the icy glare, but hopefully it would stop him kicking me out of the house.

I threw a look around at the other buildings, hunting for a possible vantage point to see into the building. There was a building opposite; a three story, old fashioned house with balconies in the middle and big windows up the top. It was a pity I couldn't get into the room up there; I'd be able to see into pretty much every building around, from there.

I kept walking, nice and slow, until I was nearly at the bottom of the street, then turned back toward Hobart when I was parallel with the highway. If it really was where Daniel was holed up, there was no sense in giving myself away by taking too long—or by turning back, for that matter. That left me not much else to do but come back tomorrow.

Regretfully, I headed back toward the grocery store. Someone had put a couple more blood bags in the fridge since yesterday morning, and if I was going to make the blood snacks I'd promised for Jin Yeong, I would need to get a bit more pastry.

THE HOUSE WAS QUIET WHEN I GOT BACK; NO PSYCHOS anywhere in sight. I chucked my coffee-stained travel mug in the sink and made myself another mug of coffee so I could stop yawning before I got to work on Jin Yeong's blood snacks. That didn't seem like enough to keep my hands busy, so I made a few for Zero, too; ones that were more mincey than bloody, and a lot easier to make. The trick with Jin Yeong's snacks was to precook the pastry in little knots before I added the blood mix so that they were still properly bloody; I was a bit worried at how good they smelt to me, and I was glad not to have the scent of them cooking, too. Mind you, with vampire spit coursing around my body, it might have stopped smelling nice once it was cooked. Zero's pastries didn't smell anything like as nice to me, and they were decently cooked.

I made a face at Jin Yeong's plate of pastries and made myself yet another coffee. At least coffee always smelt good—and it covered the smell of the blood. I didn't want to be salivating at the smell of human blood.

I was pulling Zero's pastries out of the oven just as Zero and Jin Yeong came home, arguing all the way. I heard it first through Between, like the squeaking of tree-limbs rubbing together outside the window, and as Between opened to allow them out, I could hear words and recognise voices.

Jin Yeong's voice, startling in its comprehensibility, said something like, "...raze it to the ground to find him. It's here or there, and if we slash deep enough, go quickly enough—"

"If we slash deep enough, we still risk not being quick enough to find him," said Zero. "We need to know exactly where he is. With the two of us, we're spread too thin."

"The Pet?"

"The Pet needs far more training before it's ready to join a raid."

"It will have to free Athelas before we can reach him," warned Jin Yeong, his voice fluttering through ahead of them. "It will have to come with us to that extent."

I grinned. There was definitely something Betweenish involved in how Zero and Athelas could understand Jin Yeong—when he chose to be understood, that is. If I wanted to understand him when he didn't want to be understood, I would have to keep learning Korean.

As he stepped through into the living room, Zero just a step after him, Jin Yeong cut himself off mid-sentence, eyes narrowing on my grin. "*Ku olgul wae?*"

"This is how I usually wear my face," I told him. Oh yeah. I was definitely going to keep learning Korean, if only to annoy him.

"*Hajima.*"

"You can't tell me what to do with my face. Oi, Zero."

"What?"

"They know you're looking for Athelas now? The ones who've got him?"

"They know. There has been no demand for any kind of ransom, however, so we can be certain it's information they want."

"That mean they're gunna kill him?"

"Yes. Whether or not they get information, they'll kill him—or sell him on to someone who wants him more than they do."

"And you reckon he's in one of two places?"

Zero nodded, a deep cleft between his brows. This last week was the most human I'd ever found him to be—he never spoke this much. He also never showed this much emotion.

"So we can go to either one and potentially rescue Athelas—but if he's not there, we've tipped them off that we know where to look. If we don't go, we risk leaving him there to be tortured and killed."

"Jin Yeong didn't find a hint of him at the station," said Zero. "And the fact that you're dreaming so specifically about the station would suggest either that someone wants us to focus our attention there, or that they don't know we've got a way in."

"So what do we do?"

"We dream again," said Zero.

He didn't much like it, I could tell; which meant he was talking about leveraging the dreams.

"I'm gunna dream again whether or not you want me to," I told him. "You got a plan?"

"If you're willing to help, yes."

"'Course. It's better than doing nothing about it. Maybe if we do something about it now, I won't have to keep dreaming the same flamin' thing over and over," I said.

Zero hesitated, and I got the impression that he was trying to think of a way to talk me out of it—which was stupid, because he needed the information and I was going to dream anyway. He said, "It will be dangerous."

"Yeah, well, so is being killed in my dreams, apparently," I said. "I'd rather stop it happening as soon as possible than keep trying to avoid it."

I thought about it for a bit, and asked, "How dangerous, anyway?"

"If someone is giving you these dreams, and they find out what we're doing, they could kill you outright."

"That'll be a change, anyway," I said. If it came right down to it, I'd almost rather be actually killed by a malevolent stranger than virtually killed again by Athelas. I glanced across at Zero, and he looked more tired than I'd ever seen him. I would have given a lot to know why he'd changed his mind, but I didn't think he'd tell me if I asked, so I didn't. Instead, I started to make dinner.

I WAS REALLY TEMPTED TO JUST GO TO SLEEP ON THE COUCH that night, like I'd been doing for the last few days. At least then if I woke up from a dream of Athelas, Zero and Jin Yeong would be there. They'd probably just be staring at me silently, but that was still better than waking up after being killed in my dreams without anyone being there.

But I hadn't been dreaming about Athelas every night so far, and I didn't want Zero to think I couldn't do it, now that I'd said I would. I got up and headed for the stairs.

"JinYeong, go with the Pet," said Zero's voice, from his study.

JinYeong raised a brow, but he stood regardless.

"Go with me—what? I'm going to bed."

"JinYeong will sleep with you tonight."

"*Heck* no!"

JinYeong's eyes became liquid. "*Musen il, Petteu?*"

"JinYeong will help you if there's another dream."

"I dreamed last night. Don't reckon I'm gunna dream again."

"We don't know that. You said you were willing to help."

"Can't I just rescue Athelas through the dream, or something?"

"Yes and no," said Zero. "He needs to allow you to rescue him, but we'll also need to find where his physical body is."

"Yeah, I know that. But what's it got to do with JinYeong sleeping with me?"

"We need more information."

"You said they might be listening. How can I get information from Athelas without tipping 'em off?"

"That's why I or JinYeong will come with you."

"Hang on, you mean come with me into the *dream*? That's what you meant?"

"Yes."

"You can *do* that?"

"We can try. We won't be able to come all the way, but we should be able to go through a few layers with you if we're connected when you start to dream."

"Connected, how?" I demanded, deeply suspicious. It was bad enough that I would have to sleep next to either of them; if it involved any more spit, vampire or fae, I was gunna punch someone. Not Zero or JinYeong, but someone.

"Skin to skin," said Zero, and there was that lighter blue to his eyes.

"Don't you laugh at me," I told him, but it didn't come out as adversarially as I meant it to, and the faintest crease came to the corners of Zero's eyes.

"No spit this time," he said. "You just need to be holding my hand or Jin Yeong's."

"Yours," I said at once.

"*Ya!*" said Jin Yeong indignantly. "*Nae son wae andwae?*"

"It's too pretty," I told him. "I'd probably break it or something. Oi, Zero. Is that why you said if they figure it out, they might kill me?"

Zero was serious again in a moment. "Yes."

"What about you?"

"What about me?"

I frowned. "It won't hurt you if they kill me, will it?"

"There's a possibility."

"How much of a possibility?"

"I don't know," said Zero. "I haven't had much experience with the dreams of a Sandman. Considerably less than that of a human dying under the same circumstances, I imagine."

"What about Athelas? Will he be able to see you?" A sudden hope lit in me. I'd thought of trying to get Zero in there with me, after all—I'd thought it would encourage Athelas to trust me, or at least to tell me where he was.

Zero shook his head. "No one but you will be able to see me."

"And maybe the bad guys."

"No, the bad gu—the people who have Athelas won't be able to see me. They might sense me, however."

"And try to kill everyone," I nodded. "All right. But you're just gunna have a poke around and see if they're watching us."

"That, and try to find out where Athelas' body is."

"Okay, but you'd better give me the thumbs up if they're not listening."

"The what?"

"The thumbs up," I said, and demonstrated. "So I know it's safe to ask any questions again."

Was that a touch of suspicion to Zero's face?

"What questions do you want to ask?"

"Dunno, just questions. He won't answer about important stuff 'cos he doesn't want to give them any answers, so you don't have to worry."

"Yes," said Zero, but he still sounded wary. "Don't ask too many questions, Pet. It's not safe."

CHAPTER EIGHT

"Don't wriggle," growled Zero, a huge rumble of sound that reverberated through my ribs.

"There's no room for me," I muttered. "Why are you so flamin' big?"

"I asked you if you wanted to sleep on the bed—"

"Pets aren't allowed on the bed. And mine's not big enough for you."

Zero sounded exasperated. "Then don't complain."

"Yeah, but you're so flamin' big! I can't even scratch my leg without falling off the couch."

"Don't scratch your leg."

"Yeah, but now that I'm not allowed to scratch it I need to scratch it *more*."

"*Pet.*"

"You got a spell for itchy legs?"

"Go to sleep, Pet."

"I can't sleep sitting up."

"You're not sitting up, you're leaning on me."

I huffed a breath against his arm. This couch was just the right size for me and Jin Yeong—long enough so that I could sit away from him if I wanted to, short enough so that I could throw stuff at him if I wanted to—but it was nothing like big enough for me and Zero. If I leaned against him I could just fit my backside on the seat of the couch, but I was in danger of falling off if I wriggled too much.

"Don't think I can sleep," I muttered.

There was a big silence, then Zero said, "You drink too much coffee."

I would have pointed out that coffee wasn't preventing me from being able to sit on the couch comfortably, but that would only have brought us back full circle to the whole bed or couch issue, and if it came right down to it, I'd still rather sit uncomfortably on the couch with Zero than sleep on the bed with him.

Like I said to him, Pets shouldn't sleep on the bed.

The heavy silence grew and spread out in the darkness, and maybe Zero was doing something with it, because I started to get sleepy again despite my itchy leg. I floated in creamy half-light for a while until it occurred to me that the opposite wall wasn't the opposite wall anymore. So gradually I hadn't noticed it happening, it had become billowing, creamy silk instead of a wall; almost as if Between had opened to let me see what it could be instead of what it was here in the human world.

"This is a dream, not Between," I said to it. "Why are you doing that?"

I got up anyway, and a huge weight dragged at my shoulders.

"Oi!" I said in surprise, turning back to look at Zero. "Stop it!"

But he was still on the couch—asleep, snoring—and so was I. Well, I wasn't snoring, but I was asleep, and there, but still here. That weight dragging me down must be the version of Zero that was as nebulous as my current consciousness.

Was that why I was here instead of in the hallway? I didn't know, any more than I knew if it was really Zero pulling me back, so I started walking toward the wall that was no longer a wall again. It billowed to meet me, soft and cool, and drew me in.

I lost sight in the coolness and softness of it, and when I was able to process sight again, whiteness was all around me like a cloud, nothing solid beneath my feet, nothing solid to the touch around me. I was still pretty sure that I was on my way to the hallway where I would find Athelas, but there was nothing touchable to prove it. Maybe it was because I drifted to sleep instead of falling asleep, a sort of nightmare-bound Alice, trailing a Zero-shaped weight behind me. Maybe it was Zero that was the problem.

Whatever it was, it had me drifting through unresolved whiteness for long enough to make me think I'd actually been killed by Athelas' captors before I'd really begun. To my relief, the whiteness resolved itself into halls just as I began to really worry about that.

Behind me, a huge warmth grew up, not quite with me, but not too far away. When I turned around, there was a version of Zero there, as big and impressive as he was in real life, but not quite as present.

"We made it!" I said, grinning at him. My grin didn't feel quite straight, so I stopped pretty quickly, and added, "We didn't die."

The Zero presence frowned and mouthed something.

"Can't hear you," I said. "Is that meant to happen?"

Zero shrugged, which was a bit worrying.

"Thought you knew what you were doing?" I said accusingly; and he must have been able to read my lips, because I swear he looked guilty for the briefest moment.

It was only a moment; the next, he jerked his head toward the wall that I had twice passed through to get to Athelas. Right. Down to business.

It must have been enough that we were connected physically back in the waking world, because when I moved toward the wall, Zero drifted along with me without the stepping motions that I was still using to move around. Did the floor feel as real to him as it did to me, or was he not real enough here? Did the frigid air tickle his nose uncomfortably the way it did mine?

Zero looked at me enquiringly, and I jerked myself back into motion. I was going to have to learn to think and walk at the same time. Especially now that I was stepping through the wall—another Between-like action that felt odd here in the dream world now that I thought about it—and especially now that I was going to face Athelas. I could ask questions, but they had to be safe ones. Just in case my being here was someone's plan—just in case someone was listening. Stuff about myself, maybe. That ought to be safe enough.

Just until I knew whether or not it was okay to talk. I looked over my shoulder instinctively to see if Zero was still following me into the room, and heard Athelas' voice say, "Ah, and so it begins again."

I looked across at him warily. Mentally, I was aware that he must be in a lot of pain, and a distant part of me wondered how he could function so fully. Emotionally, I could only feel sick because I knew there was a very good chance I was going to be killed again, and even if it didn't stick, it was still horrible.

It cheered me a little to think that Zero was here now, too. I could see the not-quite-presence that was him drifting around the room, and maybe I was a bit too obvious about watching him, because Athelas said, "Do we have another visitor, Pet?"

"No," I said. "I'm just creeped out. I don't like being killed in white, airconditioned rooms."

"Do you not? One wonders why it is you keep coming back, in that case."

"Just the pleasure of seeing your face, I s'pose," I said, and he laughed. "If it bothers you, you can always flamin' stop killing me! I'm just trying to rescue you."

"Your *rescue* is somewhat lacking," said Athelas, turning his head stiffly back to the ceiling. He was almost yellow today, and I wondered with a pang if someone else had been visiting him again. "Even if you free me here, what then? I kill you, escape to the waking world, and find myself captured between floors once again. Why go to the trouble?"

"Why not just escape to the waking world *without* killing me?"

"I've told you often enough that I am imprisoned—"

"Yeah, in moonlight, and hell bars the way. That doesn't mean anything to me."

Across the room, Zero stopped circling the perimeter of the room and drifted nearer to observe Athelas. There was a line between his brows and a sorrow to his eyes that I wasn't used to seeing, but he studied Athelas more coolly than I expected before his eyes rested on me instead.

"Anyone listening?" I asked.

"The same as before, I believe," Athelas said. There was more weariness in his voice again today, with just a thread of his usual amusement.

Behind him, Zero shook his head, and gave me an uncharacteristic thumbs up. Heck yes! No one was listening. I could ask questions again—if I could only get Athelas to answer them.

"You just gotta tell me where this room is," I said, as Zero crouched by the strands of moonlight. "Simple. Then we can come get you."

"We're not in a room," he said. "It's a construct. You're a construct, too; not a physical being—a thing created by the Sandman to play with me."

"That's not an answer," I said, but I was distracted enough to ask, "Is that why I didn't die properly when you killed me?"

Athelas' head dropped back with an exhausted laugh. "Even so."

"Why bother to kill me, then?"

One of his shoulders moved slightly. "Why not?"

"Athelas," I said. "It's me. Actual me."

"Even if it were *actual you*—what then? I can't kill a pet?"

"That's flaming rude," I said resentfully. "But I'm gunna be the bigger person and still ask you where you are again."

"I don't know where I am," he said. "Why should I?"

I frowned a bit. Did he really not know, or was he lying? If he was lying, why? Did he think they would move him if they thought he knew where he was? Did he not want to be moved for some reason?

"I don't believe you," I said, experimentally.

There was only silence from Athelas, and when I drew closer, I saw the deeper lines beside his eyes. His eyes were closed, too, which worried me. How tired was he? Was it possible for fae to die from torture?

I didn't want to find out, but I was also pretty sure that there was only one way of prodding someone like Athelas into strenuous life, and that was to really get under his skin as the person he thought I was. I didn't want to do that.

If I did...if I did it...

If I did it, Athelas would be absolutely merciless in his killing of me this time. And he would likely never trust me again, either.

On the other hand, Athelas already didn't trust me, and I'd freed him from his imprisonment twice now. He was also at the edge of what he could endure, I was pretty sure—he needed something to push against.

I glanced up at Athelas and found him watching me; behind him, Zero looked, I dunno...apprehensive. Athelas looked more like someone had winded him, all silent, contained pain.

"What?" I asked, alarmed. "Something happen?"

"I'm curious," said Athelas, and his voice sounded just slightly stifled, too. "What conclusion is it you just came to? If you were really the Pet, I would be feeling distinctly worried at this point. She has such a way of doing exactly the wrong—or exactly the right—thing when she looks like that."

"You know a lot about the Pet," I said.

"Ah, are we giving up our pretence?"

I shrugged and crouched by the outer strands of moonlight. I had to free him one way or the other, so I might as well get on with it. "You don't believe I'm the Pet, anyway."

"Oh, are we still doing this? An interesting choice!"

"Might as well, since I'm here," I said, setting my jaw. It hurt a bit, so maybe I'd already been clenching it without thinking about it. "I'm only gunna let go of your body, though. Not your arms."

"Do you really think I can't kill you thus?"

"Dunno," I said, refusing to look at him. "But it's gotta be better than letting you have your arms. What's your problem with the Pet, anyway? Why are you so happy to kill her?"

"A clingy little thing, the Pet," he said, ruminatively. "Always following someone, always stuck to someone like a limpet. Very useful."

"She was alone in her house for four years," I said, stung. "No parents, no safety. She's probably just trying to survive."

"Perhaps the Pet's parents should have thought of that before giving their lives."

"It's not like they died on purpose."

Athelas made the faintest suggestion of a shrug. "No? Perhaps not. But humans don't die in that manner merely because they lived a quiet life."

"There's some sick humans out there as well as sick Behindkind," I said. "And what do you know about the Pet's parents, anyway?"

I was too careless with the moonlight in my anger, and Athelas gave a ragged groan.

"Sorry! Sorry, sorry!" I said, releasing the threads I was holding. They held for a moment, then shivered away into twinkles of moon-dust.

"The Pet's parents," said Athelas, panting. "Were killed some time ago."

"Z—Lord Sero knows about it?"

"He knows its parents were killed. It was living in our house before we took it as our Pet—a very susceptible house, as it happens."

"You really think it was Behindkind who killed the Pet's parents? What Behindkind?"

Athelas exhaled a small laugh. "I see," he murmured. "You haven't got the Pet! I've become too careless, it seems. Allow me to congratulate you on some very fine interrogation at last! It would work far better if I had anything to tell you, of course, but you weren't to know that."

"What are you talking about? 'Course we've got the Pet; how else did I know all this stuff?"

"As you're always telling me," said Athelas, his voice mocking, "you're the Pet! Of course you would know."

"Fine," I said. "Be like that. I'm not gunna let you down, then."

"Are you not? That will make for an interesting change. Perhaps the people who put you in here did not make you sufficiently well aware of the terms and conditions for getting out: It is, of course, far easier to get in than out."

I wrapped my arms around my legs and caught Zero's eyes. He was frowning, but I was pretty sure it was because he couldn't hear what was going on—he could only see that I'd stopped freeing Athelas.

"What terms and conditions?" I asked.

"Surely you felt the difference in the room the first two times you freed me? There's no easy access to Between for mortals like you; it's all high stakes and widdershins walks to edge you in carefully."

"I don't need those things," I said. Actually, I hadn't felt the change to the room, but both times I'd been here previously, I'd been pretty busy being killed at that point. "You know that."

"It is not something I know. The Pet is human—though I'm beginning to suspect that you think it something else entirely—

and humans do not make their way deliberately through Between or Behind."

I grasped at a last straw. "What something else entirely?"

"I'm certain you know that better than I," Athelas said. His eyes, reflective and frightening, rested thoughtfully on me. "Do you really think that my lord wouldn't know if he had a changeling in the same house? Ah! Or do you go further and suppose him to be harbouring an Heirling? For what possible reason?"

"Beggared if I know," I said. I didn't even know what an Heirling was, and why on earth would anyone think I was a changeling? "'S'pose he can have one in the house if he wants to."

"Allow me to remind you that Lord Sero's fate is to sit on the throne of Faery as Lord of Behind. An Heirling is a direct challenge to that claim. He would be a fool to allow such a human to live, Pet or otherwise."

Right. So Heirlings were humans?

"And if you had the Pet as you would like me to believe, you would be utterly convinced of its humanity," continued Athelas. "I therefore conclude that you are merely throwing bait—though for what purpose, I can't imagine. If you are the Pet, you will need a human way out. Will you free me or not?"

I stood again as strands of moonlight dissolved to dust at my feet. "What human way out?"

"Freeing me is the first step," said Athelas, and he smiled. His eyes didn't smile along with his lips. "I'm sure you knew that much already."

"Yeah? Well, maybe I don't want to be killed again."

"Then you must take your chances, must you not? There is no other way out for you."

"We'll see," I said. If Athelas was telling the truth, and the room somehow changed to open access to Between, maybe I could sneak out after he was free. Already his lower body was drifting toward the ground, free from moonlight but tethered by the strands still piercing his upper body.

If I was quick enough. If I didn't die first.

I stared down at my shoes, reminded of—dreading—the inevitable. Athelas' feet settled to the floor just a pace away from mine, accompanied by a dripping of blue, and I heard his breath, ragged in and out, as his arms stayed pinioned above him.

I gritted my teeth against the regret. I couldn't release his arms straight away; he'd only kill me. Watching the blue spread toward the toes of my sneakers, I said quietly, "I'm sorry."

There was a flutter of movement to my left, and I turned my head to see Zero leaping for Athelas, fast and furious. Leaping for Athelas, whose arms were free, whose right hand came up to cup my cheek without being disturbed by the passing of an insubstantial Zero right through it.

I said, very softly, "Ah heck."

"Thank you, Pet," said Athelas, smiling a blue, bloody smile at me. He wasn't standing straight, but this time it wasn't to fool me into thinking he was weak.

Run, said my thoughts. *Run, fight, while he's weak.*

But I knew it wouldn't change the outcome, and instead, I heard myself say, "Can't you trust me?"

I knew I was pleading, but I couldn't help it. I hated to die by his hand again. "Can't you just...trust me? This once?"

"How could I do so?" asked Athelas, his eyes as dark and glittery as a moonlit well. "Knowing I'd be betrayed?"

"At least it wouldn't kill you," I said, and there was some bitterness in my voice.

"No," he said, and a blade of pain slipped between my ribs, cold and piercing. "That would really kill me."

I felt the hand cupping my cheek catch my head as it dropped; as I died.

I woke to see Zero's face. "Dry your tears," he said, and propped me up against the back of the couch with the hand that had caught me before my head hit the seat. He settled back beside me without objecting when I leaned against him with my arms wrapped around his, and said, "Tell me what you remember."

I WOKE UP THE NEXT MORNING, STILL SITTING ON THE COUCH with my arms wrapped around Zero's huge forearm and my head cushioned on his shoulder. I would have been content to go back to sleep, feeling safe—and above all, dreamless—but someone was throwing small pellets of something at me.

I opened my eyes and glared at JinYeong, who sat on the coffee table with half a slice of bread in one hand and a narrow, stormy look to his face.

I shook my head slightly to dislodge the pellets of bread that had fallen there, and a hot, angry *something* woke in me. "What the heck?"

"The morning has come," said JinYeong, in painstakingly understandable Korean, picking another pellet of bread from the half-torn piece he was holding. "Get up."

I opened my mouth to say something I would probably have regretted, but the movement woke Zero. He stared at the opposite wall, then turned his head to look down at me.

"Now you woke him up!" I said angrily to JinYeong.

He shrugged.

"I've already slept too long," said Zero, brushing away pieces of bread with a faintly questioning look at JinYeong, who only looked innocently back. Zero's eyes turned to me and lightened a touch; he got up and went into the kitchen.

That left JinYeong watching me with narrow eyes, so I narrowed mine at him. "What? Going for creepiest psycho? How long have you been staring at us?"

"*Ireona*," he said.

He'd probably been staring at us for at least ten minutes, willing us to wake up, before he went for the bread.

"*Wae*?" I asked, copying him. There was a sharp edge of restlessness to me, and I was very willing to pick a fight. What could he do to me? Kill me? I'd already died three times.

"*Hajima*," he told me. *Stop it.*

I opened my mouth to say *wae* again, this time more mockingly, but Jin Yeong leaned forward, his nose unnervingly close to mine, and said very softly, "*Ha. Ji. Ma.*"

"What?" I asked. "Haven't had your coffee yet?"

"*Ireona, Petteu.*"

"Whatever," I said, but I did as I was told and got up, following him as he stalked toward the staircase. His socks disappeared at the top of the staircase as I got there, and when I got upstairs, he was waiting by the first painting on the wall. Ah. So he'd finally realised what was wrong with them. It was about time —it had been more than a week since I went around the house, misaligning them all by a millimetre or two.

I stood next to him and said, "Yeah, this one's nice, isn't it? We picked it up in a car boot market in Queensland. Only five bucks."

"*Petteu*," said Jin Yeong warningly. He said something else that ended with, "*Balli!*" which meant he was telling me to hurry up and do something.

I could guess what that something was. I looked at him coldly, then at the picture. "What's wrong with it?"

Jin Yeong said a single word—probably, "Crooked," and since it still annoyed him to be understood by me if he didn't choose to be understood, I decided to understand anyway.

I would understand, and be very, *very* helpful.

"Oh, is it crooked?" I asked, grinning savagely. "Hang on, I'll fix it."

I gave it a good shove up on the side that was down. "There you go!"

"*Kurotji mala.*"

"Not like that? Oh, I did it the wrong way?" I gave it another good shove the other way and left it out by about five centimetres.

"*Petteu*," said JinYeong, his voice soft and silky, "*Chugolae?*"

"Why not?" I said. "You're already dead, and I've died three times already, so it's not like we don't have experience. Go for it: Kill me."

JinYeong turned his head to one side, gazing at me.

"What?" I said. "Trying to decide how to do it? Ask Athelas; he's got some flamin' fantastic ideas!"

He looked at me for just a bit longer, then unexpectedly reached out and patted me on the head. "Bad Pet," he said in Korean, and sauntered back toward the stairs with his hands in his pockets.

"Oi!" I yelled after him. "You can't do that!"

His chuckle curled back to me as he descended the stairs, and somehow there was a wetness falling down my cheeks, hot and cold at the same time. I crouched underneath the painting and cried until no more tears came out with the sobs, and until I heard the sound of the jug being boiled downstairs.

Then I patted my cheeks dry and went to wash them off.

I was still feeling a bit raw and cranky when I got to the kitchen to make the coffee, though my cheeks were dry and not so red, and when I saw a mug of coffee waiting for me, with Zero and JinYeong already sipping from their own mugs, I felt a warmth in my eyes again.

"Don't make me coffee!" I said to Zero. "I can make my own!"

He put his hand on my head, and for a minute I thought he was going to pat my head, too; but he pressed down until I was sitting on one of the bar stools in front of the kitchen island, and pushed the mug into my hands.

"I made it," he said. "Drink it."

Maybe the tears had taken away the edge of recklessness I'd felt earlier. I propped my feet on the cross bar of the stool and drank my coffee, and when JinYeong dropped a plate of biscuits in front of me and said "*Moggo*," I picked one up and dipped it in my coffee, too.

I didn't like the way they were both watching me, so I asked, "What are Heirlings, anyway?"

JinYeong said in a deeply satisfied purr, "*Ooah, Hyeong! Jaemissoyo!*"

I looked from him to Zero. "What's so much fun about it?"

"It's not fun," Zero said. "JinYeong simply likes things that cause trouble. An Heirling is any fae, or mix of fae and another race who is powerful enough to challenge the current rule and take control of the world Behind."

"Someone who isn't Fae can rule Faery?"

"It's not Faery," said Zero. "It's Behind. And any Behindkind with a drop of the right Fae blood can rule Behind."

Flaming heck. So when Athelas said something about Zero being the heir, he meant the heir of *the whole of Behind*? Not just a country somewhere?

Still blinking about that, I asked, "Not Between as well?"

"Nobody rules Between," said Zero. "That's what Between is —a lawless section neither here nor there."

"How do they know which Heirling is the right one?"

JinYeong chuckled, deep and low.

"I'm guessing it's a bloodbath, then," I said.

"Very nearly," Zero replied. "If there's more than one to begin with, there is usually only one left by the end of the succession discussions."

"That's some discussion. 'Zat why you left your family and became a cop?"

"I didn't leave my family and become a policeman."

"No? Looks like it from where I'm sitting. I thought your family was the mafia or something, but they're more like royalty?"

"They're not royalty."

"What, just you?"

"No one knows where the blood will out."

"Pretty sure that's not how blood and DNA works," I said. Maybe it was the coffee, but I was beginning to feel warm again. "We gunna have people turning up to try and kill you?"

"It's unlikely," said Zero. "There have never been more than rumours of Heirlings—and if there had been more, the Family would have sought them out and killed them."

"What about you?"

"What about me?"

"Well, can you just leave like that?"

"There's already a ruler Behind."

"Yeah, but if you're his heir—"

"Behindkind live a *long* time."

"What a surprise," I muttered. "So your family wants you to be king, and—"

"My family wants the power associated with me being Ruler Behind. Once there, it would be a constant struggle to remain free of their machinations."

If they were anything like as twisty as Athelas, I could understand Zero's reluctance to have his family anywhere near him while he was on the throne.

"So what, you're just gunna give it up?"

"I have no interest in ruling Behind."

"Reckon your family's gunna give up that easily?"

"No." Zero put down his coffee mug, and there was a faint line between his brows. "But that is my own issue to resolve."

JinYeong chuckled again, and the look he shot at Zero was malicious.

To my surprise, Zero actually grinned. He said, "Until it becomes otherwise, it's still my issue to resolve. That's not what's important right now."

"What is important right now, then?" I asked, not really expecting him to tell me.

"The kind of dreams you're having," he said, and paused.

"They're not being caused by Athelas' captors, though they are indirectly a result of a Sandman's work with Athelas."

"Yeah, you said that if it wasn't that, it was because of a connection or something?"

"Exactly so," said Zero, and the line between his eyes deepened.

I thought about that for a little while. "Yeah, but hang on—"

"Exactly so," he said again. "What connection do you have to Athelas?"

"Beggared if I know. Maybe it's the house. You said it's susceptible to Between, and so did Athelas. Maybe it seeped into me, or something."

"Perhaps," said Zero, but I could tell he didn't believe it.

Jin Yeong made a dismissive "*Tch*" of sound.

"What do you know?" I demanded. "It could be that."

"*Ani.*"

"What, I can't dream a dream?"

"*Andwae*," agreed Jin Yeong. "*Petteuga kunyang Petteuya. Inganiya.*"

"What about Heirlings?" I said. Maybe I was a bit smug, but if so, it made a nice change from Jin Yeong being smug.

He scowled at me.

"Technically, Heirlings aren't human," said Zero. "They're a fae and human hybrid."

"Like vampires and were—lycanthropes?"

"No. I've told you: Vampires and lycanthropes are mutated versions of humans. Heirlings and Harbingers are born."

"Ha!" I said to Jin Yeong. "Zero says you're a mutant."

Zero said a very faint, startled, "What?" and Jin Yeong threw a biscuit at me. Reckon he must have forgotten I was still pumped up on a bit of vampire spit. I caught it without having to think about it and dipped it in my coffee.

"More for me," I said, grinning a crabby grin into my coffee. I don't know how, but I was starting to feel better.

"I didn't—I didn't say that," Zero said, and I wasn't sure if the pause was because he was trying not to laugh, or because he was still so bemused. "What are you doing, Pet?"

"Getting up," I said, draining the rest of my coffee. "I'm going for a walk."

JinYeong and Zero exchanged a look, but Zero only said, "Pay attention while you're out."

"Got it," I said. "Thanks for the coffee."

That wasn't what I'd meant to say. I tried again, and this time it came out. "Thanks for trying to stop him. Athelas, I mean. I forgot to say that."

"Next time, you'll know to be more careful."

"Yeah," I said. I mean, it wouldn't stop me dying, but I'd know.

CHAPTER NINE

IT WASN'T UNTIL I WAS OUTSIDE THAT I LOOKED AT MY PHONE. The entire screen lit up with a series of texts from Detective Tuatu, leaving me to wonder exactly how the sound of them arriving hadn't woken me. Dying repeatedly wasn't really an excuse when you woke up alive.

6.15—Pet, the dryad won't let me leave the house.

6.31—Please come and get me out.

6.43—I don't know what's happening and the dryad won't let me make a phone call. Please come and get me out.

6.55—Wait. Don't come and get me. The dryad is shrinking again.

7.02—Looks like I had some visitors a couple minutes ago; they're gone now. Don't know why the dryad won't let me make a phone call, though.

7.45—Okay, I think I know what's happening. Someone's bugged my house, but they're not normal bugs.

7.46—Actually I think they're normal bugs, because they can crawl, but they've got listening equipment sort of, I don't know, built in?

7.55—Insect spray kills them.

8.42—There are leaves *in my hair, and I don't think they're the dryad's.*

I grinned down at my screen. Maybe it was mean of me, but it was kinda nice to interact with someone who was more out of their depth than I was. It made the world feel a bit normal again.

I texted, *Sorry, I was asleep. You need me to come around?*

No, it's fine. I'm collecting dead bugs at the moment. Will the leaves come out of my hair?

Yeah, but it might take a day or two.

All right. Don't call me for a couple of days, though, all right? I need to check for more bugs.

This got something to do with Zero coming to visit you?

This time there was a longer gap between messages before the reply came, *No.*

"Fibber," I said aloud, and put my phone back in my pocket. I'd have enough time later on to be figuring out what was going on with Tuatu and my psychos. Right now, I just needed to check on Daniel and maybe figure out a way not to die next time I dreamed.

Right now, it was just nice not to die.

This time, when I walked down the street, I only went as far as the house that might hide Daniel, and turned into the entrance of the building across the street like I belonged there. It was obviously some sort of shared living, and it had a pretty leafy garden where I could maybe keep out of sight. Of course, keeping out of sight wouldn't help me to be able to see into any of the windows of the house across the road, but I didn't see the front entrance of a shared building being unlocked, so it was unlikely I'd get a chance to go inside.

Just out of view of the street, sheltered from the front windows of the lower floor by a tree trunk, I threw a look around the garden. Lots of places to hide, but not that I'd be able to get a good view from. I looked up at the leafy foliage above me, wondering how well I'd be able to see from up there—and how likely it was that this place would start getting busy as the morning went on.

What was it that Zero had said about surveillance? That's

right: *It doesn't matter how well you're hidden; someone will always see you. Make sure that it doesn't matter when you are seen.*

So hiding in the bushes was out, and so was climbing one of the trees. Being seen in a tree or climbing down from a tree was definitely something that would matter.

I moved slowly toward the front wall by way of the path; nice and slow, just a normal occupant of the building having a wander around the front garden a bit too early in the morning. There was a nice little cut-away section between the last window on the left and the corner of the building; deep enough to hide me from the windows when the curtains were opened. If I propped myself up against that with my phone out, I'd look just like a normal teenager. There was a small window there, oval and sunk back into the creeper that started to take over the building at about shoulder height, but when I took a quick look into it, there was only an empty room there as far as I could see. Someone's bedroom, probably.

I nudged my shoulder into the corner to avoid the oval window, and found that I could see through the windows across the road a bit better. Not the lower ones—like the ones in this building, the curtains there were still drawn; but the upper ones were flung open, and I could see a section of ceiling and what looked like one very broad shoulder in a suit.

Pity I couldn't see any more than that. I was starting to think that I might have to find a way to sneak into the place itself, after all.

I was still thinking about that, trying to decide if it was worth the wrath of Zero when—if—he found out, when I saw a flash of movement over my shoulder. I shrank away from it, but it was just a girl's face in the tiny window; small and pale, with huge eyes and hair that was too black for her face and definitely too black to be real. Her lips were painted black, too, and there was a lot of eyeliner around her eyes, though I wasn't sure if the dark circles beneath that were on purpose or because she hadn't had enough sleep.

"Hey," she said, and her voice was a bit too breathy to be healthy.

I squinted up at her. Beggar me. There went my good hiding spot.

Hang on. Where was she, though? I wasn't looking at a person through a small window like I'd thought at first; I was looking at a mirror, tilted toward another mirror further up on the outside of the house, just beside an elkhorn. There were probably more further up, but if there were, they were too well hidden for me to see.

"Where are you?" I asked, in astonishment.

"In my room," she said, her pale face bright with enthusiasm.

"Is there a speaker down here somewhere?"

"Yeah," she said. "I don't know exactly where it is, though. If you're trying to keep an eye on what's going on over the road, you can do it from my room."

"Yeah?" I said slowly.

"It's okay," she said, more quietly. "Cops use my room a lot— there was one here just a week ago. There's a *lot* of crime around here, and I've got a good view. Windows on both walls, so I can see into most of the houses around here."

She must be younger than her makeup and the dark circles beneath her eyes had made me think: A bit naïve, too. "How'd you know I'm a cop?"

"I wasn't sure at first," she said. "You're a lot younger than most of the ones I've had here for surveillance. But you're doing all the same things that they usually do, so I figured it was a good guess."

Then she grinned. "I thought it was worth saying it, too; thought you'd be impressed if I got it right, and if I was wrong you'd only think I'm a bit weird. Most people already think I'm a bit weird."

"All right," I said, grinning back up at her. "I'll be right up. What room?"

"I'm number fifteen, top floor. It's unlocked."

The front entrance was unlocked, too, which made me kick myself a bit. I should have checked. By now, I could have been somewhere in the place, looking out of a convenient window and not caught by a thirteen-year-old. I wondered if the girl had seen me sizing up the tree to decide whether or not to climb it, too. Probably.

I trotted up the stairs pretty quickly; it wasn't exactly necessary for people not to see me, but I thought I'd prefer as few people to see me around here as possible. Across the street there had been the feeling of Between fairly crackling on the air, and even the house didn't look exactly the same from minute to minute, but over here there was barely a touch of it around. Maybe enough to make me think the balustrade could be a tree branch, but that was about it.

There were only three rooms up on the top floor, and number fifteen was the only one on its side of the hall, which made me raise my eyebrows a bit. The building wasn't exactly a small one; she must have the equivalent of half a house up here. Where were her parents?

I knocked, and the same breathy voice called out, "Come in!"

The door was unlocked, just like she'd said, and the first impression I got when I walked in was that I'd walked into a cloud. It was all blue and white and airy; windows bright and light on two walls, with conveniently-sized areas of painted brick between them from which to peer out at the world without being seen. The rest of the room was taken up with stuff that might be exercise equipment, but wasn't like any kind of equipment I'd seen before, and a computer setup that must have cost more than a year's rent in this room. Oh yeah, and the giant, mirrored black telly that was suspended from the ceiling where it wouldn't get in the way of anyone's view from the windows.

I tore my eyes away from that to look for the girl, and that was how I saw the bed right in the middle of all the other stuff, right where it had the best view from the windows. The girl was sitting in it—well, slumping a bit, really. There was a mountain of pillows behind her, and what I'd thought was a black, lacy shirt was actually a black pyjama top.

Maybe she got back in bed after she came over to look at me. Weird, but she looked like a bit of a weird kid.

She didn't ask me for my ID or anything, just gave me a huge smile that was far too cheerful for the goth thing she had going with her makeup, and said, "I'm Morgana."

"Pet," I said automatically. I could have kicked myself, but it was too late now. I should definitely think about making a fake name for situations like this.

"It's a good view, isn't it?" she said, eyes bright. "I can see into most of the buildings around here because of the incline of the street, and if I use binoculars—"

She stopped guiltily.

Grinning, I asked, "You spend a lot of time looking out there with binoculars?"

"Maybe," Morgana said. She added hastily, "Not looking through people's curtains or anything—well, sometimes by accident, but I don't do it on purpose."

"See anything across the road?" I asked.

"Yeah, someone new came in last night."

"Not last night; about a week ago."

Morgana gave a small snort of laughter. "Someone new came in then, too. I don't think he was happy to be there, though; there was fighting and a dog, and someone broke the window. I thought the dog was going to jump out, but the beefy bloke who stands at the window grabbed it by the tail."

"There's a dog there, huh?" Heck yeah! I'd found him!

"A *really* big one," she said earnestly. "I thought it was a wolf at first."

Yep. I'd found him.

"All right if I use your window for a while, then?"

"That's who you're after?"

"Nah, I'm after the dog," I said, and she grinned.

"If you need anything, I'm just over here," she said. "And there's water and stuff in the fridge. You can use the kitchen if you want, too; it might be a bit dusty, though. I mostly have food delivered."

"That's not healthy," I said; but if she had the money to eat out all the time—not to mention the money for a place as big and well-stocked as this one—she was probably flush enough to be buying good food.

She only shrugged at me, and when I settled by the window, carefully out of sight, she said, "The other cop that did surveillance here was interested in that building, too. It's a kind of Mob hospital, isn't it?"

"There's no Mob in Tasmania," I said.

"That's what he said, too. All right, Triad, then."

"We don't really have the Triad here, either," I told her, though if it came right down to it, she wasn't that far off. She just didn't know the extent of it. "It's a kind of hospital, yeah. And the people who go there aren't...well, they're not exactly law-abiding citizens, if you want to put it like that."

Morgana must have been satisfied with that, because when I turned back to the window, I heard her tv switch on in a flash of static. She wasn't wrong about her view, though; when I turned my gaze out on the window she'd pointed at, I could see the impressively large shoulder of someone who was nearly as big as Zero. I repressed a grin: He must be there to prevent Daniel trying to turn wolf and leap out the window again.

I could see Daniel, too; and the sight of him lying in bed with a scowl directed at the big bloke in the window made my heart feel lighter all of a sudden. Athelas might be waiting to kill me again, and I was bound to fall asleep much sooner than I wanted, but at least the consequences of my last escapade were less awful than I'd thought they were. Daniel didn't look too healthy—he was too pale and thin from what I remembered of him—but he was alive and obviously chirpy enough to be trying to escape, and that was cheering.

I STAYED THERE FOR WHAT WAS PROBABLY TOO LONG, WITH THE mumble of Morgana's tv in the background, until I remembered that I was supposed to be out for a walk—and until a text from Zero *ping*ed me awake from watching the small square of scowling life across the road.

It said, *Come home.*

"Bossy," I muttered, but I got up.

Morgana, who hadn't moved from her bed, looked away from the tv in surprise. "Aren't you staying?"

"Nope," I said. "He doesn't need constant surveillance—I'm just here to make sure everything's going all right. I'll probably be back a few times a week, if that's okay with you."

"All right," she said. As I was on the way out, she added, "If I'm asleep, just come in anyway. The door's always unlocked."

I stopped at the door, frowning. "'Zat safe?"

"Yeah," she said. "There's the kids out there."

"Okay," I said, and kept going. It wasn't my business. It wasn't my business to tell her that kids weren't a safety feature. It wasn't my business to worry about whether or not her neighbours were noticing enough people to see if she got into trouble—or to wonder why she didn't have any visible parents living with her.

Not my business.

Not. My. Business.

Maybe when I was done with the whole thing of sneaking in to check up on Daniel, I could ask Zero to have a look at the security of the building. That's all. Didn't have to do anything else.

I spent the rest of my walk home trying to figure out exactly how I would broach that with Zero, and came home to find Zero and Jin Yeong waiting for me in the living room. Jin Yeong looked accusing, Zero pretty much as normal—cold and very slightly disapproving. That was nice; he'd been a bit too crushed and worried lately for my liking.

"Why are you smiling?" he asked me. Now there was a faint touch of worry to his pale brow again.

"Didn't do anything," I said automatically, sitting down on the couch, and Jin Yeong made a very small choke of laugher.

"*Kojitmal*," he said.

"Rude," I said; but it wasn't like I hadn't accused him of being a fibber before, so fair enough. "What's the go? What do you want me for?"

"First," said Zero. "Lunch. Then it's time to sleep again."

"Oh, right," I said. I was tired enough to sleep at the drop of a hat, but somehow I'd expected a bit longer to recharge and recoup. "You coming with me again?"

"Every time," said Zero shortly. "They don't know we're in; it's the best avenue for information that we can get. I want to try and find where he is again."

"All right," I said, yawning. There was definitely something about the quality of sleep I was getting while I was dreaming of Athelas—it was like I hadn't had any sleep at all. I'd had three mugs of strong, black coffee today; there was no way I should be falling asleep like I was.

"*Hyeong, chunbihaesseoyo?*"

"Ready," agreed Zero. "Go now."

"Where's he going?" I asked into another yawn, as Between swallowed Jin Yeong and left behind a brief shadow that faded into a pattern in the wallpaper.

"He's going to check a possible place for signs of Athelas when you free him this time," said Zero. "Once the prison is gone—"

"Once I die," I muttered, wrapping my arms around my legs.

"—he'll be out of the Sandman's influence and in the real world," Zero continued. "I could find no trace of him while I was there, but if they'd had him in the construct again since last time, I wouldn't have been able to do so."

"Is it the station?"

"No. The station is peopled by humans; dream or not, it's impractically dangerous for them to keep him there. He could slaughter them all at one go if he got out."

"Yeah, but the dream—"

"If there's no sense of him this time, JinYeong will try the station next."

That was better than nothing, I supposed. And Zero was right —what kind of Behindkind gave someone like Athelas to a bunch of humans to torture? "If JinYeong senses him, can he go in?"

"I told him not to do so," said Zero.

"That's not an answer," I said, nudging up against his arm. "He's gunna go in if he senses Athelas, isn't he?"

A barely-audible sigh made the air heavier. "It's possible."

I nodded. "So you might have to leave pretty quick. I'll be fine. You can leave when you need to."

He nodded silently, and I got the feeling that maybe he felt bad about it. That was kind of nice, even if I would have preferred to wake up with him there instead of dying alone and waking up to an empty house.

When it came, the dream was just a little bit different again. This time there was no interim of sleepy floating, no wafting walls, and no white halls; I fell asleep in one moment, and woke the next in the white room with Athelas opposite me and the drag of Zero's passage fading from somewhere around my shoulders.

Zero moved around from behind me and silently began to

circle the room again, but I marched up to Athelas and yelled, "Stop flamin' killing me!"

Athelas' head turned slowly, his eyes taking too long to focus on me. "Must you shout, Pet?"

"Yes, I flamin' must! And while we're at it, where are we?"

"No matter how loudly you shout," murmured Athelas, "I can tell you nothing more than I know myself."

"Fine," I said. "So you're not gunna tell me where you are because—reasons. And you're not gunna tell me anything else 'cos you think I'm not myself."

This time, Athelas didn't answer, as silent as Zero stalking the room and looking at things I couldn't see.

I said to him, "What, you're sulking? I'm the one who should be sulking! You've killed me three times!"

He might not have spoken, but his eyes flickered toward me for the smallest moment.

"And it's no good saying *and yet here we are* because it's not like I've got any choice about it," I told him. "I just fall asleep and here I am. If you don't want to keep killing me, it's not like you have to keep doing it!"

A faint breath of air escaped Athelas. As if he felt he might as well speak now that the sigh had got out, he said, "On the contrary. I certainly do have to keep killing you. If you don't care for it, the remedy is in your own hands."

"Speaking of hands," I said suspiciously, "what have you got this time? A flamin' razor blade?"

"It has barely been ten minutes since last you visited," said Athelas.

"It hasn't, you know," I said. "It's been more than a day. Dunno what they've got you on, but it's definitely been longer than that."

He laughed at me, the sound bubbling as if he was breathing blood. "I think not. I killed you only ten minutes ago."

I gazed up at him. Was that why he was looking so

haggard? Someone else had been in here again with my face, and he'd killed them.

"You really don't like killing me, do you?" I asked. Maybe to someone else he would only have looked like he was worn from the torture, but I didn't think so, and somehow that cheered me more than I expected.

"It's somewhat tiring," Athelas said, turning his eyes on me fully; and the ice in those eyes made me shiver. "However," he continued, "I will kill you with alacrity every time you come back to me. I very much enjoy ridding my presence of you."

"Yeah," I said, because he hadn't said he enjoyed killing Pet— just the person he thought I was. It didn't mean I was looking forward to being killed again, but it did mean I didn't feel so sick about it.

"And it will be my pleasure to craft a new method of killing you each and every time," added Athelas.

"Thanks," I said. "Beaut. I'll look forward to that."

He laughed. I didn't know whether that was a good or a bad thing. Whichever one it was, it definitely meant he was getting stronger again quickly: Whatever wounds he had suffered in his mind from killing me last time, he was mentally preparing to do it again.

I huffed a sigh and sat down at the base of the moonlight. At least now I knew he would be able to free his own arms. Maybe I could leave him like that and it would be enough to get me out before he freed his own arms enough to kill me.

I pulled in another big sigh, reached my hands out to touch the moonlight, and asked him, "What's the go with Zero and Jin Yeong, anyway? If I'm gunna die, I want to get something out of it."

"I would assume you know as much as I," Athelas said.

"You'd assume wrong, then. What's the deal with him and Jin Yeong?"

"I would very much like to know what you expect to learn

from any such information," said Athelas. He sounded amused again, which was probably a bad sign for me. "I assure you that it won't help you in the slightest. It won't help you to learn anything about my lord that you didn't already know—you can be certain that I won't provide any useful information for you."

"You don't have to provide useful information," I said. "And I'm pretty flamin' sure that what you think is useful information and what I think is useful information is something different."

It couldn't help being different: Athelas thought I was part of Upper Management—whoever they actually were—or maybe even something else entirely. In any case, the things I wanted to know weren't even slightly the sort of thing that an information-gathering group would want to know.

"It'd be nice if you used your brain," I said sourly, and saw Athelas' eyebrows slightly quirk.

"Perhaps I shall tear out your tongue," he said.

He said it so lightly, so easily.

"Fine," I said, shoving my hands into my pockets and hunching my shoulders to stop the shivers. "I won't try to free you, then. We'll just flamin' stay here forever."

"You won't have to do so. I shall free myself."

"Yeah? How come you haven't escaped yet, then?"

"It would be a mistake to assume that I'm not here according to my own will," said Athelas, and when he looked over at me again, his eyes weren't just cold, they were amused.

I tried not to shudder. Somehow it was worse to think of Athelas being still strung up like that because he had a plan, than it was to think he had been captured and put there. Was it even possible for someone to put themselves through something like that for the sake of being undercover?

If it was, Athelas was about the only person I could think of actually being able to do it. Mind you, it wasn't like he was actually a person, so there was that.

"What about Jin Yeong?" I asked. "Can I ask about him specifically, or will you threaten to tear out my tongue about that, too?"

"Knowing about Jin Yeong can't possibly help you in any way, either."

"Never said it could," I said. "Just wanted something to talk about other than you ripping out tongues and stuff."

"There's no enjoyment in that."

"Speak for yourself. Right, if we talk about Jin Yeong, are you gunna get your knickers in a twist?"

Athelas half-shrugged, and hissed at the pain it caused him. "It's nothing to me what you learn about the vampire."

"Nice," I said. It wasn't like Jin Yeong liked Athelas much, either, but it was different knowing that and actually seeing one of them willing to give up information on the other without a struggle.

"What exactly would you like to know about Jin Yeong?"

"Dunno," I said. I didn't actually care to know much about Jin Yeong, but if it was the only information Athelas was going to spill, I might as well learn what I could. "How come he's travelling around with Zero, I suppose?"

"I've already told the pet this," said Athelas, his eyes narrow and mocking.

"Yeah," I said. "But you only told me he wanted to make sure no one else kills Zero except him. It's not like Zero needs help to survive, though, is it?"

"Perhaps not, but it seems that he's destined to have help he neither desires nor needs," Athelas said. "He has mine, after all."

"What happened with Jin Yeong's sister, then?"

"She made the mistake of becoming fond of Zero."

I frowned. "How's that a mistake?"

There was that mocking gleam to Athelas' eyes again. "As I also informed the pet, Zero is fae. He can't love in the same way that humans and vampires love."

"Hang on, vampires can love people?" I demanded. Skinny,

nose-in-the-air Jin Yeong in love with someone? "Rubbish! Jin-Yeong's too much in love with himself to fall in love with anyone else!"

"Good gracious, you're making a thorough job of it this time, aren't you? Vampires were once human, just like lycanthropes; the change to either form of superhuman amplifies rather than dampens the emotions. It's why very young vampires need to learn control very quickly. It is also why most young vampires don't live long enough to learn that control."

Well, that explained the mess Daniel and Erica made of the supermarket a while ago. I'd thought Daniel was young and stupid —turns out he's just a normal lycanthrope.

Normal. Yeah.

"Anyway," I said, "I didn't mean that. I mean, how is it a mistake that ended up with her being dead? Don't reckon Zero killed her because she fell in love with him."

"In this world, as I'm sure you are aware, and especially more so in the world Behind, there are people who use pain and terror as a method of control."

He was mocking again—not me, but the person he thought I was.

"Behindkind of that sort were interested in controlling Zero, and they found a particularly effective method in Jin Yeong's sister."

"What happened to her?" I asked, though I was more than half sure I didn't really want to know the answer. "How did Zero end up killing her?"

Another amused, side glance from Athelas. It must be common enough knowledge that he thought it amusing that I asked about it.

"She was captured by Behindkind who thought to use her as a way to draw Zero to themselves, but I don't think they bargained on how much she would fight being used as leverage. She made a bargain with one of the other denizens of the house and burst from her prison as a new vampire. Had she been a little better able to control the beginning frenzy, there might have been some hope for her."

"She went mad?"

"A clumsy way to put it, but close enough to the truth. My lord caught up with her as she was drinking her way through a household of humans, and in the struggle that ensued, she was slain. Jin Yeong arrived just too late to help."

"Oh," I said uncomfortably. I'd asked for the information, but I hadn't thought about what it would be like to get it. It was a weird thing to feel sorry for Jin Yeong.

"Dear me, are you sorry you asked? He's merely a vampire, after all. Not even an original Behindkind." Athelas watched me, darkly amused. "Or are you showing me what you think the Pet would feel?"

"'S'pose Jin Yeong took it badly," I said. I would have. Even if my parents had turned evil for a bit, I still didn't think I'd be able to forgive someone for killing them.

"You could say that," Athelas said. "So young and passionate! He has mellowed somewhat with age."

"Mellowed flaming *what*?" I muttered. If Athelas thought Jin Yeong was mellow these days, what the heck had he been like when he was first turned? I glanced across at Zero, and found that he was looking at me, frowning, instead of observing the room.

Hopefully he couldn't lip read well enough to know what we were talking about. I was pretty sure he wouldn't appreciate me asking questions about him. But if I stopped, what chance was there that Athelas would finally come to understand that I was the Pet? He had to realise at some point, right? If I just kept going? I wasn't good enough at pretending to be someone I wasn't —not when I didn't even know who I was supposed to be pretending to be.

"What is it you're looking at, Pet?" Athelas' voice was soft and thoughtful.

Almost Athelas-as-normal. Almost like we were back at home in the living room, and he was trying to find out something I was hiding from him. It had me opening my mouth to answer before I thought about it.

I thought better of it in the act, and since my mouth was already open, I used it to say, "Oi. Don't do that."

This time it was Athelas who gazed at me with his lips just slightly parted. "I could return the sentiment," he said. "But no doubt you'd claim complete ignorance."

"Don't have to claim anything," I said. "And you wouldn't believe me, anyway."

"What are you hoping to achieve here, Pet?"

"Get you free. Not die, I s'pose."

"My meaning was more direct," he said, looking down as well as he could at the bands of moonlight that I had persuaded to curl around his chest instead of through him as we talked.

"That? Why would I tell you? You'll just use the information to try and kill me."

"A fair point."

It struck me that this conversation was as close to a normal conversation with Athelas as I'd had since he disappeared and I began to dream about him. I couldn't help beaming at him, which made him blink and look away.

"I assume you're attempting to secure time for yourself in order to escape," he said. "A useless endeavour."

"Yeah?" I said, shivering the last thread of moonlight into dust.

Athelas settled into the embrace of the moonlight, and I took several steps backward, looking around me for any change in the room that I could use.

There was no change. No gleam of Between, no hope of escape.

And in the middle of the room, Athelas shrugged off the moonlight as if it was nothing, as if it was exactly what it was:

Moonlight. Zero crossed the room with him, a step or two ahead, but Athelas wasn't in any hurry. He knew I had nowhere else to go.

Zero put a hand on my shoulder, where it made a faint warmth and sank a little bit into the skin, unable to quite touch. And in front of me, Athelas came to a halt, smiling faintly.

"This has been an interesting meeting, but you should go now," he said. "I have my own experiments to conduct."

There was nothing in his hand, until there was. Then it was something sharp and short and diamond shaped that twinkled past my ear and bit my neck where Athelas' hand cupped the base of my skull.

"Ah heck," I said, and died into the real world.

My eyes flickered open into darkness, sleep-gummed and unreliable, and I had a muffled moment to wonder how it had taken hours for me to dream what happened in such a short amount of time, before they shut again.

I fell asleep.

I fell asleep, and I was there again.

"What the heck?" I said in shock, and across the room, through the strands of moonlight that held Athelas, I saw Zero, his eyes startled and his mouth open in a warning.

Too late, I saw that there was nothing to the moonlight but moonlight itself, the idea of Athelas' shape disintegrating into moon dust along with the moonlight as one of Athelas' arms wrapped around me from behind.

"How interesting," said his voice. "This construct has a little more flexibility to it than I thought."

There was no time to be afraid, or sorry; just time to fall asleep, or die, or whatever it was that ended up with me waking with my head against Zero's arm.

The house was dark and cool with Betweenness, a feeling of peril around us that was familiar and almost comforting.

"Not fair," I said, and felt my chin wobble. "I already died once."

"Sit up," Zero commanded, reinforcing the command by lifting me up with one hand behind my neck. "It's not useful to fall asleep again yet."

"Yeah," I said, yawning hugely, "but I'm flamin' tired and I don't think I can stay awake."

"Stand up. Make coffee—or cook something."

"Pancakes," I said, because the clock said it was morning when I looked up at it. Two in the morning, but definitely the morning.

I swayed into the kitchen and bumbled around for a bit, yawning and trying to find the right frypan, but by the time I'd managed it, I could feel the house getting all Betweeny as JinYeong came home. I trotted back toward the living room, and JinYeong's cologne came curling into the room ahead of him, wafted along by a Between breeze that didn't belong in the house or even probably in the human world.

I didn't need the Between-translated words to tell me what his face already told me, but I listened anyway, leaning up against the doorway so I'd stop swaying back and forth.

I heard a meaning that said *Sandman was there; had to go away before it saw me. Couldn't risk staying*, and said, "'S'okay. We'll try again tomorrow," instead of yelling at him like I wanted to do.

Even pains-in-the-neck like JinYeong have their problems, if what Athelas said was true.

JinYeong looked at me suspiciously, which was pretty rude, and when I asked wearily, "Want coffee?" he looked even more suspicious.

"Coffee," I said again, and went to make it. One thing was for sure—I wasn't sitting down on that couch again until I was good and ready to fall asleep for the next dream.

CHAPTER TEN

I COOKED PANCAKES FOR ZERO WHILE I DRANK ENOUGH COFFEE to drown a small kid, then buzzed around the kitchen making apple pie while Zero and JinYeong argued in the living room. Maybe it was because I was so sleepy, or maybe Zero was doing something to the sound, but either way, I didn't seem to be able to understand what they were saying.

I tried once or twice, my pride piqued, but I was definitely too tired for that, so I gave up and concentrated on cooking instead. Once the apple pie was in the oven, I cleaned the kitchen from top to bottom and migrated to the bathroom to do the same.

When six o'clock came around, I started on a kimchi fried rice that had JinYeong glancing often at the kitchen through the doorway as the smell of it rose in the air. It slowed down their argument, too; they'd been arguing incomprehensibly every time I wandered past, by the looks of JinYeong's bared incisors and angry eyes.

By the time I dumped the kimchi fried rice in front of JinYeong, he looked more suspicious than angry, and demanded of me, "*Wae?*"

"Made it for you," I said, yawning into my arm. "Better brush your teeth after, though; it's loaded with garlic."

"*Noh mwohya? Mwoh haesso?*"

"Didn't do anything to it," I said, shuffling back toward the kitchen. "Flamin' suspicious little vampire, aren't you?"

Maybe they thought I was trying to listen to what they were talking about, because Jin Yeong still looked suspicious when I came out again with a full glass for him.

"Got you some blood," I said. I put it on the table and headed back for the kitchen so they'd know I wasn't trying to hear what they were saying. Over my shoulder, I said, "Drink it and don't pick fights with Zero, all right?"

A hand on my collar dragged me around to face Jin-Yeong who, his eyes very narrow, said,

"*Noh mwohya?*"

"Dunno what you're saying; speak English," I said. "Can you let go of my arm? I still need it for cooking, and if you don't let go, I'm gunna lose it from lack of blood flow."

Zero, his eyes light with amusement, asked, "Did you put something in Jin Yeong's blood?"

"Nope," I said. "Just trying to stay awake."

"*Nomu soosanghae,*" muttered Jin Yeong, but he took a sip of his blood.

"Take yourself for another walk," said Zero, which was suspicious. "Jin Yeong and I have matters to discuss. Don't fall asleep. Don't forget to pay attention to your surroundings."

My first instinct was to complain, but I definitely didn't want to fall asleep again, and I could always use the time to visit Morgana again. It would be nice to check on Detective Tuatu, too; and as much as I wanted to help Athelas, I didn't want to die again just yet.

"All right," I said. "I'll be back in a couple hours."

Let them plan their little plans. I would be busy with my own.

I left the house just a bit after seven, texting Detective Tuatu on my way out to ask him how his bug-spraying was going, and about ten minutes later he texted back.

Don't talk to me. This is your fault. Before I met you, I didn't have a dryad or *an infestation of bugs.*

I grinned at my phone and replied, *You're welcome* as I sauntered into Morgana's building. I expected to run into some of the kids she'd mentioned last time, but maybe they were at school or something. I never could remember the school terms.

There was no one in the halls, and no one on the stairs, either, and Morgana's voice sounded glad when she called out, "Come in!" to my knock.

She grinned at me from the bed, same as yesterday; all black pyjamas and black lipstick that looked not quite right with how brightly she smiled.

"You're just in time!" she said.

"Yeah?"

"Yeah, this is the time they usually bring him something to eat. If he doesn't like it, things get really energetic for a while."

I snorted a bit. "Yep, sounds about right. You want coffee? I want coffee."

"Help yourself," she said, tipping her head in the direction of the open kitchen. She leaned back into the piled-up pillows just like she had the first time I came into the room, and the suspicion that had been growing in my mind that she *couldn't* move from there, prompted me to ask while the jug was boiling, "You sick or something?"

"Yeah," she said, but she sounded cheerful enough. "I'm mostly in bed. Some days I can walk a bit, but not often. I could walk more if I did the exercises I'm supposed to do. Apparently."

"That what the doctor says?"

"Yeah, but I've never felt any different when I do them. Just more tired."

I wanted to ask her how she got to the toilet if she couldn't leave the bed very often, but that felt like it was a bit too much to ask on such a short acquaintance. I couldn't see signs of anyone else living here, but her parents must live over the hall or something. Maybe they cooked in their own rooms and brought it over.

Weird, but that's how some families are, I suppose.

I gave Morgana her coffee, and she took a sip, but judging from the slight wince of black lipstick, she was just being polite by taking another.

"You a tea drinker?" I asked. If I wasn't so sleep-deprived, I would have thought to ask *before* I made the coffee.

"I like both," she said. "Just...with some sugar and milk, maybe."

"Oh, sorry," I said. "I'll get some."

"There isn't any milk," she said. "No sugar, either; I don't have too many visitors, apart from the police, and they usually want their tea and coffee black. I'll ask the kids to get some later on."

I propped myself against the brick wall, sipping my coffee, and sure enough, Daniel was throwing soup at someone. I saw the bowl fly across the room, and then a piece of pottery flying, but the bloke at the window didn't even move.

I grinned. Poor Daniel.

"Who is he?" asked Morgana. "Did he do something really bad?"

I looked across at her, but she wasn't looking at me; she was looking at the dressing mirror opposite her. Beggar me. I'd thought it was weird that she had a dressing mirror right across from her bed when there was stuff in the way of standing; she wasn't using it to see herself, it was slanted at just the right angle for her to be able to see out her window. What's the bet it was angled to see all the bits she couldn't see directly out the windows?

I thought back to the face I'd seen in the mirror and wondered how many other setups she had like that. A heck of a lot, probably. How, though?

I got up and sat on her bed instead of at the window, and there he was again. Daniel, scowling at the ceiling, scowling at his guards. Pretty normal, for Daniel. He scowled at me a lot, too. Mind you, I annoyed him a lot, but it was still a pretty clear indicator of his general personality.

"Who did that?" I pointed with my chin at her mirror.

"I bribed the kids," she said, with a sparkle to her dark eyes. "They spent all morning up here with wire and string, making holes in the wall and climbing out the window."

"Why'd they need to climb out the window?"

"I don't think they did," said Morgana. "But they know I can't stop them, and none of the adults come in here, so they figured they were safe."

I grinned. "Serve 'em right if they fell. It's a pretty soft landing down there, anyway. What you bribe 'em with?"

"Lollies, mostly. Most of the parents here are into kale and green smoothies."

"The kids do the speaker as well?"

"Yeah. I put it together, but they wired it in down there. They're pretty clever kids. Hey. You want to play poker while you wait?"

I threw another look around the room, for the first time seeing all the reflective surfaces that gave Morgana a panoramic view of the world outside—even of the street. I couldn't even see as much from where I'd been sitting at the window.

"Heck yeah!" I said. "I don't know how to play, though."

"That's what everyone says," said Morgana suspiciously, but she explained it to me anyway.

"Ha!" I said, watching Daniel snarling something at his guards. "It's like Yahtzee."

"He's a cranky sort of bloke, isn't he?"

"Yeah."

"You didn't tell me if he did something bad."

I thought back. "Kinda," I said. "But he was more stupid than bad. He was trying to do what he thought was right, he was just... I dunno. Dumb."

"Oh good," said Morgana. "That's what I thought he looks like. I've seen him a lot the last week—he keeps trying to get out of bed and they keep putting him back in. I don't think he's a very good patient."

"Yeah, sounds about right," I said. "Hey, I thought you said there were kids around here."

"There are. Didn't you see them on your way in? They were just up here visiting before you came in."

"Maybe they climbed out the windows when they heard me," I said.

Morgana shrugged, as if that was pretty likely. "They like to spy on people," she said. "Maybe they're teasing you."

"Maybe," I said.

I kept an eye out for kids on my way out, just in case. I already had an old crazy bloke following me around, and a Sandman who occasionally liked to find out what I was up to; I could do without a couple of kids, too.

The kids would probably be safer not following me around, too.

I didn't see anyone on the way out, though, and I even used the bit of Between that made the stairs a bit more like alive wood to try and pick up the vibrations of footsteps. I could feel my own footsteps echoing loudly despite how carefully I was stepping, but there was nothing else.

If there were kids around, they were flamin' good at hiding their footsteps, I decided, and went home to find that Zero wasn't there anymore.

Rats. That meant I would have to stay awake until he got back home. I didn't want to go to sleep and dream, but at least dying with Zero there was a bit easier. I huffed around the kitchen for a bit, annoying Jin Yeong, who was prowling around the place, then decided to cook something else. At this rate, we were going to have more food than we needed to eat in the next week.

After a bit, JinYeong's prowling started to annoy me in return, so I made him kimchi fried rice again and ate some myself in self-defence. That left us looking at each other across the table, which was weird, but at least I didn't have to talk to him. I got up after I started falling asleep over the last few bites of fried rice and did the washing up, but that only meant I was falling asleep over the washing up instead.

I went and brushed my teeth instead, hoping to see Zero when I came out again. What was he doing? Even if he was out looking for Athelas, wouldn't he be back before I went to sleep again? Even if he couldn't be there in the dream with me like he'd said he would be, wouldn't he come back before he had to go out again?

But he wasn't back when I came back out with shiny clean teeth and the faint remembrance of kimchi fried rice burning at the back of my throat. I didn't realise I'd been looking expectantly around the room until JinYeong raised a brow at me. I sighed, then yawned involuntarily and curled up on the couch, hopelessly sleepy. Best get it over with. Sleep, dream, die, wake.

But through the murkiness of sleep, someone poked my cheek.

"*Mwoh hae, Petteu?*"

"I'm going to sleep," I told him, without opening my eyes. I couldn't hold it off to wait for Zero to get back home. "Leave me alone."

"*Ani. Catchi ca.*"

That made me sit up. "What? You're coming with me?"

He shrugged and said something that came with the meaning, "*Hyeong*'s orders. Get up."

"Why should I get up? If you're coming into the dream with me, we can sleep here."

"I do not," said JinYeong, his Korean very slow and stately, "sleep on the couch."

"You don't sleep at all. You're flamin' dead."

This time, he showed both incisors in his snarl, eyes stormy.

"Zero doesn't care about sleeping on the couch," I complained.

He was also comfortable to lean against, and he didn't smell like a bottle of perfume. Is this what he and JinYeong had been arguing about yesterday, or today, or whatever it was now? Had Zero gone out to find a sign of Athelas next time I dreamed?

"*Hyeongun obseo.*"

"I know he's not here, I wanted to know *why*."

JinYeong shrugged. "*Caja, Petteu.*"

"Fine," I said grumpily. "But if you snore, I'm gunna kick you."

I was pretty sure I was right about the reason for Zero's absence; JinYeong's failed mission to the first site would have to be repeated, and although the Sandman had seen JinYeong on another occasion, he hadn't seen Zero.

I just didn't know why it was something they'd argued about— or why they hadn't want me to listen to them. When my psychos didn't let me hear what they were up to, it was a sure sign it was something I would want to know.

"I sleep on the wall side," I said, as I climbed the stairs. "You'll have to sleep on the open side, and if you fall off, don't blame me."

"*Ne, ne, ne,*" said JinYeong dismissively, passing me on his long legs and going ahead into my bedroom.

I opened my mouth to tell him that he'd need me to open the secret door for him, but then I remembered he was the one who'd snuck in there the first time and closed my mouth again. I was definitely too tired for my own good.

When I caught up with him, JinYeong was already hanging his suit jacket on one of my hangers and hooking the hanger on one of the wardrobe handles. I left him to remove his cufflinks and dropped down on one knee beside the bed.

"*Mwoh hae?*" asked Jin Yeong, sauntering up behind me, rolling his cuffs.

"I'm checking under the bed," I said, looking at him over my shoulder.

Both of Jin Yeong's brows went up at the very edges, and I saw the faintest touch of a smile begin in the corners of his lips. Of course. He was scarier than anything I would find under the bed.

I ducked and looked anyway, a tiny, darting glance that showed carpet with a short cityscape of shoes beneath the shadowed edge. For as long as I could remember, I had checked under the bed every night that I slept in it. I couldn't remember a time when I hadn't, and I couldn't remember starting to do it, either. It was just something that happened every night I slept in my bed, with more regularity than brushing my teeth.

Maybe that was another layer to why I preferred to sleep on the couch.

When I climbed to my feet again, the smile was stuck on Jin Yeong's face, but the amusement was gone. Great. I'd probably offended him again, somehow. Flamin' uptight little vampire.

"*Mwoh?*" demanded Jin Yeong in outrage, and I hastily shut my mouth.

Whoops. Must have said that aloud.

"You can sleep on top of the covers," I said to him, by way of tempering the outrage with another, worse one. "You won't get cold, anyway."

He muttered the Korean equivalent of *whatever*, and stretched out on top of the covers closest to the edge of the bed, bare feet elegantly angled toward the window. I wanted to grumble too, but I was tired and the bed looked comfortable, so I just climbed over Jin Yeong, without being too careful about not elbowing him, and wriggled under the covers as far toward the wall as possible.

I went to pull the pillow closer to me, but Jin Yeong said, "*Hajima*," warningly, and since it was better to be without a pillow than share one with him, I shoved it further toward him instead.

He adjusted it smugly enough to make me think he'd antici-pated that, then said "*Son*," autocratically, holding up his own hand.

I muttered, but threaded my fingers through his and let our arms flop down between us. Jin Yeong's hand was warmer than I expected from a technically dead person; warm, and softer than my own, which were roughened from hours of double knife prac-tise with Zero. S'pose that happens when your teeth are your weapon.

I huffed a pent breath into the air and tried not to wriggle. Unlike Zero, the weight I was pulling tonight wouldn't be too heavy, so there was that. I just wished that Jin Yeong wasn't so warm—or maybe that he wasn't quite so close. A single bed wasn't big enough for two people, even when they were as skinny as me and Jin Yeong.

Some time between trying to resist the urge to scratch my nose and wondering if I'd have to get up and go to the toilet, I fell asleep.

There was no sensation of falling, or movement; I was just there in the room. A slightly ghostly Jin Yeong silently muttered a word I was fairly sure was the Korean equivalent of "finally!" and looked around the room with bright eyes. I watched him go, wondering what it was he was doing, and Athelas' voice sighed, "Ah, here we are again! I wondered how long it would take!"

"Sorry to keep you waiting," I said, and this time I didn't look at the moonlight that was pretending to be Athelas.

Instead, I turned around, and there he was. He was just standing there, but I didn't trust that. I looked instinctively over my shoulder to see where Jin Yeong was, and he was already striding back across the room.

"We're gunna rescue you," I said, before Athelas could say anything else. It was far too late for games and questions. I just needed one piece of information. "When you get out this time, try to keep hidden or something so they don't find you again.

We'll be there as soon as we can. You just have to tell me where you are. Even if you don't tell me anything else, just tell me that."

"Ah," said Athelas. He was laughing again. "Alas, my current bodily state is much the same as my constructed state in here. I may escape this room, but not that one. Ah, I do wonder!"

"What do you wonder?" I asked, a bit grimly. JinYeong stood beside me, and I looked up at him. He wasn't Zero, but he was a bit of comfort. Even the expression on his face was sort of comforting; that half-snarl of distaste, or maybe just irritation. I went to stick my tongue out at him by way of cheering myself up but remembered in time that I wasn't supposed to be looking at him at all.

"A question for you, Pet—who is it you keep looking at?"

Flaming heck.

I exchanged another look with JinYeong, then sighed, and said, "JinYeong. He came with me tonight. You can't see him because he's only partway here—Zero said if they came too close the blokes who've got you would know."

"Who was it last time?"

"Zero."

"I see," said Athelas, gazing for a moment at the shiny white floor.

I would have liked to have known what he saw—and if it was likely to end with him not killing me again.

"I'm going to tell you something, Pet," he said.

"You gunna tell me where you are? 'Cos that's all I want to know."

"No."

"Oh," I said gloomily. "Then it's probably what weapon you've got this time."

"It's related," he said. "Do you know how it is that I manage to have a new weapon every time you come in?"

"Something about constructs, probably."

"Exactly," he said.

"Hang on—you've been *making* the weapons, haven't you?"

"Indeed. I waited for you to come to the conclusion yourself, but apparently I overestimated your intelligence."

"Nothing new there," I said. "That mean I can make weapons, too?"

"Indeed."

I looked suspiciously at him. "Why are you telling me that?"

"Arm yourself, Pet," he said.

"I don't want to," I said, but he was already drawing steel from nowhere, and as he did it, I could see how to do it, too.

I ran for the other side of the room, snatching two pieces of moonlight as I went, and in my hands they became two familiar knives, long, strong and thin. I turned in time to meet a lunge from a single-edged sword, slightly curved and slender, and just barely deflected it. Distantly, in the background, I saw Jin Yeong snarling something at me—advice, probably, or his disgust at how badly I was fighting—but I didn't have time to parse it out.

Athelas pressed me back and back across the room with slash and lunge, never quite touching skin but never far away, and I stumbled through the moonlight, sending sparkles of dust everywhere.

It distracted Athelas, but only for a moment. I had one gasping second to breathe before he lunged again. I slashed down; a clumsy parry that should have used both knives but was too lopsided and put me off balance, unnervingly close to Athelas in his lunge. "Stop trying to kill me!"

"Then kill me," he said in my ear, and pushed me away.

The push steadied me, and I put my guard back up, but it shook. "Can't," I said.

"Of course you can. It's hardly your first kill, now is it?"

"Haven't killed anyone before," I said, panting as I slashed down on another lunge. "Didn't mean that. Haven't got the skill."

I didn't have the breath, either.

A moment of swift, stinging back-and-forth later, I lost one of my knives. Athelas tossed away his single sword and stepped close, tempting me to lunge with my other knife, but my hand dropped to my side. While he was armed, I would defend myself, but I couldn't attack him.

He looked at me; a long, expectant look, and I sighed.

"I'm not going to attack you," I said, dropping my own knife.

"Unwise of you," he said, and there was a gleam of silver in his right hand again.

I'd almost expected it; at any rate, the knife wasn't a surprise.

"Please," I said. There was the faintest of warmths behind me; the faintest of movements, as if I could really feel Jin Yeong at my back. "It's me, Pet."

"I know," he said.

I felt a shock of hope. Was he not going to kill me?

"They've got me between floors at the police station," he said softly, and with a single stab through the heart, he killed me. I felt him catch me as I fell, scooping me beneath the arms to fall against his chest, then I was awake.

I felt warmth before anything else, and a voice buzzing up near my temple about *once twelve is twelve, twice twelve is twenty-four, three twelves are thirty-six* in a continuous murmur. It was Jin Yeong's voice, but it had pushed so far Between that I understood it without having to think about it—without being distracted by the fact that the Korean he was actually speaking was longer.

Was Jin Yeong reciting the twelve times table to me?

"...ten twelves are one hundred and twenty..."

Yep. He was.

The arms around me weren't Athelas', they were Jin Yeong's; and that was weird.

"Why are you telling me the times tables?" I asked, my voice muffled against his neck. I was pretty sure Zero wouldn't approve of me being close enough to bite Jin Yeong's neck while I still had vampire spit in my system, but I was warm and alive, and the multiplication tables were somehow soothing. A mathematical kind of security blanket.

"Sleep," said Jin Yeong, instead of answering me, the words making English shapes with Between edges. "No biting."

"Wasn't gunna," I mumbled, and then, somehow, I did fall back to sleep.

CHAPTER ELEVEN

I woke up slowly, warm and scented and not dead.

Hang on. Scented?

Why could I smell Jin Yeong in my room?

"What the—?" I muttered, and opened my eyes. Someone's jawline was there where I should have been able to see my far wall, the colour of milk coffee but not as welcome. There was a warmth around my left hand, too, and somehow or other I had rolled onto my side during the night with my far arm resting on Jin Yeong's chest.

Athelas' mocking voice said in my head "...always clinging," and I scrambled to sit up, surprising a huff of air from Jin Yeong when I accidentally elbowed him in the stomach.

"*Wae?*" he groaned.

I was off-balance enough to say, "Sorry," automatically, but when I pushed my hair away from my face, I caught the distinct scent of Jin Yeong's cologne in my t-shirt sleeve.

Flaming fantastic. Now I smelled like Jin Yeong.

"Next time, take a shower before you sleep in my bed!" I complained. "Everything flaming smells like you!"

Jin Yeong smiled lazily at the ceiling. "*Ne,*" he said. I would have said he sounded smug rather than apologetic, but that's pretty normal for him.

I glanced at the clock on the wall. Six thirty? I'd slept that long? I didn't feel as tired, either. That was nice. It also meant that my brain was working a bit better than it had been.

"Hang on," I said. "Where's Zero? Shouldn't he be back?"

"*Ah*," said Jin Yeong, sitting up in one swift, sharp movement. Between whispered a meaning that said surprisedly, "Where did the time go? I slept."

"Thought you couldn't sleep," I said, shoving my feet into my sneakers. "C'mmon, let's go get Zero."

I'd only just got my shoes on when I felt the house shift a little bit to let Zero back in. I went dashing down the stairs to meet him, Jin Yeong striding after me, and caught him just inside the door.

"He said they've got him between floors at the station," I said to Zero, gasping a bit.

For the first time in the last couple days, I saw his shoulders square up. "Are you sure?"

"Yeah," I said. "Dunno why he told me—he still killed me—but I'm certain he was telling the truth."

"Why didn't you come and tell me? We could have been there by now."

This time the question was aimed at Jin Yeong, who surprised me by shrugging one shoulder, his eyes liquid and dangerous, and tossing a reply at Zero which I couldn't understand via either of my usual methods. Judging by the tone, it was rude.

And this time, instead of treating Jin Yeong like a child, Zero's ice shattered for the briefest moment. In a snarl, he said, "We do not have time for your childishness! I'm aware that you and Athelas have no love for each other, but you of all people should know how he's been kept for the last week!"

"Sorry," I said, and my voice cracked. We didn't have time for them to fight; there was no *reason* for them to fight. Not now that we knew where Athelas was.

I tugged at Zero's sleeve. "It was my fault; I fell asleep again. But Zero, if he's at the police station, why can't he get out? It's just Between, isn't it?"

Zero took in a deep breath through his nose, and his face was clear and smooth again.

"Athelas will still be bound," he said. "Free from the construct, but not the moonlight. They would be fools to allow him to wander Between on something so easy as an open widdershins way. Jin Yeong—"

"*Chunbihaettda,*" Jin Yeong said, grinning wide and deadly, and entirely without humour. "*Petteu?*"

"Yeah, I'm ready. Let's go."

THEY DIDN'T EVEN STOP TO TELL ME I WASN'T COMING—WE went directly Between, with a flash of yellow that Zero took loose in his hand instead of over his back. It wasn't the first time I'd seen him wield that particular sword, but I didn't often see him take it out of the house, and I wondered why he hadn't brought his usual weapon instead.

Between, I could see it flicker from its chosen form of a huge yellow umbrella to its real form of a massive sword. I looked around us nervously, somehow worried that it wasn't okay for him to be doing that here, and saw Jin Yeong glancing warily around us, too.

Well, *that* was flamin' comforting.

Zero strode ahead of us without pause; a fierce, unstoppable force that glowed in the darkness of Between and might have worn a crown if a crown was made of pure light. I was thankful for him, because the part of Between we streaked through was dark and wild, and I saw writhing things that coiled back away at the sight of him and his crown.

Some of those things resolved themselves into chains between bollards in a parking lot, and that was even more of a relief, because we must be nearly out of the Between part of the journey —for now.

We came out in the Maccas parking lot, just on the far side of the bollards and their chains, but Zero didn't stop to wait for us. He strode on, his crown gone but his walk still purposeful and murderous, and in the human world he swung a yellow umbrella with each stride.

I ran to keep up, Jin Yeong at my side, and the front entrance of the police station opened of its own accord without a touch of Between. I didn't know if that was Zero using magic, or if someone inside had seen us coming, but it spooked me. It was too easy to forget that my psychos had a range of different skills that weren't necessarily connected with Between, and were even less explainable.

No one stopped us as we swiftly passed through the hall, nor when we took the stairs to the seventh floor. I saw our shadows ripple across the floor, but there was no sound, and that was chilling, too.

Not even the door at the entrance to Upper Management stopped Zero. It exploded inward at one look from Zero's icy eyes, and there they were; human heads poking up out of cubicles with their eyes wide.

I don't know if they saw the sword or Zero first. Someone yelled, "Evacuate!" and they bolted *en masse* down the hallway toward the widdershins way. Jin Yeong sprang forward with a delighted chuckle that was frightening in its joy, and Zero swept after them, the umbrella flickering just once more before it swung into being as a sword, finally and utterly.

I dashed after them, forgotten and trailing, and I was only a few steps behind them when Zero roared, "*Quickly*, Jin Yeong!"

Jin Yeong said something sharp and hasty that sounded bad, and I heard him say, "Ah! Too late!"

I caught up and saw in disbelief that they were right; the humans had vanished down the widdershins hallway. Properly disappeared, too; not just retreating with the sound of scuffle and fear, but entirely vanished without sight or sound. When I followed Zero and JinYeong further down the hallway, it was just a hallway that led right back to the main room.

"What's happening?" I asked. "Why is it a normal hallway? How are we supposed to get to Athelas like this?"

"They've closed it," said Zero grimly.

JinYeong said something swift and surprised.

"Not possible, but it's happened," Zero said. "Someone has been teaching humans a few tricks. They've closed it, and they'll be running."

"*Hyeong, ottokaeyo?*"

"We'll find another way in."

"It's Between; can't you just go there?"

"There's no entrance here. The widdershins hall was fashioned to give humans a way in, but it was also fashioned because there was no natural way in. We'll find another way in; if we can't, we'll force our way in."

There was a sickness of failure to my stomach. "Yeah, but can we do it in time?"

We couldn't be too late. We *couldn't* be; not now that we knew where Athelas was—not when we were so close to rescue. Athelas had undergone too much. I had died too many times. We had to get to him before they did.

I had—hang on...

"Quick!" I said. "Put me to sleep!"

Zero didn't say *what*? but he did say, "Why?"

"'Cos that's how I can get in!" I said excitedly. "I'm right, aren't I? Dead cert, I'm right! Right here, right now, that's the only way to get through into the floors Between. You said it was a different kind of Between—sorta Between awake and asleep instead of Between here and there. That's our way in!"

"No," Zero said, frowning. "Athelas will kill you again. And if he kills you while you're actually Between, instead of in a construct of it—"

"Yeah, I figured," I said soberly. "Reckon I won't be a construct this time, either; I'll actually go Between, just like the widdershins hall, right?"

"I'll go."

"Yeeeah," I said doubtfully. I wasn't any too happy about that, either, but as sure as I was that I had to go to sleep to pass through into the floor that held Athelas, I was equally sure that Zero wouldn't be able to get through with me. "Pretty sure you can't get in, though. It's only humans allowed, and they've closed off the widdershins way. Sleep'll get me in, but I'm pretty sure it'll only be me. It's all geared toward humans, right? Because it was humans torturing him and they didn't want you two to be able to get to him if you found out."

"How am I to put you to sleep?" he demanded, but it was more of a stall than an actual question. He knew I was right—had probably known since he saw the humans fleeing toward the widdershins hall.

"Dunno," I said. "Hit me, or something."

"*Ne!*" said Jin Yeong cheerfully.

"Don't hit the Pet," Zero said, in a low, warning rumble.

"*Ye, ye, hyeong.*"

"You've got a spell, haven't you?"

"Nothing that won't interfere with the job you're trying to do."

"Oh," I said. "Well, Jin Yeong better bite me again, then."

Jin Yeong's brow went up, and he exchanged a look with Zero. "*Ne?*"

"It'll put me to sleep, right?"

"No," said Zero. "You've had too much recently; your body is beginning to get used to it. It might make you sluggish for a while, but that's all. You'll have to ingest it."

"Flaming heck!" I said crossly. I didn't have time to persuade Zero to hit me instead. "All right, hurry it up."

Jin Yeong shrugged, and there was an upturn to one corner of his lips that should have worried me. It didn't, because the worst I was expecting was for him to lick his finger and shove it in my mouth again.

He didn't.

He took a swift step toward me, grabbed me by the ears, and kissed me. There was a tickle on my upper lip that must have been his tongue, and I tasted something familiar.

I didn't even have time to glare at Jin Yeong; first I was being kissed, and then I was in another place completely. I should have expected that it would be the same room even Between; the same white shininess, the same grotesque display of torture that was Athelas suspended in moonlight, and yet it was still a horrible surprise to find myself there again. The only difference to the real room Between as opposed to the dream construct was that there was a door.

Somehow, despite what Athelas had said, I'd kept hoping that when he came out of the constructed dream, he was just imprisoned or something. Zero must have known all along—and now I thought I might really understand that slow, defeated look he'd worn so lately.

"Man, I hate this room!" I said bitterly.

"What a coincidence," rasped Athelas. His real voice was much rougher and softer than I expected. "I find that I don't care for it myself."

I drew in a breath and said, "I'm going to let you down, all right?"

"Are you really? How bold of you."

There was a noise outside, someone at the door, and my mind flew to the staff members who had escaped through the widdershins way. They were coming for Athelas, just like Zero had said.

I ran for the door, sweeping bars of moonlight up and out ruth-lessly as I ran. Athelas cried out, sending the tears to my eyes as I slammed those bars against the door, and then there was a silence that almost deafened me before I heard Athelas' ragged gasps.

"How appropriate," he panted, and then he laughed. "Well done, Pet!"

"I'm sorry," I said huskily. "It was all I could think of."

"Not at all," he said, with an affected politeness that didn't come close to masking his pain. "It was well done."

"We'd better be quick," I said, wiping away tears as I hurried back across the room. "Zero's waiting, and I think he wants to catch them all before they get away."

It was time to free Athelas for real. After that...

After that...

Well, maybe it was just best to get on with it. I reached out a hand to the moonlight, and for a wonder, that hand didn't shake. With a smooth, flowing touch across each one, so much easier in real life than it had been in the construct, I disintegrated each thread into sparkling dust.

This time when Athelas settled to the floor there was real weight to him, blood spilling out in blue rivulets, and he closed his eyes. My foot edged closer, but I didn't allow it to take a step forward. I couldn't trust him not to be faking it. So I waited, tortuously, until he opened his eyes again and blinked at the ceiling, then over at me.

"I really wasn't sure whether to expect a corporeal form of you," he said, almost as if he was talking to himself. "But here you are. So. Very. Interesting."

"It's me," I said. "I know you don't believe me, but it's actually me."

"You do it so convincingly!" he sighed. "And yet, I'm unsure! It seems so unlike Zero."

"Zero wasn't really happy about it," I said. Frankly, I added,

"I'm not very happy about it myself, actually; if you kill me this time, I'm really dead. So please stop flamin' killing me!"

"I'm aware," said Athelas, dragging himself up into a sitting position near the far wall. "It seems as though my lord trusts me somewhat more than I expected."

I didn't help him—I didn't dare. I didn't know if he'd kill me, and there was no Zero to help me in here.

He fell back against the wall, and I couldn't help the way my hand twitched to help him. Maybe he saw it, because he laughed a spurt of blood.

Wiping it away, he said, "Didn't I tell you I was bound by moonlight and that hell barred the way? There's only one way out of this room."

"Yeah?" I hung back where I was. I still didn't trust him. "Don't suppose you're going to tell me what it is?"

"I've told you over and over," he said. "And considering that you're frequently accusing me of withholding information from you, I find your attitude appalling."

I dissolved into a sputtering mass of giggles. "Flaming fae! Always getting so flamin' cut when someone can't understand them through layers of lies and blarney!"

"One wonders what human children are taught in school, these days," said Athelas. His eyes were getting lighter; probably a good sign for his health, but I wasn't sure about my own.

"Wouldn't know," I said. "Haven't been to school for years."

"You're claiming reasonable grounds for your ignorance?"

I huffed a sigh. "You and Zero seriously need to work on saying stuff nicely."

"I say things nicely when there's sufficient motivation," Athelas said. "As for Zero—well, let us just say that sufficient motivation for him requires a great deal more than worrying about the feelings of one pet."

"Fine," I said, giving up. "But I still don't know what you're talking about."

"Ah," sighed Athelas. "And to think I'd hoped that your humanity would cause you to take the hard road!"

"What road?" I demanded. "And what's it got to do with humanity?"

"My pride won't allow me to repeat it," Athelas said. His words were harsh, but his eyes were amused as he said, "You're a very stupid pet at times."

"What, you've finally decided I'm the pet, after all?"

"No," he said. There was still a laugh in his eyes, but I was pretty sure he was laughing at himself. "I'm no longer sure what to believe. But I've decided not to allow such a small thing to affect my actions."

"Dunno why you can't trust me," I muttered.

"I do, Pet," said Athelas; and for the final time, I saw there was a knife in his hand.

"Ah heck," I said. Where the heck did he get *another* knife from? We weren't in the construct any longer! "Athelas—"

"There's no use protesting," he said. "It really is the only way."

"You said you trusted me," I said. After everything I'd gone through, he was just going to kill me. *Again.*

And this time, it would stick: Even Zero couldn't help me.

"Isn't it ridiculous? For all I know, you're not the pet. But I'll trust you."

"Then put the flamin' knife down!"

"That's no way to break out of a prison of moonlight," he said, softly chiding, and climbed to his feet.

I didn't know I was backing away until I felt the wall behind me, hard and cold, and very certain about being a wall.

"There's no way out like that, either," said Athelas. He didn't seem to take a step, but he somehow approached, slow and gliding.

How could he even walk after being pinioned by millions of strands of moonlight? Maybe that's why he seemed to glide instead.

He put a hand on my shoulder, and if I'd thought about it, I probably would have expected to cry. I didn't cry; there was an empty, aching sense of futility to me that dried me right out. Athelas, in the end, hadn't been what I had always hoped for him to be, and there was no need to cry. All there was, looking up into his tired face, was an aching sense of how much of a *shame* it all was.

Athelas' fingers tightened in a sudden rictus, and he gasped. I didn't understand until his head dropped an inch, his eyes falling from mine, and I saw the blue staining through his shirt and dripping onto the floor. There was a knife in his chest.

Then I didn't understand again, because the knife was angled upward, and the hand around the hilt wasn't mine—or even Zero's. It was Athelas' own hand, fingers white and strained, then loosening as he fell against me.

I tried to catch him, but he was so heavy and limp that even the wall behind couldn't help, and we slid to the cold, bloody floor together. I pulled him across my legs, but I didn't know whether to take out the knife or leave it in, and I'm not sure Athelas knew what to do either, because he looked down at the knife and then at me, and there was confusion in his face.

"Tell me quickly," he gasped. "Are you really Pet?"

"Why are you worrying about that now?" I howled. "What the flaming heck are you doing, stabbing yourself?"

There was the barest thread of a laugh from him, bloody and soft. "Ah, it is you. Don't let go of me, will you?"

"I'm not going to let you go!" I snapped, wiping tears away from my eyes. "Just shut up and concentrate on healing!"

"That would defeat the purpose," murmured Athelas.

"What purpose?" I demanded, but his head dropped against the crook of my elbow, and there was no fanning of breath on my skin. "Athelas!"

Nothing.

His cheek was too cool against my skin, but that didn't mean he was dead—it was too quick to mean he was dead.

I felt for a pulse in his wrist, but there was nothing there, either.

Didn't mean he was dead, I thought, my chin crinkling. Maybe fae didn't get a heartbeat to their wrists.

I felt for a pulse at his neck instead, but there was nothing there either, and it occurred to me far too late that the only sort of training I'd had from Zero had involved learning how to kill things, not how to save them. I didn't even know CPR.

With a hand that shook, I pulled out the knife. It couldn't do any worse, now.

My voice shook, too, when I said, "Athelas? Athelas, you can't die. You gotta hang on for a bit longer."

He didn't reply, and there was something missing from the Athelas that the last of my temporary vampire abilities had been able to sense a few minutes ago. Something less of shadow, or maybe less of darkness.

Athelas was really dead.

CHAPTER TWELVE

THE ROOM WAS ALREADY A BLUR AROUND ME, SO WHEN IT GOT blurrier, it took me a while to notice. When I did, I said, "What the heck?" and reflexively tightened my hold on Athelas even though there was nothing I could save him from now.

It wasn't until everything mizzled into grey uncertainty and began to reform in a white corridor that I knew what was happening.

"What's the use of doing that *now?*" I snarled, hugging Athelas to me. "It's too late!"

I might as well have spared my breath; the room was gone completely, and I sat with my back against the far end of a familiar hallway, Athelas sprawled across me in a slick of blue blood and the hallway stretching away in front of us.

Still Between, but no longer trapped. What a waste.

"Do you think, Pet," said Athelas' voice faintly, "that you could refrain both from abusing the world at large and holding me quite so tightly?"

I yelled and dropped him into my lap.

"And perhaps you could add to your goodness by *not* jolting me?"

I looked down at him in shock. Although his head still lolled against my knee, blood wet and staining his shirt, his eyes were half open—and in those eyes there was a distinct gleam of amusement.

"What the heck?" I said. "You're alive? But you died! How are you alive? And how the heck are we out?"

"Pet, I believe the correct response to an acquaintance being alive after being thought dead is congratulations, not complaints," said Athelas, unconsciously echoing me.

"Yeah, that's what I said to Zero," I said. "Congrats, but how the heck are you still alive?"

"Ah, must I explain it again?"

"Yeah. I don't know what it means when you talk about moonlight barring the way, so if—"

"Hell, not moonlight. I really must speak to Zero about your education. Moonlight and incarceration, for your information, inevitably require self-sacrifice to break free."

"For someone who's killed me five or six times, you're pretty flaming matter-of-fact," I said sourly.

"Ah yes," said Athelas. There was a shadow of grey to his face again, but this time I knew why it was there. "I would like to point out that if you hadn't kept coming back to me, I wouldn't have had to kill you so many times."

"Don't even think about blaming it on me," I said, but I knew that as much as it hadn't been my fault, it also wasn't really Athelas' fault. He had just been, for the first time since I'd met him, wrong. Very, *very* wrong. And somehow that was possible, though it had never occurred to me that it was. "Can't you—can't you just say you're sorry?"

"With what possible motivation?"

"That's how it goes. You say sorry, I forgive you. Nice and easy —it doesn't hurt."

"Pet," said Athelas, and he sounded exasperated. "Don't forgive me."

"You three can tell me to do a lot of stuff, but that's not one of the things you've got any control over," I said.

"I know," he said. "Perhaps that's one of the reasons we find humans so repulsive—there's always one hidden element to them that we can't control."

"You could just apologise," I told him, grinning. "It's better than choking on your spleen because you were rescued by the pet, isn't it?"

Athelas struggled to sit up and gasped a little bit of blood again.

"What are you doing? Lay back down! You're not even healed yet!"

But he fought until he was sitting; and, from that position, bowed to me. Head low and eyes down, for far longer than I was comfortable with.

"Stop it, Athelas," I said uncomfortably.

"If you will forgive me against my will, you must accept such apologies against your will," he said.

"Is that what that is? Apologies?"

"Something akin to it," Athelas said. "The closest thing of which I'm capable. I tell you again, Pet—don't forgive me. It won't do either of us any good."

"What do you know?" I said, putting my nose in the air. "You're just fae. You don't know about human stuff."

Athelas laughed, helpless and disbelieving, and dropped back against the wall by my side. "Remember that I warned you, Pet. Why shouldn't we continue as adversaries, side by side?"

"I dunno how fae do it," I said, "but in the human world adversaries don't walk side by side."

"Do they not?"

"Not if they've got brains. Someone who walks beside you isn't an adversary; they're an ally. Look, can you please just flamin' lie down again until Zero gets here? You're getting blood on my jeans."

"I need some time to recover," said Athelas. "I do not need to be rescued."

I might have snorted. I tried to turn it into a cough but didn't manage it in time. Since it was too late anyway, I said, "Yeah, I s'pose that's why I had to come in and rescue you?"

"What I mean, Pet," Athelas said amusedly, "is that my body has already begun to heal itself, and now that I don't have a constant stream of moonlight coursing through different parts of my body, I should at least be able to stand in a few minutes."

"Lucky you," I said. "You don't need vampire spit."

"Ah, so that's what is so different about you. Jin Yeong bit you this time, I take it?"

I stared at him. "Can you tell?"

"Not precisely," he said. "But it is why I sensed a Behind-kind edge to you—and a great part of why I killed you so many times."

"That flamin' vampire," I said. I felt vindicated. "He's always making stuff harder!"

Athelas laughed once more, and this time there was no rattle, or wetness to the sound.

"Hey!" I said in surprise. "You're healing!"

"There are certain benefits to being fae—and more so when one is fae born to service. We're so very useful."

"You were born into service?"

"No," said Athelas, with decision. "We've been maudlin for quite long enough, I believe. I shall not regale you with stories of my childhood and exploits. Do you think you can resist being sarcastic for as long as it will take to help me to my feet?"

"S'pose," I said. "But that's no fun."

I saw the creases beside his eyes as I leaned over to help him up. He said, "Perhaps you should remember that we are by no means out of danger at this point, Pet."

"Don't think I'm ever out of danger," I said, a bit dryly. "If it's not Jin Yeong biting me, it's you stabbing me. Oi."

"Yes, Pet?"

"Did you apologise so you wouldn't owe me anything?" I demanded. "'Cos I'm pretty sure that killing someone six times means you should be answering some questions and stuff later."

Athelas made a very strange sound, and I grabbed at his arm, but he was only laughing. He laughed until he was fairly crying with it, dropping back down on one knee and ignoring every attempt I made to help him back to his feet.

After the first minute, I crouched back on my haunches, gloomily resigned to waiting until he was finished. Flamin' fae. You couldn't ever pick how they were going to react. At least JinYeong was pretty consistent—if he wasn't annoyed by me, he was pouting at me.

And as Athelas laughed, shadows gathered at the end of the hallway, in the main room. I didn't worry too much about them until it occurred to me that we weren't in the dream-hallway anymore, and that shadows in an actual hall probably heralded actual people or actual Behindkind.

By the time I looked down properly at the shadows at the end of the hallway, they were attached to people. People, and a Behindkind or two to round out the ugly. The humans hadn't been running to escape; they'd been running to get reinforcements. And now they had guns, which worried me because even if I could have accessed my knives, what good would they do against guns? The two Behindkind only had teeth, but somehow they were still more frightening than the humans. Maybe that's because their teeth were each the length of my forearm, but still.

I wished, very earnestly, that Zero and JinYeong were also here.

Athelas, the laughter still on his lips, looked up with a wild, dark satisfaction in his eyes. "Fools," he said. "They've opened the widdershins way again to bring in reinforcements."

"It's open again? Zero can get to us?"

"Ah, at last!" he sighed, more to himself than me. "Something I can really enjoy killing!"

"There's nothing here for me to fight with," I said, shivering. I didn't know if I was more afraid of the bunch at the end of the corridor with their guns, or Athelas and his laughing fury.

"Oh, there's no need for you to fight this time, Pet," said Athelas. "I can take care of some humans and a stray Behindkind or two. Stay behind me, but not too close."

"That's not very specific," I said, shivering again. "Don't—don't enjoy yourself too much, Athelas."

"I am very much afraid," said Athelas, "that that is not possible. Close your eyes."

"But—"

"Pet," said Athelas, rising to his feet with deadly grace, "I've already killed you six times. Close your eyes."

I wanted to protest, but there was nothing I could say that made sense, and he was already moving. I closed my eyes.

For a moment there was only the softness of my own breath settling in the air around me. Then there was a delicate footstep, and another; footsteps that continued and fell closer and closer together as Athelas began to run.

Gunshots, and the slither of steel; Athelas' footsteps swift and brief across the hall. I dropped to the ground at the sound of gunfire, covering my head instinctively though it wouldn't have done much good against bullets; and with a howl that made me cower even lower, the fight tore into being.

I know it sounds stupid, with everything I've seen, but I didn't dare to open my eyes. I didn't want to see the Athelas that was beneath the smoothness; Athelas stripped down and bare by torture: Himself. I didn't dare look.

Instead, I crouched where I was, covering my ears against the sound but unable to stop the warm, salty smell from entering my nostrils. There was a dull roar that wasn't gunshot all around me, and three or four times something swept past me, stirring the air. I was trying hard not to look, but I was pretty sure it was Athelas. And each time that something swept past, another something made a dull thud nearby and ceased to move.

I don't know when the movement stopped, or when the gunshots ceased. I don't know when the fight moved past me and down the hall—or even which direction it took, widdershins or deiseil. Soon, my hands were aching too much to keep covering my ears, so I wrapped my arms around my legs instead, eyes still squeezed tightly shut.

Some time after that happened, I heard someone say, "Pet."

It was Zero's voice. I let out my breath in a dizzy rush, and as I opened my eyes to a haze of red, a cool, slender hand covered them again, blocking my sight before I could make sense of the jumbled scarlet.

"Take the pet out," said Zero's voice. "I'll go after Athelas. He's gone deeper."

I didn't have to ask who he was talking to; I could already smell Jin Yeong's cologne. I let go of my legs and blindly started to stand up, but my legs were weaker than I thought they were and another hand grabbed the back of my collar just in time to stop me falling over.

"Zero?" I said, uncertainly; but I could already feel that he'd gone. Now there was only a slight presence behind me—Jin Yeong and his cold hand that was edged with red.

"*Obseo*," said his voice. "*Choshimhae, Petteu.*"

Not here. Be careful. The floor was slippery beneath my feet, and I didn't want to think about that too much, so I asked Jin Yeong, "How'd you know where to find us?"

And as first one foot and then the other moved across the slick floor, instead of listening to the Korean Jin Yeong spoke, I tried to listen for the meaning he spoke.

"...left foot; a bit of a slip there..." The Korean made no sense, but JinYeong's murmur was warm behind me like his presence, and it continued on with something like "suddenly opened...no sign there. *Hyeong* said we should try another level..."

Right foot; something spongelike gave way beneath it.

I stopped dead, shivering, and JinYeong walked into me.

"*Mwohji?*" he said. "*Caja, Petteu.*"

I couldn't. I knew it was possible—I knew I could physically lift my foot again—but I couldn't bring myself to do it.

"*Mwohji?*" said JinYeong again, this time surprised, and I realised that I was crying. "*Igae mwohya?*"

"Can't," I said, very tightly. If I tried to say anything else, I was pretty sure I would break down.

JinYeong gave an experimental sort of push at the back of my neck, but I folded with it and dropped back to my haunches, wrapping my arms around my legs again. There was a nightmare hovering at the corners of my mind, and even though JinYeong's hand was somehow still over my eyes, his warmth still behind me, the red that haloed it seemed to seep through the cracks in his fingers.

There was a mutter behind me that could have said, "What's wrong with it? Was worse than this before?" then the hand over my eyes went away, as did the warmth behind me.

JinYeong said something in Korean that I was pretty sure was, "Stay, Pet," and suddenly my arms were being separated and pulled forward until I fell onto the familiarly slender back in front of me.

I locked my arms around his neck before he could change his mind, and JinYeong rose. There was no sense of slipperiness when he took a step forward—almost no sensation of movement at all—but I kept my eyes shut anyway. I felt the stairs as he walked down them, heard the swish of the electric door at the entrance of the station, but my eyes wouldn't open. Even as I felt the world change around us from red to green, they stayed shut.

Unease gripped me. Between. We were going Between again?

I clung more tightly around Jin Yeong's neck, and there was a low murmur of "*Wae irae, Petteu?*" from him. It was stupid to feel comforted because I could feel his voice vibrating against my ribs, but somehow I did feel comforted.

"Where's Zero?" I asked, because I didn't *want* to be comforted by a vampire. I wanted Zero.

Jin Yeong *tsk*ed gently and his words had the meaning of, "Patient, patient, Pet."

"I don't want to be patient, I want *Zero!*"

Surprisingly, Jin Yeong didn't snarl at me; his voice continued to murmur in Korean with very little meaning but vibration and warmth until I felt the atmosphere change around us again and I smelled the smell of my own house.

Jin Yeong put me down on the couch and took my sneakers away, and to my relief it became possible to open my eyes again. I was on my own favourite couch, with the house normal and tidy around me, and both Jin Yeong and my sneakers were gone.

I saw the tips of my socked toes, and tucked my feet up beneath me on the couch. In the kitchen, the jug began to boil, so when I figured out that I wasn't shivering any more, I put my feet down again and went there to make coffee. Jin Yeong came back while I was doing that; he had my sneakers in one hand, and they were somehow clean. He tossed them at me and sauntered off into the living room again.

Over his shoulder, in Korean, he said, "Coffee, *Petteu.*"

I could have stuck out my tongue at him, but somehow I didn't feel like it. Instead, I brought two cups of coffee into the living room and plopped down next to him, slinging my sneakers next to the coffee table. I meant to drink coffee, and Jin Yeong must have drunk his, because I remember the repetitiveness of his mug rising to his lips and being put back on the coffee table, but I fell asleep instead.

I woke a little when Zero and Athelas came home, filling the house with warmth and familiarity that seeped through into my sleeping mind, along with a murmured conversation. I didn't wake up properly; just enough to wriggle a bit against the softness of an arm in a fine business shirt that moved to accommodate my wriggling by draping itself over me instead. There was a heavy silence all around me, but when I tucked myself under that arm and curled up again to sleep, Athelas' voice floated gently through the fuzz.

"A bold move," it murmured. He gasped a little, and I saw a brief flutter of movement through my lashes as Zero lowered him into his chair. "If they had been giving her the dreams, they could have killed her for that."

There was a time of fuzzy sleep before Jin Yeong's laugh sounded, bumping my head. "Ah, will you fight? What fun!"

Between, I thought hazily. He wanted to be understood.

"Not everyone fights at the drop of a hat," said Athelas, but his voice was cold.

Zero said, "If they had been giving her the dreams, it would have meant they knew about her and were actively seeking information about her. That information could potentially have come from you, as well as other information. The dangers were even."

"There was some interest in the Pet." Athelas sounded more like himself again.

"How much is *some interest?*"

"Enough to use her face to attempt to trick information out of me about her. Most of the interest focused on you, but it could pay to be wary with the Pet."

"Perhaps you could suggest some ways of being *wary*," said Zero's voice, with an edge of frustration. "It keeps doing unexpected things. I never know what to guard against. And now that Upper Management knows about it, too—"

"Hmm," said Athelas, and there was some dark amusement in his voice. "At least there will be no need to worry about any information being lost from our friends at the police station."

Because he killed them all, said my thoughts, fuzzily.

JinYeong's voice buzzed against the ear that was pressed against his ribcage. "Did you get the others, *hyeong*?"

"They were already gone by the time we got there," said Zero. "It was to be expected. Upper Management will regroup, but I doubt they'll try to use humans again."

"What of them?" asked JinYeong. "What did you discover there?"

"Not as much as I should have liked," said Athelas. "But enough to know they were behind the waystation we cleared out a little while ago. I thought it was a touch too well-organised to be a single cell operation."

"I see." Zero's voice could have chilled me properly awake if it wasn't for the warmth of JinYeong against my cheek. "I would have moved a little more quickly if I'd known of that particular connection."

"And I was in no fit state to be useful in the chase," Athelas' voice said, with a deep regret. "Perhaps, had I been quicker—"

I lost some time in sleep, and when I woke again, Zero's voice said, "It's no use repining, Athelas; your injuries were left for too long as it was. Upper Management will appear again, soon enough."

"Do you think so?"

"*Ne*," said JinYeong, without hesitation. "Even if a starfish has many arms, it doesn't like losing them."

"Starfish arms grow back," I mumbled, before I was awake enough to keep pretending to be asleep.

"*Mwohya?*" said JinYeong, lifting his arm again. "*Kkaenae?*"

"I can still understand you," I told him, sitting up, but it was more of a habitual dig than because I actually felt like irritating him. There was more warmth to the house now that my three psychos were back together, but my very clean sneakers were still sitting on the ground beside the coffee table, and there was also a kind of creeping discomfort to the reunion.

Maybe I'd feel better when I had a full night's sleep, I thought,

but I reached automatically for my coffee, grimacing at the cold-
ness of it when it touched my lips. Zero took it from me and went
into the kitchen without a word, and I heard the sound of the
microwave.

"Where'd you go, anyway?" I asked Athelas, curling my toes
into the carpet beside my sneakers. "You left me in a hall full of...
of *stuff*."

"Ah," said Athelas. "That was necessary."

"Yeah? How's that?"

There was a brief pause, and in the kitchen, the microwave
dinged. As Zero came back into the room, Athelas said, "You were
in the way. It was troublesome to fight around you, so I took the
fight further away. When I did so, it became apparent that there
was more cleaning necessary."

I took the newly hot mug that Zero gave me and clasped it
between my two hands. "And when you say cleaning, you mean—"

"Yes," Athelas said, smiling faintly. "I was quite busy. There
were some familiar faces that needed to be attended to, and I
was...inspired."

"Well it wasn't very flaming tidy!"

"Go back to sleep, Pet," said Athelas. "Drink your coffee."

"Heck no," I said. There was something about it—a weird
smell, or feel. I put it down on the coffee table. "There's something in it."

I turned accusingly toward Jin Yeong, and one of his brows
went up in surprise at the look.

"Did you put something in my coffee?"

Athelas' eyes flicked past me to Zero, who said, "Drink your
coffee, Pet."

Jin Yeong, indignantly, said, "*Na aniya!*"

"What, you're offended?" I stared across at him. "You're the
one who stuffed spit down my throat! *And* you flamin' kissed me!
Don't think I've forgotten about that."

"*Keugae wanjon dala!*"

"How come?" I argued. I was in the mood for a good argument; maybe it would help fight off the feeling of horror that still somehow clung to my insides. "How is that totally different?"

"*Kunyang*," said JinYeong, after a brief pause.

"Pet," began Zero.

I was afraid he was going to tell me to drink the coffee again, and now that I was sure there was something in it, I didn't want to. I stood up, jostling the coffee table, and the cup tumbled to the floor in a shower of not-quite-coffee.

Pity it didn't splash JinYeong. To him, I said, "Just you wait. Got something nasty for you."

JinYeong's other brow went up. Then, to my surprise, he grinned. "I'll be waiting," he said, in easy-to-understand Korean.

Athelas sighed. "It was nothing more than an inducement to sleep, Pet."

"Don't you know that Pets don't like medicine in their food?" I told him. "Anyway, I already slept."

"Not," said Athelas, his eyes studying my face, "for quite long enough, I believe."

Zero, leaning against the back of the couch, asked, "How did you know it was drugged?"

"Perhaps *know* is a little too strong," demurred Athelas. "After all, the Pet *is* human. Perhaps it would be more pertinent to ask what gave her the impression that you had er, added to her beverage."

I looked accusingly at Zero. "*You* did it? Don't you know you're not supposed to put stuff in people's drinks? It's flamin' rude!"

"I don't have time to tend to your nightmares tonight," he said. "It would have made you sleep soundly."

"Nobody has to tend to my nightmares," I muttered. "I can look after 'em myself."

"Do as you please," said Zero, and vanished into his study.

If I didn't know better, I would have thought I'd hurt his feelings. If it was JinYeong, I would have been sure—JinYeong tended to sulk. Even now, he was watching me with his mouth pursed.

I threw a cushion at him. "You mickey-finned me," I told him. "You're no better."

JinYeong folded his arms and muttered a stream of sulky Korean into the other side of the room. I ignored it and went to the kitchen to get some paper towel to clean up the coffee spill. Lucky the carpet was dark; it wouldn't stain, at least.

"A piece of advice, Pet," said Athelas, when I got back. I expected to see his face all quiet and amused like it usually is when he talks to me, but when I looked up from my coffee stain, he was quite serious.

"What?"

"Don't bite the hand that feeds you."

"The only feeding that's going on around here is me feeding you lot," I pointed out.

"A fair point," said Athelas, and now he was smiling faintly again. "However, do you think you could refrain from offending my lord?"

"Don't speak for me," said Zero's voice. "If there's a need for me to speak, I'll do it myself."

His voice was harsh, so I was surprised to see that Athelas' smile had grown. "My mistake," he said.

"Yes," said Zero.

"*Hotsori*," muttered JinYeong, and stalked away upstairs as if he were done with the nonsense.

Athelas gazed after him, and the amusement in his eyes grew. "Life becomes more and more interesting every day," he said.

"Yeah? Don't suppose you're gunna tell me why?"

"I think not."

I looked around me at a room that wasn't as darkly uncomfortable as it had been when I first woke, and at an Athelas who was no longer dripping in blood and horror.

"Oh well," I said. "Looks like we're back to normal again, anyway. Whatever that is."

CHAPTER THIRTEEN

I DIDN'T MEAN TO FALL ASLEEP AGAIN—I MEANT TO STAY awake, with one eye on Athelas, for as long as it took him to drop off to sleep. I must have fallen asleep at some stage, though, because I woke up from a refreshingly dreamless sleep, still on the couch, while the clock told me it was ten in the morning.

Flaming heck. I'd really slept in today.

I could feel the movement of Zero upstairs; along with it a flicker of Jin Yeong's presence, but Athelas was opposite me on the other couch, his eyes closed.

"Ha," I said, with slightly satisfied crankiness. "So much for super fae healing."

"My healing is coming along quite nicely, thank you Pet," said Athelas, without opening his eyes. "And for your information, healing veins and muscles takes significantly more time than healing outer wounds."

"'Zat mean you were running around the place bleeding on the inside yesterday?"

Athelas opened one eye. "Perhaps you would be good enough to make tea, Pet?"

"You were!" I said in astonishment. "You were running around slaughtering Behindkind and making trouble while you were bleeding internally! Why didn't you let Zero deal with it?"

Athelas opened the other eye and turned his head to gaze at me. "Are you planning on mounting a strike to protest your treatment?"

"All right, all right," I grumbled. "I'm flamin' going!"

"Some things," said Athelas as I headed for the kitchen, and his voice was meditative and soft, "are personal. Those things should be handled personally."

"Revenge, you mean," I muttered to myself as I tapped the button to boil the jug. I mean, fair enough. They *had* suspended him on strands of moonlight and tortured him for a bit over a week. I'd be pretty cranky at that, too.

Hang on. I was the one who'd died six times. I was already flamin' cranky. It didn't help that it was humans who were responsible for that—it was the sort of thing I was used to from Behindkind, and I didn't like the feeling that humans had been capable of something just as horrible as Behindkind, given the right tools.

I didn't like the fact that there was a group out there like Upper Management, *giving* them the tools to do it.

I thought Athelas had gone back to sleep when I came in with the tea, but he opened his eyes as soon as I put the tray on the coffee table. Maybe he smelled the biscuits. I dunno. I helped him to sit up, and maybe he found that suspicious, because the look he gave me when I passed him his tea as well was nearly worried.

"Pet," he said. "Have you put something in my tea?"

"What?"

"I hesitate to think it of you—"

"Yeah? Doesn't sound like it."

"Well, if the truth must out, I did wonder if your forgiveness included pranks directed at myself instead of Jin Yeong. I had the distinct impression that Zero gave you some bad ideas last night."

"Heck no," I said. "It's too much fun messing with Blood-Breath. Told you I forgive you."

"Indeed," said Athelas, and sipped his tea. "Then perhaps you could pass the biscuits."

"They're not your favourites," I warned him. "And before you think *that*'s a subtle bit of payback, you can blame the vampire for it. He found where I was hiding them and ate them. I don't think he even likes them; he just ate them because they're yours and because I hid them."

Athelas smiled into his tea. "Certainly. What else would you expect of him?"

"Nothing good, anyway. How long are you gunna be lying around the living room?"

"A few more days, I expect. Why?"

"No reason," I said, to give him something to think about. *Not* revenge. But Athelas is always thinking about stuff, and when he's not guessing what I'm up to outright, he's getting too flamin' close. I wanted to give him something to think about. Not that I was gunna be up to anything. Not around the downstairs living room, anyway. I was going to be doing all my getting up to things outside the house.

Keeping tabs on Daniel from Morgana's window, for instance. Probably training with Zero again, now that Athelas was back home and Tuatu hadn't been arrested. Figuring out how to help Tuatu when he didn't want help and Zero didn't want me to help.

Athelas settled a lingering look on me, and said at last, "I don't believe you."

It surprised a laugh out of me. I filled his teacup again and said, "Okay. Think what you want."

"Ah, where's the enjoyment in that? I expected hot repudiations."

"Sorry to disappoint you."

"Are you? Again, I take leave to doubt it."

I dissolved into ridiculous giggles. "Maybe that's my revenge! Driving you mad with tiny doubts."

"If so, your revenge has well and truly been completed," he said, and put down his teacup. There was a distant look to his eyes that I didn't like. "In the moonlight I had a thousand tiny doubts that never made up enough to allow me to be sure one way or the other."

"Yeah, and that's weird, too," I said, without thinking about it.

He smiled, waking from that glazed look. "Indeed? And what seems strange to you, Pet?"

"Nothing," I said. "Just...I didn't think you could make mistakes."

I hadn't exactly thought he was infallible. It was more that I'd thought he couldn't be wrong. Dying six times had proved that wasn't true. Athelas, just like any human, could be so blinded by what he thought he knew, that he couldn't see the truth even when it was right in front of him.

And if Athelas could be wrong about that, there was a slight chance he was wrong about other things—even fae things.

"I've made many mistakes in my time, Pet," Athelas said, smiling faintly. "Some of them I rue more than others—some of them are more dangerous than the others. Some of them are perhaps not the mistakes I thought them to be."

"Got no idea what you're talking about, now."

"I'm happy to hear it."

"Typical," I said gloomily.

JinYeong, padding downstairs at the sound of hot drinks and biscuits, shot me a malicious look. I ignored it, and him. I didn't want to feel sorry for him, and this morning it was hard to feel the same level of antipathy toward him that I was used to feeling. Maybe I could think of a prank or two to pull, make things feel more like normal again. Apart from the guerrilla kiss, he'd been pretty nice last night. More than that, I'd seen the way the golden fae treated him, and now that I knew how he'd been turned, it seemed like a tenuous connection between our respective human and once human states had been formed.

I didn't much care for that.

And speaking of connections, there was something I'd been wanting to ask Athelas for a little while now. Maybe I could ask it suddenly enough that he wouldn't be ready for it. With that aim in mind, I said abruptly, "Zero says there's a connection between us."

There wasn't even a flicker of reaction from him. He said smoothly, "Does he? Why so?"

"Because of the dreams," I said. "He said we had to be connected in some way for that to be possible."

"How interesting," he said. "No doubt my lord will have further words with me, in that case."

There was silence for a moment, before I asked what I'd really wanted to ask. "*Is* there a connection between us?"

"Certainly. You're my pet; I'm your owner."

"Yeah, but that's true with Zero and Jin Yeong, too. I don't go dreaming about them."

"Perhaps they have not been in as significant an amount of peril."

"Isn't it weird that I'm dreaming *at all?*"

"Unusual, certainly," said Athelas. "But not unprecedented. You've lived for most of your life in a house teetering perilously on the edge of this world and the one Behind. Certain things— certain abilities—leach more than others."

"I've been contaminated by Between?"

"As non-felicitous a way of putting it as I could imagine," he sighed. "But effectively, yes. I will discuss the matter with Zero."

"Oi!" I said indignantly. "I want to discuss the matter now! *And* I want to know why Upper Management were asking about me!"

"Pet, *must* you yell?" Athelas sighed.

"Oh, sorry," I said, remembering in time that he was still injured. "You want more tea?"

"I would like to point out that not all problems can be solved by tea," said Athelas. "And yet, at the risk of undermining that, yes, I would."

Lucky I asked; when I got to the kitchen to make another pot of tea, there was one last packet of Athelas' special shortbreads hidden beneath the box. I grinned my satisfaction at the teapot and took them with me when I trotted back out with a teacup and three cups of coffee.

Jin Yeong, nosey thing that he was, looked bright as soon as he sniffed the biscuits.

"Found you some more shortbreads," I told Athelas, setting the tray down. "Don't let Jin Yeong have 'em; he's had blood and snacks and he's still moping."

Jin Yeong said an offended, "*Mwoh? Petteu, wae irae?*"

Zero, coming down the stairs in time to hear, said, "I see the Pet is awake," and went on to the bookcase to pick out a book.

I trotted off to the kitchen while Jin Yeong protested from the living room about his lack of shortbreads. He was still going when I got back with Athelas' teapot, so I told him, "I got them for Athelas, not for you," and gave him a cup of coffee instead.

"*Ah, wae?*" pouted Jin Yeong.

"'Cos you weren't tortured for a week and a half. Also, you're mean to me."

Jin Yeong's mouth dropped open. "*Ya, Petteu! Nan moggolae!*"

He made a dart for the plate of biscuits, but I snatched them away and ducked behind Zero. "Well, you *can't* eat 'em! Zero, the vampire is trying to eat Athelas' biscuits!"

There was a snarl from Jin Yeong that sounded like *Don't call me the vampire!* as he dodged around Zero and after me, but I leaped the couch without even thinking about it, and stuck my tongue out at him from behind Athelas' couch.

"Yeah, you forgot I've still got vampire spit, too, didn't you? Told you you're getting old!"

"Don't taunt the vampire," said Zero, looking up from his book-choosing.

"The house is so lively these days," sighed Athelas. "Pet, do you suppose I could have one of those biscuits at some stage? Since you got them for me, after all."

"Coming," I said. I feinted right, but Jin Yeong wasn't having any of it. He leapt the couch in a moment, fingers snatching where I'd just been. My feet flickered over the coffee table and I landed softly on the carpet, rolling through the gap between Athelas' usual chair and Zero's spot. Not one of the biscuits dropped, and I laughed in glee.

Across the room, I felt rather than saw Zero's put-upon sigh: he sat down on the couch Jin Yeong and I regularly and warily shared without trying to go to his normal seat, and opened his book. Jin Yeong cleared that seat in a second, and I nipped around Athelas again while he was diving for my ankles. There was a chance; I took it. I dived for Zero and safety, ducking under his arm and into his leather jacket, tucking in my feet just as Jin Yeong snatched at them.

Legs, safe. Biscuits, safe. Good thing that Zero was so flaming big, or I would never have been able to get away with it.

Zero put down his book. "Pet—"

"Sanctuary!" I panted. "Sanctuary!"

Athelas' soft laugh danced across the coffee table toward us. "Well done, Pet!" he said. "But what now?"

"*Nawa, Petteu!*" said Jin Yeong, prowling back and forth in front of the couch. There was a glitter to his eyes that wasn't the dark, dangerous one I was used to.

"Nope," I said, peering at him from my leathery hiding place. If I didn't trust the dark glitter because I knew what it meant, I didn't trust the one I didn't know the meaning to. "I'm not coming out while you're standing there."

"Pet," began Zero again, but he must have run out of words, because nothing else came out. Or maybe it was just that I'd knocked over his coffee while I was leaping over furniture. At length, he simply sighed and went back to his book, his arm stuck out awkwardly where I had taken shelter.

I stuck my tongue out at JinYeong.

"And yet I still await my promised biscuits," said Athelas. There were crinkles at the corner of his eyes. "Pet," he said. "Come."

JinYeong made the smallest bite of satisfaction at me, the edges of his teeth showing.

"No fair!" I protested. "Behindkind all ganging up on the pet!"

"Pet, Pet!" sang JinYeong, and he must have meant me to understand, because the meaning came through perfectly. "Come here and don't leave me waiting!"

"Bite me and I'll bite you back!" I warned him.

In a voice that was very close to a purr, he said, "*Hae bwa*."

"You're flamin' weird! Zero, make him go away!"

"JinYeong—"

"*Hyeong*," said JinYeong, still in that soft, purring voice, "*Haji-masaeyo*."

"Stop chasing the pet around the living room."

JinYeong looked at Zero, then at me. Very deliberately, he bared his fangs at Zero and said, "*Shileo*."

Now there was a dark, dangerous look to his eyes, and I didn't know if it was aimed at Zero or me. Whichever way, I didn't like it.

"Is he allowed to say *don't wanna* at you?" I demanded, looking up at Zero. "If I'm not allowed to say *don't wanna* to you, the vampire shouldn't be able to!"

"Don't bait the vampire," said Zero, and stood up.

"Oi!" I protested, but Zero only touched me briefly on the head in passing with a zap of static electricity and walked away into the kitchen.

Jin Yeong was on me in a second. I squeaked and tried to dive away, but something pushed me sideways and sent Jin Yeong flying across the room. He collided with the opposite wall, shocked and dishevelled, and rolled back onto the floor in a tumble of slender limbs.

I expected him to get up straight away, but he didn't; there was a glassy look to his eyes where his head rested on the carpet, his hair tumbling across his forehead, and a small gasp trembled on his lips.

Uncertainly, I stood up. "Jin Yeong?"

"No doubt he'll pick himself up," said Athelas amusedly. "Unlike my poor biscuits, which are incapable of picking themselves up."

Jin Yeong rolled onto his back with difficulty, his right hand dropping to the carpet, and drew in a rattling breath. His eyes, dark and bloody, glared up at Zero as Zero came back out of the kitchen with another mug of coffee and went toward the staircase.

"Zero," I said, but he didn't stop, leaving my uncertain, "Zero —Jin Yeong is—" hanging in the air behind him as he climbed the stairs.

Jin Yeong muttered something wet and angry, and coughed a bit of blood onto his chest.

I don't think I actually meant to walk over there, but that's what happened. Jin Yeong's glassy eyes roamed my face, and I saw a smile come and go on his bloody lips.

I slipped my hand into his inner suit pocket, prompting a rasping, surprised, "*Wae?*" from him, and pinched his handkerchief. Trust him to have the exact same type of handkerchief in the exact same pocket I'd seen him put the other one in.

"You're all mucky," I said to him, patting away the blood on his lips and then at the bit that had splattered on his suit. "Better get that off so I can wash it straight away, or it'll stain."

"*Appaseo; mothae,*" said Jin Yeong, pouting.

That was a good sign. If he was well enough to pout, he must be recovering.

"You'll be fine," I said, and grabbed one of the fallen biscuits. I shoved it in his mouth. "Here, have a biscuit."

Maybe it took him by surprise. He just blinked up at me while I unbuttoned his suit jacket, and let me tug the sleeves off his arms without either struggling or helping. He didn't cough up any more blood either, which was nice.

"That," said Athelas, retrieving a biscuit that had been flung on the coffee table, "is far more trouble than it's worth, Pet."

"It's only a small stain," I said. "I can fix it."

"I've no doubt you can," he said mildly. "But that's not what I meant."

"Well, maybe you should talk properly instead of riddling people," I told him, pulling the last of the jacket out from under Jin Yeong, who was still gazing up at me with the biscuit in his mouth. "Maybe then people would understand what you're talking about."

"Now where would be the fun in that?" asked Athelas, and he went back to smiling at the ceiling.

Still, Jin Yeong seemed to be recovered by the time I came back with his bloodless suit jacket. He was sitting on our couch with a cup of coffee and three of Athelas' biscuits tidily on the knee that was crossed over the other leg, his top two buttons undone as though he meant them to be that way instead of the plain fact that the second from the top had popped off. I could have told him again that the biscuits weren't for him, but I didn't have the heart.

Besides, he seemed to be expecting me to say something about it; he kept watching me through his hair, which was now somehow artfully ruffled instead of just plain messy, and it was no use having a go at him if he was expecting it. His gaze was off-putting enough that I went into the kitchen to avoid it and spent the rest of the morning making pancakes for Zero and tea cake to go with our evening coffee.

I couldn't help smiling a bit, though. As much as JinYeong didn't seem to doubt it, I didn't doubt that Zero had put a spell of some sort on me when he went away. Now that I was sure JinYeong wasn't more than passingly injured, I could enjoy the warm little feeling of being looked after. I might just be a pet, but I was still being looked after.

To my surprise, JinYeong didn't have a go at Zero when Zero came down for dinner. He seemed almost mellow, in fact, though he didn't eat any of the dinner. Instead, he wafted off toward the shower with his going-out clothes on a hanger.

Zero saw, and raised his brows in Athelas' direction, but as much as JinYeong had seemed intent on making his presence felt earlier, Zero appeared to want to be out of sight. He went away upstairs again as soon as he finished eating, leaving Athelas and me to eat tea cake with tea and coffee by ourselves.

Athelas was content to sit upright by now, to my secret relief, reading a book and drinking his tea almost as if he had never been tortured or injured. I picked up an omnibus of *Footrot Flats* that was somehow still around the house after all these years and let myself relax, too.

Maybe JinYeong felt like he wasn't getting enough attention, I dunno. He sauntered out of the bathroom in just his trousers—and, more irritatingly, in a cloud of cologne that made me gag behind my book—and held up two ties for Athelas' approval.

"Neither," said Athelas, after a brief look. "Top two buttons undone, as before. Unless, of course, you are trying for an uptight look."

JinYeong made a *pft* noise, but he went back to the bathroom looking thoughtful.

I raised my brows and flopped backwards on the couch.

"What's up with him *now*?" I asked Athelas, over the top of my book. "He's going out?"

"One assumes that the blood in the fridge wasn't fresh enough," suggested Athelas. "Or perhaps that it lacks a bouquet JinYeong finds appealing. Or perhaps he simply regrets being forced to give up this morning's sport. I believe he's going to hunt tonight."

"Is he allowed to do that?" I demanded, sitting up again. "Didn't Zero—"

"Zero objects to humans being brought home to be fed upon," Athelas said. "JinYeong is free to hunt where he chooses."

"What if he kills someone?"

"Oh, I think it very unlikely," said Athelas. "Zero, after all, also objects to bodies in the streets. Things like that draw unwanted attention."

"Yeah, but I don't think JinYeong thinks like that, and he likes annoying Zero. Wouldn't be surprised if he really wanted to annoy him, after this morning."

"JinYeong is very good at drawing the line exactly where it should be drawn," Athelas said gently, lifting his teacup. "I wouldn't worry if I were you, Pet."

I went back to my book, but I wasn't completely convinced; and when JinYeong emerged from the shower in a cloud of scent and steam, his lips red and his eyes glittering, I made a face behind my book, hissing a small, disgusted puff of air into the pages.

Seriously, what a pong. Even JinYeong didn't usually stink to that extent.

I was still wrinkling my nose when my book was summarily swept away. JinYeong's face replaced it, narrow and tilted too close for comfort.

"*Mwohya?*"

I looked back at him unblinkingly. "Didn't say anything."

"You breathed disparagingly," Athelas said. "It seems that

JinYeong has taken offence."

JinYeong tilted his head just a little more, his eyes roaming my face. "*Chal duro, Petteu*," he said, and gave vent to a swiftly flowing stream of words that meant nothing to me. When he was done, he smiled a small, smug smile at me that held more than a little mockery, and, tossing my book back into my lap, sauntered away toward the front door.

"*Mwohya?*" I complained, imitating him. He was deliberately speaking too fast for me to understand him.

"He said," murmured Athelas, "that although you dislike the scent now, in time you will come to associate it with him. He says that one day you will find yourself smiling, although you don't know why, because you smelled this scent and involuntarily thought of him."

"Ew," I said, making another face. I called out to the widening section of Between that had opened to allow JinYeong to pass through, "That stinks just as much as your perfume!"

MAYBE WE WERE ALL A BIT TIRED AFTER EVERYTHING. ZERO came back downstairs with a book after JinYeong left, but he didn't look up from it for the next four or five hours—didn't even go to the loo, which was normal for him but still weird—and Athelas sat back on his couch, dreamily looking at the ceiling in a way that made me think he saw more there than just the ceiling. Maybe it was his kind of dreaming.

I drifted in and out of sleep, hazy and content. The twin threats of Zero and Athelas would keep any bad dreams at bay; they were a warmth and a warning that couldn't be ignored, and I slept in the security of them.

I woke only because I felt the contented drifting of JinYeong approaching the house. Maybe he was a bit drunk, because there was a happy, satisfied feeling to his approach that seeped through Between ahead of him. I hoped there wasn't an equal and opposite reaction out there in the form of a body drained of blood, but I got up to make coffee and cut cake, anyway.

Athelas smiled at the ceiling as I passed; because he was looking forward to tea, or from some reason of his own, I wasn't sure. Zero put down his book and glanced at Athelas, who smiled dreamily at Zero instead of the ceiling for a change.

"Stop talking to each other in code," I said over my shoulder. "It's rude."

I started the jug boiling and dug out some of Jin Yeong's snacks from the fridge. Even if he was pumped up on someone's blood, he'd probably still like them. Athelas had his special biscuits, after all, and Zero had more pancakes to look forward to tomorrow morning. Or tonight, if it came to that. When you don't sleep for more than a couple hours every night, morning and breakfast don't mean much to you.

I'd just put everything onto the usual tray when something tickled the edges of my mind that wasn't Jin Yeong. Frowning, I trotted out into the hallway, and there in the hallstand, leaning harmlessly against the wall, was a bright yellow umbrella.

"Heck!" I said softly. It *looked* like an umbrella, but I knew better. That was no umbrella—it was a sword; and for the most part, it was a sword that preferred not to be seen.

"Zero!" I yelled. "Reckon there's something coming! The sword let me see it again!"

At the same time, the whole house went sideways or maybe turned inside out, and Jin Yeong said something from just inside the front door that was definitely swearing.

"Such an intrusion," sighed Athelas, and the sound of it was somewhere beneath my feet until there was a Zero-shaped *twitch* and the house went right again.

Slender fingers pinched my right ear, tugging me away from the sword, but my fingers were already wrapped around the umbrella handle that felt like a sword grip, and I staggered sideways, pulling it out of the stand.

"*Manjiji ma*," said Jin Yeong, tugging lightly on my ear again.

"Look, the sword told me to pick it up, so who am I supposed to listen to?"

"*Na*," he said, threateningly.

"Yeah, but if I listen to you, what about the sword?"

Jin Yeong sighed, then reached over me and grabbed the umbrella sword. To my disappointment, it let him take it. I mean, I dunno what it would have done to stop him, but it would have been nice to see him get the magical equivalent of an electric shock again.

"*Darrawa, Petteu*," he said, and pulled me back toward the living room by one wrist.

"I can walk by myself," I said, but then I saw who was in the living room with Zero and shut my mouth. I might also have scooted just a *smidge* back behind Jin Yeong, whose fingers tightened around my wrist.

It was the golden fae, and this time he'd brought a couple of friends. Around Jin Yeong's arm, I saw the tightening of the fae's mouth as he saw Jin Yeong holding the umbrella.

"Why does *that thing* have the Heirling Sword?"

I opened my mouth to say something rude, but I thought better of it a split second before Jin Yeong's fingers crushed my wrist.

I kicked the back of his shiny shoes, then poked him in the ribs for good measure. I heard him mutter a complaint beneath his breath, but when I looked up at him, his cheeks were sharp in a dangerous smile directed at the golden fae.

"Oi. Ask him if he wants anything to eat," I muttered, tugging at a pinch of his suitcoat.

Jin Yeong's cheeks sharpened just a touch more, and his lips parted.

"Hello," he said in Korean that was layered through Between and very carefully understandable to the golden fae. "Would you care for something to eat?"

Printed in the USA
CPSIA information can be obtained
at www.ICGtesting.com
LVHW010817200923
758533LV00013B/339